THE POSTMODERN ADVENTURES OF

KILL
TEAM
ONE

BOOK ONE

RATED **R**

MIKE LEON

Cover art by J Caleb Clark

Edited by Rob Smales and Stacey Longo

PLEASE SEND ALL COMMENTS, QUESTIONS AND DEATH THREATS TO:

PROFESSIONAL.MIKE.LEON@GMAIL.COM

THE FOLLOWING PREVIEW HAS BEEN **APPROVED** TO

ACCOMPANY THIS FEATURE

BY THE MOTION PICTURE ASSOCIATION OF AMERICA,
INC.

R	**RESTRICTED** ⊕
	UNDER 17 REQUIRES ACCOMPANYING PARENT OR ADULT GUARDIAN
VIOLENCE, GRISLY IMAGES, LANGUAGE, NUDITY AND SEXUALITY	

"*Los Angeles*," the thundering voice of a faceless narrator bellows as the orange-hued city skyline rolls by. "*The city of angels is about to meet the devil.*"

A bald man, fifty-something, a patch over his left eye, stands on top of the Ritz Carlton overlooking the Staples Center. He wears epaulets on his shoulders and has a hook for a right hand.

"Good morning, Los Angeles." He speaks English with an accent that is foreign, but cannot be placed. "My name is Ripper Cabrón. Remember it. Fear it."

"*He holds a city in his grasp,*" warns the voiceover ominously.

"My men have hidden forty-six million gallons of VX nerve agent bombs throughout your city. At three o'clock today, I will detonate the devices unless the people of Los Angeles deliver Miss America to me. You have seven hours."

"*The police are powerless,*" booms the narrator.

"He's got us by the balls, Mr. Mayor," says the chief of police in a meeting room with a dozen men in business suits.

"*The citizens will do anything to survive,*" rumbles the unseen baritone.

A man in a brown muscle shirt stands at the head of a crowd on the steps of city hall.

"The mayor is protecting some dumb bikini model, but what about the children?" he says. The crowd cheers. Some of them brandish makeshift weapons.

"*The government has given up,*" the narrator blares.

The mayor, tall, black, dragging his hands through short, cropped hair in the same meeting room as the chief of police, shakes his head. "We're gonna have to give him the girl."

"*But there was one thing they didn't count on*," the narrator reveals.

Boom! A car explodes! It flies into the air and falls back down into the middle of the L.A. freeway.

A man in a leather jacket and blue jeans steps out of a flaming building and shoots a mohawk-sporting goon with a pistol. He takes the hand of a beautiful woman wearing a sash that says MISS AMERICA. "Don't worry, Miss America. You're gonna be safe with me!"

"Who are you?" she cries, as he shoots two more villainous henchmen.

"I'm Jack Reacharound!" he says.

Ripper Cabrón screams in the face of an underling atop the Ritz Carlton.

"You're telling me your whole squad couldn't stop one man?" Spittle sprays from Ripper's mouth. "*One man?*"

An army general speaks to the mayor at city hall.

"Jack Hardpecs Reacharound is the baddest bastard there is," says the general. "He's the only man ever thrown out of the army, the navy, and the marine corps just for bein' too tough."

"*This summer*," says the narrator.

An M1A1 tank jumps over a low-flying helicopter with Reacharound behind the steering crossbar, while Miss America screams from the open gunner's hatch.

"*Get ready for action!*" rumbles the narrator.

Reacharound swings on a rope from the top of a building, smashing through a plate glass window and onto a conference room table, sliding along the top, firing four Uzis, two with his hands and two with his bare feet, killing droves of armed soldiers along the way.

"*Get ready for desire,*" the narrator growls.

"I thought you could use a little incentive, Mr. Reacharound," Miss America says. The two of them are alone in a public restroom and she wears only a light pink bra. She undoes the clasp between her shoulder blades, exposing her back, and just a little bit of side-boob. Reacharound winks.

"*Get ready for a reach around!*" roars the narrator.

"I'm getting too old for this!" yells Reacharound, freefalling from a smoking jetliner in the distance above him. He tears a parachute from the back of a terrorist falling beside him and tosses the man a plastic explosive in trade.

"*Rex Octane is . . .*" the narrator says.

"Reacharound," says Miss America, as he holds her in his arms.

"Reacharound," says the mayor, incredulously.

"Reachaarrrooouuunndd!" screams Ripper Cabrón as a building explodes behind him.

". . . . *Jack Reacharound!*" the narrator exclaims.

And now our
FEATURE PRESENTATION.

EXT. DARK FOREST — NIGHT

The hollow man stands alone. He melds with the dark. He becomes it. The silent shadows blanket a shell filled with so much screaming rage that it seems impossible anything could insulate it at all.

"Come out, Mister Gallardo," calls a voice with an East Asian accent that would be almost unnoticeable except for the stretching of the honorific into a screeching *meeesta*. It comes from a man with spotty brown skin and black receding hair that leaves the top of his head mostly uncovered. Thick glasses reflect the beams of the flashlights each time they shine past him. "Come out or we kill the girl, Mister Gallardo."

The girl he's talking about is the twiggy five-foot tall child he hauls along in a tight bear hug: twelve-year-old Kat Way. She's so rail-thin that even the relatively small East Asian man can carry her and keep a palm pressed over her mouth. Still, she has a lot of fight in her for her size. She viciously jerks her head left and right, managing to tear free of his grasp and shout a warning into the woods.

"Run, Mr. Gallardo! It's a trap!" she shrieks.

Cute kid. Her parents call her Kitty. The hollow man is usually annoyed by children, but this one was nice to him, so he's here now. It would be a shame if something happened to her.

Kitty's father is some kind of computer big shot. He has an enormous mansion outside Redmond with two wings, chandeliers the size of minivans, and an Olympic-size swimming pool, which the hollow man was hired to attend in exchange for room and board—

all off the books, of course.

Unfortunately, all of that money seems to have attracted the wrong kind of attention. Six masked men came in the middle of the night. The hollow man watched curiously as they crept past the pool house where he stays, cut through a back door into the house, and came back out carrying little Kitty. They left a note on a table demanding twenty million dollars for her safe return.

He usually tries his best to ignore these hassles, but Kitty was always friendly to the hollow man during the many hours she played in the pool and told him about things like cootie catchers and photo bombing (which he was surprised to learn does not involve actual explosives).

There are five men left now, crackling through the woods the way men accustomed to the city always do. They make no effort to conceal their footfalls or the crinkling of their heavy jackets, or the jingling of keys. They do whisper carefully when speaking to each other, but the hollow man hears them anyway.

"We can't leave yet," the boss says, struggling to contain Kitty's flailing body. "If he has seen our faces we will all go down for this."

"We should kill the girl now and leave the country," says a slick-haired companion.

"No! We keep walking. He will follow and Chang will get behind him."

Wrong. Chang is dead. His blood has already grown tacky on the hollow man's killing hands. He inspects the men from all angles. They have shotguns and handguns, and some knives too. One carries a lead pipe. They are hardly any kind of mercenaries, and quite far from the type of monsters that pose a threat to him.

He takes one of them into the shadows with him.

There is no scream. No struggle. The mangled corpse even stops spurting blood before the others realize their compatriot is missing.

"Where did Lim go?" says the first hunter to notice their number has been reduced.

"I don't know," the boss answers.

"Lim!" another man shouts. "Where are you?"

"That idiot probably tripped and fell down the hill," the boss says.

The hollow man drops the body on top of them. It falls from the tree tops and hits the soil at their feet with a low thud. Blood splatters the shoes of the other men and one man cries out before covering his mouth.

"He's dead!" says the man with the lead pipe.

"I can see that," the boss yells.

"His throat is cut to the bone!"

"More money for the rest of us," the boss says. "Now we split the ransom four ways."

"Three ways," the hollow man says. His ghostly murmur carries through the trees and the kidnappers rapidly turn in a desperate attempt to locate the source of the sound. Even if they could pinpoint it, the hollow man isn't there anymore.

Another is already gone, taken away into the darkness. His shotgun never discharged and now it is just a heavy useless thing in the hollow man's fingers. He decides to play with them a little. He throws it back to the survivors. It clunks to the dirt and the boss picks it up while the slick-haired man falls to his knees.

"How is this happening?" the kneeler whimpers. "Where is he?"

The boss sets the girl on her feet and pulls a chrome plated Desert Eagle .50 from his jacket. It is one of the largest handguns in the world and looks incredibly awkward in the little man's hand. He's holding it all wrong. He has his wrist bent and his thumb on the backstrap and the middle pad of his index finger on the trigger. It looks like the dipshit has never fired a gun before, but none of that matters when he puts the muzzle up to Kitty's head.

"You come out or I blow her brains out," the boss yells into the surrounding woods.

"Please let me go!" Kitty screams. "I won't tell anybody! Please!"

"Where are you, Gallardo?" the boss shouts over her squealing.

"Here!" the hollow man shouts.

The boss instinctively turns in the direction of the voice and blasts off a series of hand cannon shots that rattle the trees. With madness in his eyes he pulls the trigger again and again until the pistol's magazine is empty and one of his own men is dead, his skull shattered by the very first stray shot.

Only two remain. The kneeling coward wails loudly as the boss turns, searching for the terror encircling him in the dark.

"It's a monster! It can't be real!" the slick-haired broken man wails.

"Shut up, you fool!" the boss barks.

The hollow man comes from the dark and takes hold of the boss. He jabs his fingers into the little bastard's eyes. He takes the Desert Eagle and pistol whips it right through the boss's teeth. The boss's spine makes a sickening crack as the hollow man re-orients his head to face backward. The boss looks better that way.

Kitty won't stop screaming. She doesn't run. She doesn't fight. She just keeps shrieking at the sight of the ruined carcass as it slumps to the ground with its backward head, broken teeth, gouged eye sockets and emptied bowels. She really seems to be taking it hard considering the guy was just some asshole who would have murdered her.

"Hey," the hollow man grunts. "Calm down."

That doesn't work at all. This is why he doesn't like kids.

"What are you?" the last man chokes out through snot and drool. There are bits of leaves and dirt mixed in his gelled hair now. Hair gel is a thing the hollow man does not understand. Why bother with it at all? Why not just buzz the hair down so it doesn't require such absurd maintenance?

The hollow man is not interested in this pathetic coward's questions. He approaches the broken man soundlessly and takes hold of his arm. He forces the man's head up and glares down into his terrified eyes with a hundred holocausts of hatred.

"Will there be more?" the hollow man demands. His voice is pure bass tone barbarism.

"More—more what?" the man cries. "Triads?"

"What the fuck is a Triad?"

"What? I don't . . ."

The hollow man breaks two of his captive's fin-gers. He repeats his question.

"Triads! Chinese gang!" the little coward screams.

"Will there be more?" the hollow man says.

"No! It was all Miao's idea! Nobody else knows! Please don't kill me!"

"Where do I find Miao?" the hollow man grumbles.

"That is Miao!"

He means the crumpled heap of broken bones and steaming feces on the ground beside them. Good. That means this is all cleaned up. The hollow man draws a weapon from its holster on his belt: a foot-long knife with a straight black blade and brown leather handle. He drives the knife into the base of his enemy's skull. It makes a sharp crack and the man squeaks. Then the woods grow silent.

"Who are you?" Kitty asks between short frantic breaths.

He's not Gallardo. Gallardo is just another dead man whose identity he uses. He can't explain who he really is. He never explains that to anyone. It would just put them in danger.

"The less you know, the better off you are," he says.

"What does that mean?"

"You know how to get home from here?"

Kitty looks out into the dark woods and shakes her head.

The hollow man points in the direction of the nearest road. She can't possibly miss it unless she somehow turns completely around in the wrong direction. "You walk that way and don't stop until you reach the street. Then wait for a car. Got it?"

Kitty nods.

"Good," he says. "You'll never see me again."

INT. VIDEO TIME – DAY

Lily leans on the corner of the dilapidated checkout counter, chewing on a lock of her bottle-black hair next to a small, dust-covered TV/VCR combo unit showing a fuzzy copy of *The Lion King*.

The video store has four aisles of DVDs running parallel with its cavernous length. The checkout counter is a booth by the front doors with several candy displays taking up most of its surface area. They have all the usual suspects: Snow Caps, Twizzlers, Sour Patch Kids. There is a popcorn machine and a Pepsi® cooler stocked with delicious drinks.

"So what's his name?" she asks quietly, masked by the noise of Nathan Lane belting out "Hakuna Matata," so as to avoid being heard by the subject of her inquiry— a broad-shouldered and serious-looking boy in the far corner of the store. He has dark hair, a camouflage hoodie and some ratty blue jeans. He sits at a tiny circular table, at the end of a long row of DVD cases, filling out a job application with a half-length No. 2 pencil. He is roughly her age, maybe a little older; she can't quite tell.

"Uh, Jerry . . . Jeff . . . Jeremy," answers Amy. The store manager is a few years older than Lily. She's blond and cheery and conservative—and there the differences end. In a different world, Lily thinks she could have been Amy—just like her, if it weren't for what happened back home. It's a curiosity she sometimes considers.

Lily returns to scrolling through Instagram on her iPhone like she has done for most of the day. There isn't much else to do here. Video Time only has a handful of customers each week. It's a poorly kept secret that the place only remains open as a front for the owner to launder money. It's amazing to Lily that the authorities haven't caught on yet. The place is a glaring anachronism. They have VHS tapes for fuck's sake. It might as well be a haberdashery, or a typewriter shop.

Lily feels a man's ogling eyes on her and looks up from the phone in time to catch their job applicant staring. He does not immediately shift his gaze away from her when spotted. Instead, boldly looking her over before he returns to his job application.

"I think you should hire him," Lily whispers to Amy.

"Did you talk to him?" Amy looks up from her early childhood education homework. "He seems kind of weird."

"He has eyes like a caged animal. I bet he fucks like one." Lily shoots through the lad with the sort of primal gaze a tiger gives to its next meal.

"Saying stuff like that makes people think you have daddy issues."

"I do have daddy issues," Lily says dryly.

"I don't like him." Amy grimaces and shakes her head, before poking it back in her homework.

"Come on, Amy," Lily sighs. "This town is so boring. All the guys here are lame."

"I'm not going to hire some creeper just because you think he's hot." This time, Amy doesn't even look up from the textbook spread open on the counter in front of her.

"Please? Pretty please?" Lily flutters her eyelashes.

"No."

"I'll organize the porno tapes."

Amy stops, eyebrows rising involuntarily. Lily knew the offer was too good for her to pass up without at least a second thought. The three big Rubbermaid bins of adult movies at Video Time have been in wild disarray as long as Lily can remember—primarily due to Amy's irrational fear of touching any of the videos inside. This has led to an ongoing problem: the mouth-breathing ham beasts that actually still rent porn on tape have to ask for the bins at the counter, then spend an eternity digging through them while eyeballing the girls lecherously. It's an awkward dance that could be prevented if they put the tapes in order and just printed out a list of what they have.

"Ew, gross," Amy says, obviously feigning disinterest. "You're only seventeen. I think it's illegal for you to handle that stuff."

Lily answers with nothing but a dismissive glare. That's bullshit. Aside from handling the porno tapes pretty regularly, she's probably done most of the things featured in them. Amy knows that. She's not stupid.

"No," Amy says, shaking her head in response. "I'm not doing it."

"Who else are you going to find?" Lily whines. "We haven't had anybody fill out an application for months."

"You don't know anything about that guy," Amy whisper-yells. She looks sideways to make sure he's not watching them. "He looks like he just jumped off a cargo train. What if he's a serial killer or something?"

She makes an interesting point. He's certainly dressed like a serial killer. Lily is hardly shaken. A serial killer might be exciting . . .

"I could use a little excitement in my life." Lily smiles.

"Maybe you should be careful what you wish for."

INT. VIDEO TIME – BACK ROOM – DAY

The back room at Video Time is a small space with a panel ceiling and bare concrete floor. Shelving units stacked with old VHS recorders line the walls, and unused store displays lay haphazardly on the floor. Most of this stuff has been here since the nineties, when the store was still viable as a legitimate business.

Jeremy sits quietly in a plastic swivel chair as Amy jots down notes on a clipboard. The notes aren't notes so much as random scribbling she makes in half-ass compliance with the standard interview questions. She files them away after filling them out, and she's certain no one ever looks at them after that. She should really just throw them in the trash.

"So Jeremy, what kind of skills do you have?" Amy asks.

He shrugs.

"I can kill a man with a plastic straw," he says, without any hint that he might be kidding. His voice is deep and unwavering with no accentuation. It has a frigid quality, Amy thinks.

Amy laughs nervously, but he only continues to stare at her coldly. She knows he's joking. He has to be joking, but he's way too deadpan for her to be comfortable.

"You have a sense of humor," she says, awkwardly trying to coax something else out of him. "That's a skill."

"I try." He finally cracks a smile. She notices what Lily was talking about. He's handsome in a certain way. He's dark and confident, but there's something hollow in that smile—something that bothers her.

"But really, what kind of skills do you have?" Amy moves the interview along according to the form.

"Well, I like movies."

"I should hope so." It's not a skill. It's not even a standout trait. Everybody likes movies. Amy jots down his answer anyway and moves on to the next question. "Did you go to school around here?"

"I did the homeschool thing."

"Oh, that's cool." It's not. Homeschool kids are creepy. He's creepy. "Is that why you want to work at Video Time? Because you like movies?"

"Yeah. And I'm on my own now. I need to bring in some cash to pay the bills."

"Right on. Story of my life," Amy says. Getting anything out of him is like pulling teeth. Amy skips down the form to the last question. "So where do you see yourself in five years?"

The question seems to give him pause. He thinks about this one, seriously considering it before answering, though what comes out is just as terse as all the other things he told her.

"Doing regular stuff," he says.

She looks back at him and waits for more, but it never comes. Regular stuff. That's it. What kind of answer is that supposed to be? Then she thinks of something she didn't notice before. He's wearing a camouflage hoodie. It's way too warm out for a hoodie. Amy was even a little put off by the skimpiness of the shorts Lily wore today, but this weirdo looks like he's going on a moose hunt in the Yukon. Why is she even talking to him?

"Okay," Amy says. "I think we've got enough here. If we're interested, we'll . . ."

"*Amy!*" Lily shouting from the front of the store interrupts her. Amy rolls her eyes and leans back in her metal folding chair to peek out the stockroom door.

Lily stands at the counter across from a bulbous man, dressed in torn cotton shorts and a sleeveless maroon T-shirt that leaves much of his abundant back hair showing.

"This guy wants to look at the, you know . . ." Lily looks back and forth before cupping her hand to her mouth to whisper-shout. ". . . Mommy and Daddy movies."

"So get them out," Amy says.

"But I can't," Lily says, shrugging exaggeratedly. "I'm only a minor."

Amy looks at the ghastly creature with the back hair again and it smiles at her, exposing the last few rotting teeth it has.

"Can you have them organized by Tuesday?" she asks begrudgingly.

"I think that can be arranged," Lily says. She hoists the first bin of porno tapes on top of the counter, opening the lid as she grins back at Amy.

Amy turns back to Jeremy.

"When can you start?"

INT. LILY'S ROOM – NIGHT

Lily keeps looking at the poster for *Edward Scissorhands* hanging above her headboard. She tries to imagine herself with Johnny Depp right now, but it isn't working. Maybe because of the scars on his face. Maybe because of the scissor hands. Those would be a problem. Of course, if it were really Johnny Depp, he wouldn't have scissor hands, but she can't picture him without them because the stupid poster is right in front of her.

She closes her eyes to try harder. All she can see is Krohike. That's frustrating. Oh well. Johnny isn't really her type anyway.

She opens her eyes and looks down at Krohike underneath her. He keeps squeezing her breasts, not cupping or fondling them, but twisting them sort of like a kid honks a bike horn. Chris is a nice kid, but he's useless in the sack. He's a scrawny ginger with a squeaky voice that cracks a lot. At least he doesn't drag it out for hours.

"I'm gonna come," he says. And there it is. Lily looks at the clock on her desk. Forty-eight seconds. It's a new record for him. Meh. She doesn't fuck him because she likes him. She fucks him because they have an arrangement.

Afterward, she pats him on the head and reaches across her nightstand for a Kleenex® tissue, with its gentle softness and dependable strength. He watches as she wipes herself dry, which is a little weird.

"What does wasteland mean?" he whispers.

He's talking about the tattoo on her pelvis,

WASTELAND written in Celtic script and placed so low that her underwear usually covers it. Lily likes tattoos and she has a few of them. The largest is a half-sleeve heavy metal interpretation of the chemical wedding, an angel entwined with a demon, surrounded by black lilies between her left shoulder and elbow. She also has a cliché tribal on her lower back, and a script under her right breast which reads: DEATH COMES WITH THE TERRITORY. SEE YOU IN DISNEYLAND.

"It means what it says," she tells him, as she tosses the Kleenex® in the trash a few feet from her bed.

"I know what the word means. I meant I wanna know *why*? There must be more to it."

"It's personal," she says. She throws her right arm over him, resting her face on the pillow next to him.

"Personal?" he scoffs. His voice becomes even more high-pitched—he's excited. He props himself up on one arm and looks down at her. "We just had sex. I came inside you!"

"Yeah." She shrugs. She never tells anyone what it means. "It's personal."

Krohike scrunches his face in confusion. He lies back on the bed as Lily reaches for her cigarettes: Marlboro Gold Pack in a box on the dresser next to her. She shuffles through some assorted junk to find the Zippo lighter she keeps there: a Jack Skellington key chain, a paperback of *Save the Cat!*, and an Emily the Strange coin purse.

"So why do you do this?" he asks.

"Why do I do what?" She raises an eyebrow to this question as she lights a cigarette.

"This." He motions down at them, their naked bodies in the bed. "Like, with me." He thumbs his bony chest.

"I thought that was pretty clear from the start." Lily inhales a breath of smoke. "I need someone to do my calc homework and you need someone to . . . we barter."

"I know that's what we say, but I mean . . . you, like, you don't—" he stammers, then stops altogether. He takes a second to restart. "You know my friend Rick?"

"Yeah." Rick is one of the nerds Krohike plays video games with. Lily sees them in the cafeteria sometimes.

"Okay. He's been Jenny Brunswick's lap dog since we were freshmen and she doesn't even do 'over the clothes' stuff with him. She's been going out with Chad Evers the whole time."

Chad Evers. Varsity shooting guard. Hot. Tripod, too. Lily fucked him in a closet at Mike Wilkinson's pool party last year. He was wearing Jenny's stupid purity ring the whole time. Lily halts a snicker and almost chokes.

"So?" She doesn't understand what Chris is implying here.

"So you don't really have to do this with me."

"But that's the deal we made."

"Yeah, but I think that's sort of like prostitution."

"It's not prostitution." Lily holds the cigarette away from her face and glares at him. "It's friends with benefits," she says forcefully.

"I don't know . . ."

"Are you calling me a whore?" Lily interrupts sharply.

"No!" Krohike barks, holding up his hands.

"Look." Lily puts her head back against the pillow. "We're friends, and we give each other benefits. Friends with benefits. See?"

"I know, and they're really great benefits. They really are. All I'm saying is: I know that you know that you don't have to go all the way for this, but you do anyway. That has to mean something."

"You want me to be a total cock tease bitch like Jenny Brunswick?" Lily asks with conspicuous sarcasm. He's not going to say yes to that.

"No! I think you're awesome. It's just I wonder why you do it. I think there's a reason."

There's a reason. There's a reason for Chris and Chad, and all the other boys—sometimes men. There's a reason for the times she wanted it and the times she didn't. There's a reason. It's just that the reason is hers alone and he would never understand.

"Because I'm not a cock tease bitch like Jenny Brunswick." Lily inhales a deep breath of smoke and blows it into his face. She giggles playfully.

Krohike waves smoke away.

"You know," he says. "Those are really bad for you."

"I only smoke them after sex." It's a half truth. She *usually* only smokes them after sex.

"Yeah. I mean, I don't know."

They lie there in awkward silence for a moment after that exchange. Lily knows cigarettes are bad for her. That's exactly why she likes them. She needs that dry, burning sensation to fill her lungs now more than ever. She imagines her body rotting and doesn't care.

She lies perfectly still as the insects come for her. They eat her gray decaying flesh until she's just bones. Even the bones melt away and then she's just nothing. Nothing might be better.

"What's *Tokyo Gore Police*?" Krohike says.

Lily rouses from her death trance to try and figure out what he's talking about. It's the poster in her room, of course. Her walls are covered in movie posters. There's *Die Hard*, *True Lies*, *Monster Squad*, *The Evil Dead*, *Dirty Harry*, *Star Wars*—the list goes on. All of them glow eerie silver in the light of the TV, the only light she typically has on in here besides that from the iMac in the corner.

"It's a Japanese splatter movie," Lily answers. "The girl from *Audition* is in it."

"Huh," is all he musters. Lily didn't expect much more out of him. Krohike is an honor student with a full ride to Duke. He wears American Eagle and doesn't drink. He's not the J-horror type. He's not even into movies. His job at the Cineplex concession is entirely accidental.

"Oh, so get this," Krohike says. "The Cineplex has a phantom."

"What?" Lily laughs.

"Yeah. Cases of bottled water keep disappearing from the concession. So the manager thought it was one of us, except who steals bottled water? But then the cleaning crew started finding tons of water bottles in the bathroom garbage in the morning—like they were left there overnight. So Mindy had the ushers check all the theaters at close last night, under the seats and everything. They didn't find a thing. But then Justin texted me this morning and they still found bottles in the bathroom when he opened up."

"That's fucked up." Lily dumps ash into the Bates

Motel ashtray on her nightstand.

"Casey—the AGM—swears she saw this creepy guy go in one of the projection rooms once, but when she went in there he was gone. Like poof. Vanished."

"What did he look like?" Lily has become genuinely interested in this now.

"I don't know." Krohike shrugs. "Old fashioned, I guess. Aren't ghosts always dressed in old clothes?"

"That's so stupid. How come you never hear about a ghost wearing a Metallica T-shirt or something? It's always a lady in white or guy in a Civil War uniform."

"Yeah, I guess it's pretty dumb."

"That's still really cool. You know there are lots of ghost sightings, but a full body apparition sighting is extremely rare. Most people just feel cold or think they see some orbs or something lame."

"Look at you. You're like a ghost buster."

"I just watch a lot of TV."

Krohike smiles.

"I have to go," he says, climbing out of the bed. "I'm gonna miss my curfew."

He leans over to kiss her lips, but she turns away just enough to catch it on the cheek. She doesn't like to kiss when it's strictly for business.

INT. MOVIE THEATER – NIGHT

In the darkness of theater ten, the hollow man is more comfortable than most places he visits. He picked this room, the least occupied theater, to avoid other people. They make him uneasy. In his position, his world, as he often puts it, any one of them could be a harbinger of death mixed in with the others, dressed in a disguise of designer shoes or T-shirts with pithy sayings. Any one of them could pull a gun or a knife, or something far more exotic. They could catch him off guard and then it would all be over.

He tries to forget all that for just a moment. He sits in the corner of the back row of the theater, with his back to a wall so no one can come up behind him. He tries to tell himself he's safe here, but that is probably a lie, and it goes against everything the old man ever taught him. Still, he tries.

He focuses on the movie on the hulking screen in front of him, flickering by with its upbeat soundtrack. The man in the movie, with his unusually shiny hair, has just ridden a stolen motor scooter through New York City to catch up to the woman, who also has unusually shiny hair, just as she was about to leave on an airplane for Buenos Aires. He says he loves her and asks her to marry him.

The hollow man does not know what any of this means. The credits flash on the screen and he can only grunt quietly to himself. Obviously it has some relevance or the normies wouldn't watch it. It's probably meant to spur some kind of emotional response. The hollow man does not feel anything. He never feels anything—except rage, anger, hatred. They're all just different words for the same thing: whatever he feels when he's killing. This is the only thing the old man ever allowed him to feel.

He tries to remember if he was ever sad, or afraid, or lonely, or happy. Maybe once, too long ago and too early for him to recall. He remembers not wanting to stab a sleeping child to death a few years ago. That may have been the last time he felt hesitation.

He leaves the theater and scans the hallway outside for the glowing red showtimes on the little signs outside the doors. Another showing of *Endoskeletal* starts in ten minutes. He understands that one. It's about a man with a robot skeleton who fights a man with metal skin to have sex with a pretty girl. The hollow man has seen it six times. He can recite all of the dialogue with his perfect eidetic memory.

This is his attempt to understand and be like the rest of them—the normies, normal people who understand and identify with the loud and colorful things he sees every day. He saw the importance they placed on these movies, with the monolithic structures constructed to house and display them. He snuck into this place and began watching, and watching, and watching. For the last two months he has been coming here every day, all day, and watching these things in an effort to become more like them.

Normies don't have to worry about the things he does. Normies have it easy. He wants to be one of them.

He goes to the lobby to steal bottled water. There's a closet near the concession counter which is poorly guarded by the theater workers, who are not sentries but clerks, or maybe *associates* as the normies some-times say. They rarely have eyes on the door, and the hollow man has near carte blanche to walk in and take what he wants. This time he takes two bottles, ignoring the rainbow of sugary candies and sodas stacked with the water. He only ever drinks water. That's what the old man told him to do, and so he does.

On his way back through the movie theater lobby, he stops briefly to observe a group of pretty young women talking on their way past the concession. He thinks they are older than him by only a few years, so maybe twenty or so. Women don't pay attention to him at all, except to avoid him. These women are no exception. One of them seems to notice him ogling and averts her eyes quickly.

Someone once told him there are promiscuous women out there looking for sex. The hollow man has been on the lookout for these promiscuous women ever since. So far, he has only seen them in movies.

INT. SCHOOL – CALC 101 – DAY

Calculus is a waste of life. Mr. Kimble is in what feels like the seventeenth hour of a lecture about triangles or something. Lily sits in the rear corner of the room with her head down low, discreetly reading Sergei Eisenstein's *Film Form: Essays in Film Theory* on her iPhone.

Eisenstein pioneered montage theory when he made *Battleship Potemkin* in 1925, and practically invented film theory in general. No one has been more influential to moviemaking, except maybe D.W. Griffith, who made a movie about the KKK that Lily has on a DVD she got in a Walmart valuepak for $5. She hasn't watched it yet.

She looks up from her reading to check the time, and to see if Kimble is watching her. He's not, and there are still twenty minutes left of this torture. Lily stretches her neck, which aches from looking down at her phone for the last forty minutes. She looks to her right and sees Kayla at the desk next to her, losing the battle to stay awake. On the other side of Kayla is Mike Wilkinson. He's not that hot, and he doesn't play sports, but everybody likes him, and he has great parties because his parents are drunks. He smiles and sticks his tongue out at her between two fingers. Lily flips him the bird. He chuckles. Lily smiles.

She turns away from Wilkinson and looks out the window beside her. It's sunny out and cars pass by on the street in front of the school. Someone stands by the side of the road. He wears a thick leather jacket and sunglasses, his long curly dark hair wrapped in a bandana, and rests his hand on the Harley next to him. His fiery eyes zero in on her as if the walls don't exist. There is nowhere to hide. He's here for her. Death is here for her.

She blinks and looks back at the window. He's gone. He just vanished. She leans closer to search more of the schoolyard. There's no sign of him. No Harley. No engine roaring away. It's impossible. She knows she saw him there. She's not crazy.

Lily gets up from her seat.

"Miss Hoffman?" Kimble says, halting his lecture.

Lily ignores him. She keeps walking.

"Miss Hoffman?" he says again, attempting to wave her down as she walks from the room.

The hallways are empty because class is in session all over the building. Lily hears the kids in her class laughing behind her. She doesn't care. She closes the Eisenstein book on her iPhone and opens her contacts. The first one says **MOM**. She punches it.

It takes three rings for her mother to pick up, enough time for Lily to make it to the ladies' room. The bathroom is empty.

"Lily?" her mother says. Her voice is accompanied by the low bass beat of lunchtime at the club.

"I saw him, Mom," Lily says. She leans to peek under the stall walls. She sees no feet occupying any of them.

"Saw who?" her mother asks, confused. She's difficult to understand through the music. "What are you talking about?"

"Ted! I saw Ted. He was here watching me."

"What? Hang on."

Lily waits for a moment and the bass beat fades,

then goes away completely.

"You saw him where?" her mother asks.

"At school, Mom," Lily says. She leans in the corner, where the stalls meet the sink countertop. "He was standing outside, watching me."

"Lily," her mother starts. She pauses for a moment, carefully choosing her next words. "There's no way. He's still in prison."

"I haven't had a flashback in two years. This was real," she insists. She's so sure. "He was there."

"You remember what Doctor Edgemar said. Take a deep breath. Look at where you are."

"It wasn't a fucking flashback!" Lily yells into the phone. She can't believe her mother is being so condescending. "I saw him!"

"Okay," her mother says, keeping calm. "What was he doing?"

"He was just standing there, staring at me." Lily turns and rests her elbows on the countertop. She blinks down into the empty sink in front of her.

"Just standing there?"

"Yeah." Lily closes her eyes and takes a deep breath like her doctor always tells her to do.

"And then what?"

"And then he disappeared."

"Where did he go?"

"I—I don't know." The visual of Ted vanishing into thin air like a ninja suddenly makes the whole thing seem so much more insane.

"And he could see you? In that whole school building, he somehow knew right which class you were sitting in?"

"I guess . . . it sounds kinda crazy."

"Lily, he's in prison. He's two thousand miles away. We changed our names. There's no way he found us."

"Yeah," Lily admits. She was practically falling asleep in that class anyway. She might have dreamt the whole thing. "You're right."

"I'll be home early tonight. Why don't we watch some movies and just be lazy?"

"Okay, Mom. That sounds like a plan."

Lily hears someone coming as she hangs up the phone.

The girl who walks in is taller than her by half a head, with shiny golden hair and earth-tone lip gloss matching her tan complexion. Her pink top is cut short to expose her perfect washboard abs and her skinny jeans cost more than Lily makes in two weeks at the video store. The girl fiddles with the silver purity ring that is her signature—and that of anyone who wants to hang out with her. It's Jenny Brunswick. Lily can't stand her.

"I heard you're going to prom with Chris Krohike," Jenny says. She smirks slyly. "Hot."

"That's not true," Lily says. Krohike must be blabbing to people about sleeping with her. She's gonna smack that little nerd when she sees him. "We're just friends. That's all."

"Too bad. You guys would make a cute couple." Jenny snickers. "And it's not like anybody else is gonna ask you."

"What?"

"Well, Marilyn Manson doesn't go here," Jenny says. She cocks her head to the side and smiles. "And I don't think they allow lesbos at the dance. Even lipstick lesbos."

Lily can't believe that bitch is starting this right now. Right away, she wants to tell Jenny she fucked her boyfriend. That would feel real good, but she doesn't want to make a mess for Chad. She likes Chad. She settles for saying something lame.

"Who writes your insults?" Lily says. "Your grand-pa?"

"Who did you blow to get those shoes?" Jenny fires back. "The garbage man?"

Lily looks down at her stiletto boots. *You don't dis the boots . . .*

"Jenny, your roots are showing," Lily says, pointing up to Jenny's hair. "The ones in your hair and the ones from the trailer park."

"Please." Jenny waves her hand dismissively. "You look like a mangy raccoon some hick tried to pass off as a chupacabra carcass." She circles her eyes with her fingers.

Lily steps closer and gets serious.

"You look like something a flea market shopper sharted onto one of those motorized carts through their sweatpants," she says, glaring up at Jenny.

"You look like what my dog grinds into the carpet when he has worms," Jenny says, breathing down at Lily. The bitch is a lot taller than her.

"You look like the after picture from one of those 'three months on meth' P.S.A.s," Lily says. The stench of Taylor Swift's Wonderstruck fragrance is almost too much for her to deal with this close.

"You look like the before picture from an Accutane commercial," Jenny says.

"You look like something Sarah McLachlan would

sing about. You're an abused animal that nobody wants."

"There's a Cards Against Humanity card with just your face on it." Jenny leans in so she's talking right into Lily's nose. "That's all that's on it. Your face."

"You look like Yolandi Visser," Lily says, realizing too late that Jenny has probably never heard of the South African popstar, who looks like a bleached blond and emaciated Cro-Magnon.

"Who?" Jenny scrunches her face in confusion.

"If you knew, you'd be really offended."

"I'm offended by you, sucking every dick in the school."

"At least I'm not a freezer." Lily has finally had enough of this. She doesn't know why she stood here for so long.

"If you give the milk away to *everybody,*" Jenny says, stretching out the last word for emphasis, "then who's gonna buy the cow? Cow."

Lily pushes past Jenny and out into the hall as the bell rings.

"Moo," Jenny lows at her from the bathroom door. Lily looks back at her angrily as she walks down the hall. Jenny moos one more time.

INT. VIDEO TIME – DAY

The horror aisle at Video Time is well-stocked with B-rate gems of the eighties shock video golden age. It's what attracted Lily to this place from the start.

"So are you, from around here?" she asks her new coworker as she replaces a plain white cassette case labeled *Faces of Death* behind its Styrofoam filled and skull adorned box. "I've never seen you around."

"I grew up in a commune," Jeremy says, eyeing the video cover curiously.

"Oh, like a hippie cult thing?"

"Yeah," he says. "Sort of."

"That's interesting," Lily says. She doesn't really think it's interesting. It's messed up, but she likes messed up. She wore the skinniest skinny jeans she has, very low-rise with leather stiletto knee boots and a stretched out black *Army of Darkness* T-shirt that leaves her left shoulder bare. She's trying to get his attention without going quite all in. Nothing is more disappointing than a man who needs a walkthrough.

"It wasn't for me," he says. "I bailed. Figured I wanted to be more like normal people."

"I hear you," Lily says. She makes a point to tug at her leopard-print bra strap only inches away from his chin. This close to him, she catches a whiff of something familiar. He has a smell she recognizes. It isn't clean, like aftershave or cologne. It's not musk. It's not a boy smell. It's something else—something salty?

He ignores her. He grabs a handful of tapes from

the cart and begins shelving them himself. *That's a strike*, she thinks.

"What about you?" he asks. "Are you from around here?"

"Not really." It's a half truth. She wasn't born here, but she's been here for a long time—all of this life, anyway. "My mom bought one of the clubs by the base and we moved here."

"A strip club?" Jeremy asks. There's a tinge of something in his voice. Surprise? Disapproval? She isn't sure.

"Yeah. Why? You got a problem with that?"

"No," he says, shaking his head. She isn't sure whether to believe him. Maybe that weirdo commune made him super religious or something.

"Good," she says. "I want to dance, but I'm not eighteen yet. The money is fantastic."

"Are you promiscuous?"

"The hell is that supposed to mean?" She raises an eyebrow. She thinks he's trying to be sly about getting what he wants. She can play this game.

"Nothing." His answer is cold and robotic. He continues shelving returned tapes.

The next tape Lily picks up is Paul Haggis's 2004 simpering glurgefest *Crash*, a movie so hammy it would make Nicholas Sparks retch. She makes a point to switch the tape with the 1996 Cronenberg movie of the same name—a film which features James Spader fucking an open wound on Rosanna Arquette's leg. She likes to do this when Amy isn't around, in hopes that she'll expose some church lady lame-o to a real masterpiece instead of the trash they thought they were getting.

"Why don't you want to do this anymore?" he asks.

"You mean like what do I really want to do?"

"Yes. What do you really want to do?"

Lily stops, uncertain whether to say. She always struggles with this, because she thinks it makes her sound like a stupid little girl.

"I want to be in movies," she says. "I know it's stupid, but that's what I want to do."

"Why is it stupid?"

She smiles at him, but she doesn't say anything in reply. Unless he's a blithering idiot, he's just being patronizing. She's fine with leaving it at that.

When they've finished putting back all the videos, Lily teaches him how to use the cash register. The point-of-sale system at Video Time is an ancient thing, older than dirt and half as useful. But then that seems to be the case with point-of-sale systems everywhere Lily goes.

"I'm pretty sure this shit computer is older than I am," Lily says. She smashes the cash drawer closed after her second demonstration of how to ring up a sale. The black screen displays a lime green box made up entirely of ASCII characters surrounding the words ###SALE COMPLETE###. "Now you try."

Lily sets a twenty-ounce bottle of refreshing Pepsi® on the counter. He gets it right in exactly one attempt. Press F2 to start the sale. Press F4 to pick a customer from the list of store members or F3 to enter a new one. F5 starts a generic sale for candy and snacks. Scan the tapes to add them to the invoice. Push F8 to continue. Arrow keys select the payment type. Push *Enter.* The computer asks ARE YOU SURE?

Everyone always gets stuck there because it doesn't say what to push, and the usual Y or N keys do nothing. F8 continues and prints a receipt. He gets it, though. Even all the stupid F keys. He does it just as fast as she does.

"I thought you would have more questions," Lily says. She pauses, unsure how to continue. "Do you have more questions?"

He shakes his head. Expressionless. Unblinking. He has the kind of coldness that belies either intense rage or total apathy. Lily can't decide which it is quite yet.

"Okay then." Lily frowns quizzically. "The last thing we need to go over is what to do if somebody robs the store."

"I won't give them anything," he says, shrugging absently. He doesn't say it with the sort of tough guy bravado she would expect from a cocky boy her own age.

"No," she corrects. "I mean, you're supposed to give them everything. Not like it matters. We have like six dollars in the register on our best day. Nobody comes in here."

"Why not?"

"Dude, this place is a front. You realize that, right? Marty, the owner, just uses it to launder money from whatever it is that he does. He's kind of old and I don't think he realizes how obvious it looks. You don't think people actually rent videos when there's Netflix and Amazon? Tapes and DVDs are done. Blu-ray was hardly ever a thing."

"What's Blu-ray?"

"Yeah. Exactly." Lily rolls her eyes. It's a lame

joke, but she laughs anyway. After a second, she realizes he isn't laughing with her.

"Wait. Seriously?" she says.

"Huh? Oh, no. I know what Blu-ray is," he says.

"That's good. You seem so intense all the time. I can't tell when you're joking."

"Yeah," is his only response. He continues to stare back at her with quiet severity.

"Intense." Lily can't deal with him looking at her like that for very long. It's hot, but it's also kind of creepy, like he can see through her down to the soul. "I bet your girlfriend likes that."

He shakes his head.

"I've never had a girlfriend," he says.

INT. LILY'S HOUSE - NIGHT

Lily turns the corner on to her street and sees the reflective lettering of a police car glowing in her headlights. That's unusual. The second car is a cause for fear. It's parked in her driveway.

Lily brings her purple Chevrolet Malibu to a hard stop in front of her house, cutting the engine. She leaves the movies she brought home sitting on the passenger seat as she jumps out. She stomps through the grass to her front door.

"Mom?"

The front door hangs open and the lights are on inside. As she nears the door, she gasps, putting her hand to her mouth. There is a bloody dead thing on the front porch across the welcome mat, so coated in slick red muck she can't tell what it was before—she thinks it might have been part of a horse or a dog. Above the carcass, the front door is smeared with drying blood. It spells out one word, all in caps except for the H.

WhORE

"Mom!" Lily screams.

A suited man she does not know appears framed in the lighted doorway. Tall. Gangly.

"Who are you?" she says, backing away. "Where's my mom?"

"Your mom is fine," says the man in the doorway. "She's down the hall."

Another man leans around the corner of the door, this one wearing a police cap and black and whites. She steps forward.

"The back door is open if you don't want to step over the, uh . . ." the uniform cop points at the thing on the doorstep.

Lily climbs the front steps to the porch, keeping her eyes on the door as she steps over the carcass. She doesn't want to look at it.

She clomps down the hallway toward the kitchen, her boots like bass drums on the wood floor. The house is bigger than most, with an open floor plan and sprawling rooms. The decor everywhere besides Lily's room is mundane: some cookie jars shaped like fat cats, a rainbow-colored painting over the kitchen table, a framed picture of the Beatles on Abbey Road, generally a lot of stuff that Lily's mom got at Target.

"Mom?" she says.

"In here," her mother says.

Lily sets foot into the kitchen and finds her mother at the table in front of a bottle of vodka with a glass in hand. Jeanette Hoffman is a tall woman with blond streaks in her long auburn hair. She's still wearing her work clothes—shredded jeans and a tube top. A detective wearing a cornflower blue tie sits at the table, not across, but next to her.

"Lily," her mother says. "I want you to meet Detective Burnett."

"You already met Detective Lowrey," says cornflower tie. He motions down the hall toward the guys at the front door.

"Yeah," Lily says. She scrunches her face at her mother, wondering if she's drunk. "What happened?"

"Your mother came home this evening and found some remains," Burnett says. His tone is bland. He smirks. He's going for the soft sell.

"I feel so silly about it now." Jeanette laughs.

"She called us," Burnett says. He's dismissing the whole thing already, Lily can tell. "Turns out it was just a cow head. We think it's from a butcher shop. Probably some neighborhood kids."

"Neighborhood kids?" Lily says. "Do the children of the corn live on this block? There's an animal sacrifice in the yard! Did you tell them I saw Ted this afternoon?"

"Lily, we talked about that," Jeanette says.

"It was him! I saw him!" Lily shrieks in disbelief. She doesn't understand why they won't listen.

"New York State Department of Corrections confirmed for me earlier that Mr. Smalls is currently incarcerated pending his parole hearing next month," Burnett says.

"Did you miss the front door somehow? He has a whole gang of biker lackeys! He could have sent any of them!"

"We see every kind of vandalism imaginable, Miss Hoffman." Burnett smiles reassuringly. "Just last week, a kid spray-painted 'fascists' across the front doors at the Galleria. He didn't even spell it right."

"Do they hire just anybody to be cops now?"

"We're monitoring the situation. If Ted comes here after his release and commits any crimes, we'll put him away."

"Yeah," Lily says. "That'll be awesome when I'm already dead."

"Officer Burnett knows what he's doing." Jeanette pats Burnett's hand on the kitchen table. "Do you and your partner want to stay for a while? I have some steaks I could grill up."

"I can't believe this." Lily rolls her eyes.

"What?" Jeanette asks.

"We're gonna be murdered, and you're playing badge bunny."

"Lily, you're overreacting."

"You weren't there. He didn't tell you he would hunt you to the ends of the earth for what you did!" Lily hammers the table with her tightened fists. Her mother's glass of vodka rattles. "He *told* me!"

Burnett slowly inches his chair away from the table. He looks like he really doesn't want to be here.

"Stop screaming," Jeanette says softly, holding up her hand to talk Lily down.

"Then get your fucking head out of Inspector Gadget's ass and do something!" Lily turns and stomps away.

"Lily!" Jeanette stands from the table.

Lily clomps back down the hallway and up the stairs to her room. Her mother shouts after her, but doesn't follow.

In her room, Lily throws herself down on the bed and cries into a pillow. No one is going to help her. Her mother can't do anything. The police are about as useful as horror movie cops. They don't even care. If they were anything like the heroes in the movies she loves, this would never have happened at all.

She loses herself quickly. She's back in the old kitchen, at the house where she used to live, in another life. Ted is there, and he's angry. He's like a giant in her imagination. She was so tiny then, and she feels so much smaller with him hovering over her. His breath is black smoke. His eyes are red in her memory. Her mother cowers in the corner, squealing like a frightened child.

Suddenly, the front door crashes down; the room shakes as it hits the floor. A foot comes through the doorframe from the glowing white nothingness outside. A tall man with receding brown hair and serious eyes steps into the kitchen pointing a massive revolver at Ted. It's Dirty Harry.

Ted picks Lily up from the ground, putting a switchblade to her throat. He feels weaker than Lily remembers. Like she might be able to overpower him, even as a small child.

"You'll never take me alive, Callahan!" Ted says.

With one hand, Dirty Harry raises his .44 Magnum. It's the most powerful handgun in the world (and will blow your head clean off). He shakes his head, grim faced as always.

"Go ahead," Harry says. "Make my day."

Lily elbows Ted in the balls and runs. Harry shoots him with the Magnum, not once but all six times. Then he reloads, shooting Ted six more times just for good measure.

"You okay, little girl?" Dirty Harry asks.

She's not okay. This is just a fantasy. She's alone in her room and Dirty Harry is not real. He won't be coming to save her.

EXT. SCHOOL CAFETERIA – DAY

The next fourteen hours are a sleepless mass of rage and angst and fear and nothing really coherent at all. Lily doesn't speak another word until she's five minutes from the end of lunch break and staring down a peanut butter and jelly sandwich she hasn't taken one bite from.

She quietly slipped out of the house this morning while Jeanette was in the shower. She doesn't know how long she can avoid her mother, but right now she hopes she can keep it up forever.

The gory animal head was gone when she went out the front door, but the bloody writing was still there. She tried not to look at it as she left. It called to her anyway. It taunted her. It threatened her. It made her feel powerless.

"So what'll happen if he gets out?" The question is all she's been able to think about for more than half a day, but hearing it from another person suddenly makes it so much more real.

She snaps out of her terror trance to look at Kayla, sitting next to her in the cafeteria.

"I don't know." Lily pokes at the peanut butter and jelly sandwich like a really careless scientist investigating the black goo from LV-223. "They'll probably find me dead in a ditch somewhere—if they find me at all."

"Come on," Kayla says, taking an emphatically cheery tone. It seems out of place from a girl wearing a Robert Smith T-shirt and eating out of a *Crow* lunch box. "It can't be that serious."

"The guy has his own satanic biker gang." Lily buries her face in her hands. "Literally. They worship the devil. He's been in gunfights. I think he's killed people. He carries a broken jagged baseball bat. He calls it the peacekeeper."

"You could hire a three-hundred-pound guy to follow you around like Britney Spears." Kayla laughs.

"Yeah. Not funny."

"Sorry."

The conversation crashes there, and after an awkward moment of silence, Lily begins to melt back into her solitary pit of despair. Kayla heroically changes the subject.

"So Jessica said there's some hot guy working at the video store now?"

"Oh." Lily forgot about the boy at the video store. Crushing on boys seems so trivial right now. "Yeah, he's weird. I don't know."

"What do you mean?"

"He just doesn't talk much. He said he grew up in a cult or something. I think he might be gay."

"Aw. That sucks," Kayla says. "Where does he go to school?"

"I don't think he does."

INT. MORSTON PARKING ENFORCEMENT - DAY

The hollow man walks into the office of the Morston Parking Enforcement Authority and takes a bite from the steak in his left hand as he scans the room for threats. He sees none. A sign directs him to a service window which appears to be bullet resistant. He steps in front of the window and knocks to get the attention of the obese man on the other side.

"Hi," he says. "You took my car. I'm here to get it back."

The fat little man is taken aback as he looks up from his Michael-Scott Earle paperback and says "Are you eating a steak raw?"

"Is there another way to eat steak?" the hollow man asks, with a tinge of skepticism. He loves steak, and he always eats it this way. He chomps another bite from the red meat and feels runny red juice spatter his chin. The fat man doesn't answer, so he shrugs and moves on to the next order of business. "I need my truck back. Sign said they took it here."

He means the sign near the spot where he left his truck parked this morning in downtown Morston. After only a few hours running errands and exploring the city on foot, he returned to find no truck at all. After reading a warning sign posted nearby, he concluded the vehicle must have been towed by mistake. The sign he parked next to was clearly marked NO PARKING EXCEPT TRUCK LOADING. The vehicle *is* a truck, and he was planning to load it later.

The parking attendant's face turns from bewilderment to pure lethargy. "We'll need to see your license, registration, proof of insurance, VIN number, and all fees must be paid in cash."

The hollow man sighs. He has none of those things. He took that truck from a dead man. "I don't have time for this."

INT. VIDEO TIME – NIGHT

"In local news, the Morston Police Department is looking for the man who drove a pickup truck through the fence at the city impound lot just about an hour ago," reports news anchor Don Braun. The picture on the old video store TV shifts to a little woman in a flower hat standing in front of a collapsed fence strung with police tape. A puffy black microphone hovers near her chin.

"Errbody was runnin' up in there gettin' they cars!" she says. "I said lawdy it's a free giveaway! Robin Hood came here today! Robbin' from the rich and givin' to the poor!"

Lily wonders if that sound bite is worth auto-tuning and uploading to YouTube.

She kneels in front of a shelving unit with a tough-built and reliable DeWALT® cordless power drill. She decided hours ago that the best thing would be to keep on plowing ahead. Some kind of project might help her stop dwelling on her problem. She's assembling a new shelf that they can use for all the adult movies Amy wants organized. She wanted to assemble the whole thing in the back room alone while Jeremy watched the front of the store, but he still hasn't appeared, so she's started working on it at the front of the store. She'll worry about hauling it to the stock room somehow later.

She's still working on the shelving unit, and nearly certain they'll never see Jeremy again, when she hears a thundering engine outside. She looks up to see him stepping out of a big brown Chevy pickup with no muffler to speak of and plenty of rust holes, wide enough to toss a baseball through.

"You're late," Lily says, as he comes through the door. She squeezes the trigger to drill the air threateningly.

"I got held up in a business meeting," Jeremy says. It's a ridiculous lie. Nobody who needs a job at this video store could possibly have any sort of business meetings outside of the occasional small time dope deal.

"Somehow, I don't believe that," she says.

Jeremy shrugs. He's not even trying to hide it. He just doesn't give a fuck—and there's something she likes about that.

"I won't tell Amy," she says. "But you have to move this shelving unit to the back for me when I'm done."

"Deal," he replies. He picks up a stray movie from the counter and looks it over. It's Stephen Spielberg's 1982 blockbuster hit, *E.T. the Extra-Terrestrial.*

Lily goes back to drilling. The old units they use only have peg holes every two feet, so they drill new ones every seven inches to have more shelves for DVDs. She drills another hole in the side of the unit and looks up to see Jeremy still examining the same video box.

"It's a classic," Lily says.

"It looks really strange," Jeremy says. He sets the box down on the counter.

"It's *E.T.*" Lily gives him an incredulous glare. "You've never seen *E.T.?*"

"No." He shakes his head. "Is it a horror movie?"

"No! It's a kids' movie." She pauses for a second.

"Well, actually, it started off as a horror movie, but some stuff happened with that, and then it was supposed to have a horror movie sequel . . . it's a long story."

"But there's a monster," Jeremy says, staring back at her in cold disbelief.

"Yeah, but he's a nice monster. He just wants to go home."

"That sounds stupid." He picks up another video case from the counter. *Poltergeist.*

"You really don't know what *E.T.* is?" Lily puts the drill on the counter.

He shakes his head.

"What's the best movie you've ever seen?" she asks. She leans across the counter and ogles him, waiting for a response.

He takes a moment, and when he does answer, what he says is slow and uncertain.

"*Batman?*" he says, asking more than telling. He watches her for approval.

"Okay . . . I can see that," Lily says. "Burton *Batman* or Nolan *Batman?*"

"The one with the shark in it."

"Are you fucking kidding me?" Lily squeals. "Are you kidding me right now? You're talking about the sixty-six *Batman?*" Lily smacks him in the shoulder. He means the Adam West *Batman.* The one nobody likes. "What do you have, like, a major hard-on for Lee Meriwether or something?"

"I don't know." He stares back at her ambiguously, as if waiting for her to attack or shapeshift into a twenty foot snake and snap at him. It makes her uncomfortable.

"What else?" she says, putting an end to the awkward staring contest. "What's your second favorite movie of all time?"

"Adam Sandler," he says. Lily waits for him to elaborate. He does not. She is forced to follow up.

"Which Adam Sandler?"

"The one with the brain damage," he says. It certainly narrows down which actor he's talking about, but not which movie. Lily can't think of one where Sandler plays a character who's supposed to have brain damage.

"I don't even think that's a movie," Lily says. "I have no idea what you're talking about."

He scrunches his nose at that.

"What about *Scarface*?" Lily asks.

Jeremy shakes his head. Nope. Mob movies aren't for everybody, though.

"*Terminator*?" He has to have seen *Terminator*.

"No."

"*Star Wars*?" Lily leans forward to glare at him in menacing anticipation.

He steps back as she encroaches. "No," he admits. "But I've heard of that. Is it good?"

"What. The. Fuck. You haven't seen *Star Wars*? Were your parents luddites or something? Were you, like, born blind and you just recently regained your vision through a miracle of science?"

"I can only see what they show in the theater."

"We can't let this go on," Lily says, walking away from the counter toward the science fiction movies. "I'm educating you myself."

The next step is finding a *Star Wars* DVD and loading it into the player on the counter near them.

Truthfully, she doesn't care that much if he's seen it. Assembling shelving wasn't enough of a distraction, and she's just looking for an excuse to find a better one.

The two of them sit through the first *Star Wars* movie almost uninterrupted; the sole exception being some preteens who wander in from the nearby Section 8 housing to look at the candy. Jeremy doesn't say a word through the entire movie and Lily almost forgets about her demons for a while. Almost.

When the credits roll, he turns and asks a question.

"Why did he turn off the targeting computer to fire the torpedo at the end?"

"Because he used the force. Obi-Wan says 'Use the force, Luke.' It's one of the most epic moments in the history of cinema."

"It's stupid. It's an obvious tactical misstep."

"It worked."

"So? He got lucky. It would've worked even better if he was actually aiming the torpedo."

"But then he wouldn't be using the force and the end would be boring. It's just how movies work, dude. The hero learns an important lesson during his journey and then uses what he learned to overcome overwhelming odds at the end of the story. He doesn't just have a computer do it for him."

"And the only reason he succeeds at all is that Han Solo guy just happens to come back at the right moment. What was his contingency plan in case that didn't happen?"

"I don't know."

"His plan was to fail the mission."

"You're one of those people that like itemizes fast

food receipts for your taxes, aren't you?"

"I always have a plan."

"Oh my God, you nerd." Lily shakes her head at him. "Come on, and let's close this bitch up."

As she turns again to the front of the store, someone rips the door wildly open just as she reaches for the handle. She doesn't have time to register what's happening before she's shoved to the tile floor.

She looks up at a man in a black leather jacket, dark curly hair wrapped in a bandana. He has a fading tattoo of a teardrop under his left eye. He's tall, and from her place on the floor he looks like a giant. He yells at her and waves something around. It's a gun.

"Hey! I know you . . ." she starts. He's the man who was watching her at school.

"Get on the ground, bitch! Get on the ground!"

"Seriously?" Lily says. "I can't get any more on the ground!"

"I said on the ground!" the robber yells. "Don't look at me!"

He points the gun directly at her face. It's a big black six-shooter like she's seen a thousand times in cop movies from the seventies, but this is the first time she's ever stared down the barrel for real. She flattens against the floor as much as she possibly can.

The thug turns the gun on Jeremy.

"You! Open the registers!" he shouts.

Jeremy frowns briefly. He tilts his head slightly, his eyes moving up and down the thug across the counter. He looks like he's completely spaced out—so scared he's not connected to reality anymore.

"He doesn't have the keys!" Lily says, jangling the

keys in her hand. The gun whips back to her.

"Next time you open your cunt mouth you get a lead salad in your fucking face!" the robber says, snatching the keys from her hand.

He turns the gun back to Jeremy, pointing it with his arm outstretched over the counter.

"Open the register!" he says.

Jeremy wrests the gun away and breaks the thug's arm in two places. He pulls the guy across the counter and elbows him in the face. Blood splatters all over the countertop, squirting into the air as the robber falls backward onto the tile next to Lily.

Jeremy fires a single shot through the front window of the store, missing the robber completely. Seconds later Lily hears the crunch of a car in the parking lot and realizes what he did. He's killed the robber's get-away driver.

Jeremy hurdles the counter, landing between Lily and the robber. The guy is mumbling something about his arm when Jeremy reaches down with one hand and hoists him to his feet, then slams him against the counter.

"Who sent you?" Jeremy says. He asks the question the same way people ask what the soup of the day is, or what's on the television. It's unsettling.

"My arm, man! You broke my arm!" the thug screams. The arm dangles from the elbow, held there only by soft flesh.

Jeremy grabs the man's dangling hand and plants his foot on the robber's chest, forcing him back against the counter. He growls like an animal as he tugs backward with his upper body, tearing the arm free. Lily sees strings of tendon stretching and ripping and has to look away. The robber's screams fill her ears. These are the worst sounds she's ever heard from a human being.

Jeremy smacks the robber in the head with the severed forearm. Blood erupts from the open end of the limb as it makes contact with the cowering robber.

"Who sent you?" Jeremy shouts.

"All right! All right!" the robber says. A fountain of crimson pours from his shredded stump and runs down the side of the counter. Some of it squirts onto Jeremy, but he doesn't seem to care. "Some guy in Riker's! Used to ride with Chino! Said he'd hook us up with fifty stacks if we did the girl and made it look like a robbery or some shit!"

"Her?" Jeremy says.

"Me!" Lily shrieks. "I knew it! Fucking Ted!" Ted is in Riker's. Ted rides a motorcycle. Ted wants to kill her.

Jeremy hits him again with the severed arm.

The thug slumps against the counter, either blacked out from the pain or dead from blood loss; Lily can't be sure which. It doesn't matter. Jeremy shoots the robber in the face a second later, then twice in the chest.

Then he turns his attention to her. She doesn't know what to say; what to do. Words start to form, but they don't mean anything. He stares at her with his coal-black gaze, the gun smoking in his hand. Then he comes toward her.

Lily closes her eyes as he reaches for her. She squeaks, certain the next thing she'll feel will be the icy touch of death.

He reaches past her to grab a yellow stand-up sign

propped against the wall behind her. He stands it in the middle of the ocean of blood on the floor surrounding the dead robber. WET FLOOR—PISO MOJADO. Lily can't believe what she's seeing.

"This isn't my problem," he grumbles. He turns to leave.

"Wait," Lily says. "Where are you going? Who are you?"

"Trust me," he says, turning to look back at her with those nothing eyes. "The less you know, the better."

He walks out the front door into the dark night. She remains kneeling on the floor, frozen with fright as she hears the loud rumble of his ancient Chevy pulling out of the lot.

It takes a long time for the police to get there. Someone called in about the car outside, its fender bent around a telephone pole near the street. Lily is still sitting on the floor when they find her. The first cop coaxes her outside and sits her on the back of his cruiser. Amy gets there as more cops wind yellow crime scene tape around the parking lot and Lily sits on the back of an ambulance. They give her a blanket. She doesn't understand why. She isn't cold. Amy sits down with her and immediately goes into hug overdrive.

The cop talking to her is named Dillon. He's a husky black man with glasses and a purple button-up shirt. He doesn't have a tie. Most cops have ties. She keeps hanging on that. He keeps asking her the same questions. She answers them the same way, but the answers don't make sense—not even to her.

"So he sawed off the arm and hit him with it?" Dillon says.

"No. There was no saw. He didn't have anything."

"He just pulled the guy's arm off?"

"It wasn't like he just plucked it off all *Beowulf* style. He had to tug on it—a lot. It was disgusting."

"Are you going to keep asking her the same questions all night?" Amy says.

"We're just doing our job," Dillon says.

Another investigator taps Dillon on the shoulder. The other guy has a manila folder that he keeps closed, but Lily recognizes it. It's the W-4 and other papers Jeremy filled out when they hired him. Amy says something to Lily about making it home okay, but Lily doesn't hear. She's listening to the cops.

"All of this is shit," the other cop says. "Driver's license and social belong to a Chinese kid two counties over. The address he used on the forms is the public library."

"Who is this guy?" Dillon says.

INT. MAXIMUM SECURITY FACILITY - DAY

The inside of this place is every bit as sterile and cold as Helen expected. She's never been to a prison before. The main corridor is tiled in white with little grey specks. An inmate in an orange jumpsuit mops the floor ahead of them. None of the caged prisoners on either side of the corridor whistle or hoot at her. She might be a little insulted. Pantsuits must not get them going.

The doctor is a short guy with a beer gut, gray beard, and thick-rimmed black glasses. McElroy is his name. Helen already doesn't like him, but she can't put a finger on exactly why. She follows him down the corridor with the commander.

"He's been asking to see you since he saw this morning's paper," McElroy tells the commander. "He wouldn't stop screaming. I wanted to give him a sedative but I couldn't find anyone willing to go in the cell with him."

"You give him newspapers?" the commander asks. He sounds stern, although his slight and perpetual tone of disappointment is just a little more pronounced. He's a tall man, a bit taller than Helen, and she stands at six feet. He wears a brown trench coat that makes him look terribly unofficial, but he isn't very interested in keeping up appearances.

"I think it's good to keep him stimulated," McElroy says.

"You shouldn't let him have newspapers," the commander says.

"What's he going to do?" McElroy sneers. "Paper-cut somebody to death?"

"Just stop giving him newspapers."

"You know, Mister . . ." he pauses to have the name filled in for him, but that never happens. "I'm seriously considering filing a formal complaint with the Board of Corrections over the way this patient is treated."

"He's a patient now?"

"Yes. He's my patient, and he's obviously seriously mentally disturbed. Of course, I don't know the extent of his history because every file I request that might say anything pertinent has everything except for the page numbers redacted. I have to assume your department has something to do with that?"

"Yup." The commander nods with a cocky grin.

"And what department is that exactly?"

"The NYDB."

"The NYDB?"

"Yeah. None of Your Damn Business."

As they approach the end of the corridor, Helen sees a red door ahead. A guard steps forward and offers up a sign-in sheet on a wooden clipboard. The commander thumbs at the clipboard for her to sign.

"Of course." McElroy rolls his eyes. "And how exactly am I supposed to treat this patient with no access to his medical or criminal history?"

Helen takes notice that there are no other names on the sign-in sheet.

"You don't," the commander says. "Leave him in the box and forget about it."

The commander opens the door into a large open room. A dozen armed guards stand around the outskirts along the wall. Some of them are dressed in full riot gear and carry submachine guns. They look like they're ready for a helicopter insertion into Iraq, not a shift in a correctional facility. What they're guarding is even more bizarre.

In the center of the room, encircled by a crudely spray-painted black line on the floor, is a fifteen-by-fifteen bulletproof glass cell. Inside is a pale, naked figure with a grizzly black beard and filthy hair hanging down past his shoulders. He punches the glass with a slow rhythm, again and again, each punch smearing new wet blood on the stain that is already old and dried. As they get closer, Helen can read the fading word tattooed in lopsided clumsy script across his chest: RAPEGOD.

There's something familiar about him—something she can't quite place. She knows that face somehow. She studies it through the thick black beard. She remembers: two years ago, she intercepted a photograph while working at NSA which she believed was connected to secret forces within the United States government. She was able to connect the man in the photo to an engagement inside Mecca with the Saudi National Guard, and a black box recording from a crashed Saudi airliner. As soon as she started making noise about it to the Special Operations Group, some jerks in a black van grabbed her and offered her a job working for the very same supposedly non-existent bastards she was investigating: Graveyard. She never identified the man in the photo.

"Who is this guy?" Helen asks.

"He's the deadliest man alive," the commander answers.

"He always hits the exact same spot," says the guard closest to them. "Been at it for over a year. I don't think he can break it, but God help us if he does."

"How're you doing, Sam?" the commander asks.

"I'm as good as you can be doing this gig," says the guard.

"Who painted the circle around the cage?"

"That's the ten foot line. Dick Stehlin did that after an orderly lost some fingers. A few days later the subject killed him."

Helen looks to the box for any place the prisoner might be able to reach out or grab someone. There are only some tiny air holes, not big enough for a finger, and a slot for sliding in food. Then she notices there aren't any other objects in the cell. There is no bed, no toilet—though there *is* a hole in the floor. She spies the newspapers mentioned by McElroy.

"How'd he do that?" she asks.

"He just looked at him and Dick dropped dead," Sam tells them. "I mean, Dick was getting old, but if you see the tape . . . none of us look him in the eyes anymore. I don't think you should, either."

The man inside the box stops hitting the glass and turns his glare toward the commander. Helen doesn't like this. She doesn't like this place. She doesn't like this man they keep in a box. She doesn't like his eyes. She doesn't like the way that guard said *the subject* as if his name was some unknown or unspeakable thing. She doesn't like the horrid grin stretching his face.

"I'm not afraid of the bastard," the commander says. Helen watches him step forward, right past the painted line on the floor, marching up to the bloody spot on the big glass box. She moves to follow.

"Walter," the prisoner says. "Your friend is pretty. I'm going to sodomize her."

He leans forward and licks the bloody glass. Helen decides it best to stay behind the ten foot line. She stops where she stands.

"It's been a long time, Victor," Walter says.

"You should try spending it in here."

"What do you want? I don't have all day for your bullshit."

"I know where Sid is hiding."

"And how would you possibly know that?"

"Easy."

"Prove it."

"If I told you, I wouldn't have anything to bargain with, would I?"

"And if you don't give me a reason to believe you, then you don't have anything to bargain with, do you?"

Victor smiles. He peers over Walter's shoulder and wiggles his tongue at Helen.

"There are plans, contingencies the old man forced us to prepare for. Passphrases, locker combinations, smoke signals, safe houses, locations . . ."

"He's following one of those contingency plans," Walter concludes.

"I know which one now. I can show you right to him." Victor smiles. His teeth are yellowing and filthy. "For a price."

"And that would be?"

"The Lindemann device."

"The what? I don't know what you're talking about."

"It's in your vault. I know it is. An associate told me all about it before she met with an unfortunate accident."

"You gutted her," Walter briskly counters. "I saw

the body."

Victor shrugs. "Bring me the case. It's just for my entertainment. It won't hurt anyone."

"You're a terrible negotiator, Victor," Walter says.

Walter turns his back on the cage and walks away. Victor punches the glass again.

"You know you can't find him without me!" he yells.

Walter points to Helen. "I'm going to need copies of all the newspapers he's seen in the last week." That's going to be her job." Walter turns to McElroy. "You don't give him access to anything else, right? TV? Internet? Yoga classes? A waterslide?"

"I've had about enough of your remarks and . . ." McElroy starts to say.

Walter catches McElroy by the necktie, shoving him against the wall.

Behind them, Victor laughs as he wildly pounds on the cage. "You're all gonna die! I'll kill you all! I'm gonna open you up and shit in your guts!"

"And what?" Walter barks into McElroy's face. "You'll report me?"

Victor continues to curse at all of them. "I'll stab you in the throat and fuck the hole!"

"Think about this, McElroy. Understand this," Walter says. "Every night, when you go to sleep, I get to decide whether you wake up in the morning."

Walter sets the doctor loose and the little man slinks away as Walter leaves the room. Helen glances at McElroy on the way out.

"It's true," Helen says.

INT. DEVIL'S HORSEMEN MOTORCYCLE CLUB
- UPSTATE NEW YORK - DAY

It is two in the afternoon by the time Gill Davies wakes up from last night's bender, pays the hooker on his couch to leave, smokes a little crank to get going, throws his cut on, and makes it down to the clubhouse. The inside of the clubhouse is messier than usual. A couple tables are knocked over and whiskey bottles are all over the floor. Iron Maiden's "Bring Your Daughter to the Slaughter" is blasting on the club's old wood furniture speaker system. Sweet Tits is behind the bar pouring Wild Turkey for Duck Dick and Lawrence. Poochie has a fold-out map of the West Coast spread over the bar and he's looking it over with Bald Sack, the acting president of the motorcycle club.

"You get my text?" Bald Sack asks, scratching flakes of dead skin from his beard. His eyes are bloodshot and baggy, more so than usual.

"Phone's broke," Gill says. Someone bet him he couldn't bite through it last night. They lost that bet and Gill won five dollars.

"Fingers and the prospect are dead," Poochie says.

"Holy Hell. Sack, you okay?" Gill asks.

"I look okay to you?" Sack snaps back. He does not look okay to Gill at all. "They killed my boy, Gill. My boy." The news is a shock. Fingers was a rough kid. He grew up in the club running drugs and guns, knocking over liquor stores, pimping, and dropping a few bodies along the way. He was no pussy, and everybody liked him.

"What happened?"

"They went out west looking for that harlot that locked Ted Smalls up, and somebody invoked violence from the depths of the collective unconscious on them," Poochie says. Poochie has been saying some really weird shit since he went back to school and got that philosophy degree.

"We gonna go get us some then?" Gill says.

Poochie nods. "It is impossible to suffer without making someone pay for it; every complaint already contains revenge. Friedrich Nietzche."

"Damn straight," Bald Sack says. "Saddle up. All six of us are going. It's a two day ride. We're gonna find that little slut, and when we do we're gonna do her up worse than that probie that ratted on Booger Lips."

"Let's split the bitch open," Gill says.

EXT. SCHOOL YARD - DAY

"So think about it," Kayla says. She has to speak loudly to be heard amidst the chaos of all the cars jammed up on their way out of the school parking lot. High school kids tend to drive hand-me-downs and whatever used clunkers they could afford flipping burgers. It makes the three o'clock hour noisier than it needs to be.

It's nice out today and the girls sat at a picnic bench in front of the building. Lily's iPhone hasn't stopped jingling all day. She couldn't make it ten feet through the hallways without kids she didn't even know stopping her to ask about what happened. The story grew throughout the day. First she heard it was three guys; then five. Then they all had machine guns. In the most entertaining version, Jeremy punched through one of them, ripping out his heart and eating it.

"About what?" Lily says. She tilts her head to eye Kayla incredulously over the rims of her sunglasses.

"He just shows up out of nowhere," Kayla says. "Fake name. Fake ID. Fake everything. He's mysterious and aloof. Handsome and quiet. He exhibits supernatural strength."

"Don't say it." Lily stares across the table at Kayla through narrowed eyes.

"He's a vampire." Kayla whispers the word while looking around to make sure no one else is listening.

Lily hides her face in her hands.

"He killed those men to protect you." Kayla puts her hand to her chest. "What if he's just like Edward?" she squeals.

"You're seriously retarded right now." Lily lies down on the picnic bench and stares up at the blue sky.

"Whatever," Kayla says as she rips open a bag of crunchy cheese flavored Cheetos®. "He ripped off some dude's arm. That's, like, so hard."

"I know. I was there, remember?" She closes her eyes and she can see it again, as if it's happening right in front of her. It's horrific every time she pictures it, and yet she keeps doing it—viewing it over and over all day. "I'm probably gonna be messed up forever because I saw it."

"You were already messed up." Kayla laughs.

"Yeah, well, whatever."

"I think it's the stuff you *don't* know that makes it really fucking spooky."

"What's that supposed to mean?"

"The blood and guts is gross and whatever, but it's spooky because we don't have any idea why. That's what I keep thinking about. Why was he here? Where does he come from? Where did he go? Think about it. There's this guy out there who's obviously not just a guy. He could be anywhere, and he's pretending to be one of us for some reason we don't know. How spooky is that?"

"You're right," Lily says. She thought about it plenty, but she isn't any closer to an answer. The best she can figure, he was like Viggo Mortensen in *A History of Violence*. He was a hitman for the mob and things got ugly, so he went into hiding. That story doesn't make sense, but it's the best she can do. "It's a little spooky."

"I still think he sounds hot," Kayla says. "Edward drives a way nicer car, but we can talk about it."

The comment spurs Lily to think of something she hadn't before. She picks up her *Invader Zim* backpack from the picnic table and walks away.

"Lily?" Kayla shouts after her. "Don't go. I'm sorry."

She looks back at her friend.

"It's cool, Kayla. I have to go. I'll call you tomorrow."

"Okay?" Kayla shrugs.

Lily leaves school in her Malibu and takes a detour past the mall to be sure. She sees what she's looking for. It sits parked at the corner of the movie theater lot: a rusted brown Chevy pickup truck.

INT. GRAVEYARD - DAY

It takes Helen less than an hour to retrieve the newspapers Walter wants and then she's on her way to meet him back at the building. The gate men wave her on as she flashes her security pass at them, and she drives up the only road there is beyond the ten foot fence surrounding the company compound.

The desert sun burns brightly outside, but it is cool in the Hummer H2, with the air conditioning on high. She's halfway up to the building when her phone rings, interrupting the Glenn Beck radio program. The touch screen display on the stereo says Matt is calling. She takes it on the Bluetooth.

"Hey, what's up?" Helen says.

"Guess what I got you," her husband says excitedly over the car's speakers.

"Mmmmmm," she hums. "I don't know. A vacation?"

"I'll give you a hint. It's a first edition."

"*Sense and Sensibility?*" Helen guesses. She collects rare books as a hobby and she's been looking for a first run of that one for years.

"Nope. Not that one."

"I don't know. What is it?"

"You'll have to wait and see when you get home," Matt says.

"About that," Helen says. She bites her lip. "We have this thing at work. I probably won't be home for a couple of days."

"What kind of thing?" Matt asks. He sounds disappointed, but not angry. Yet.

"I can't really talk about it." This argument has been going in circles since she took this job. It isn't going to get any better today.

"Can you talk about anything you do?"

"No." Helen sighs.

"So that's not really a surprise."

"You're the one who said you could use some space."

"Not this much. I haven't seen you in a week, babe. Before that, you were gone for five days. You're hardly ever home."

"Yeah. And you never went away with the navy."

"No. Never," he says. His words wobble with false zeal. It's a damn lie. Matt left her alone at their house in Maryland for months at a time when he was deployed with the SEALs.

"Really? You're gonna stick to that?"

"I just don't understand. When I got out of the Navy we were talking about settling down, starting a family, and then you suddenly want us to up and move to the other side of the country and you never talk to me about anything. What happened? What are we doing?"

"Look," Helen says. "I'll take some time off after this project. We can go to the cabin."

"Fine. We'll talk about this later."

Helen pulls up in front of the building.

"All right. I have to go."

She hangs up and steps out of the Hummer. Matt might not believe a lot of what Helen does even if she told him. Most people think her job is a myth, and the people who don't are usually crazy.

Helen is the number two at Graveyard, the private

military wing of the shadowy group that actually controls the world—well, at least the western half of it. Any time a farmer reports seeing black helicopters in the vicinity of mysterious cattle mutilations—that's Graveyard. When creepy guys wearing sunglasses at night show up to tell somebody what they *didn't* see—that's Graveyard. The people who actually shot down United 93, The AT&T longlines mind control project, JFK, gangstalking—all Graveyard. Slenderman—accidental, but Graveyard. MKUltra—that was the CIA . . . but Graveyard helped at little.

The company's building stands ahead of her, ten stories tall, in the desolation of the Arizona desert. The glass front appears shining black in the sun. Helen has wondered since she first saw the place just why so much of the building is constructed from glass. It doesn't lend itself well to combat or secrecy—two major interests of the company.

She enters the lobby and finds the usual two security guards manning the metal detector in front of the stairs leading to the overlooking balcony. She walks across the tile floor, briefcase in hand, and smiles at the guards. They're clad in black fatigues, riot helmets, and heavy ballistic vests bearing the company's ominous logo: a human skull with vampire fangs over crossed bones. It includes no numbers, names, slogans, or departmental or regimental markings. It is not very complex, and might even be called generic amongst military patches. Walter once told Helen that was the intention. It's a scary picture just for the sake of being a scary picture—and easily confused with a lot of other military markings.

The stairs take her up to the balcony where the

two elevators going to the other floors can be accessed. She boards one and pushes the button for floor ten.

Walter is waiting for her in his office.

"That was quick," he says.

"It wasn't hard. I went to the newspaper's offices. I probably could've gone to Barnes & Noble."

She drops the stack of newspapers on his desk. Walter keeps this room like something out of the 1960s. He has a plastic globe on a wooden stand, a rotary phone, and a green desk lamp that Don Draper would call passé.

"I've seen him before," Helen says. "In a picture I saw at the NSA. I think you know the one."

"I know the one," Walter says.

"Who is he?"

Walter opens up the first paper and begins leafing through, though scanning for what Helen can't say.

"We don't actually know what he is," Walter says. "We only know that the old man is responsible."

"The old man? You mean Ivan Hansen? Kill Team One?" Helen never met the legendary assassin in person, but she knows all the stories. No person or unit ever racked up a higher kill count. He was a one-man wrecking crew, able to compete with whole squads of soldiers. He became Kill Team One by himself after he was the only member to return alive from so many missions that the old Graveyard commander stopped assigning him teammates. He didn't need them anyway. Ivan Hansen was practically a mythological demigod to the mercenaries of Graveyard, and to a number of raving conspiracy theorists that had managed to obtain not-quite-redacted-enough documents.

He was eventually crippled in a secret operation, and retired. His current whereabouts are unknown. "You're telling me Ivan Hansen made him somehow?"

"Yeah. After Van's injury, he got pretty loopy for a while. Started talking about preparing for the future. Before I knew it, he had these kids out in a shack in the woods. I don't know how, but I don't think they're entirely human. We don't know what he did—if they're genetically manipulated or mystically empowered. I'd visit them and I would see things ... toddlers stabbing men to death, shooting at live targets. We provided him with detainees from Iraq and Afghanistan for a time. He would put them in a cage with the prisoners and say 'kill.' Early on the victims would be tied down. Later he stopped tying them down. Then he started adding more men. You ever seen a ten-year-old get in a cage with a dozen grown men and rip them all to pieces? That's a rhetorical question. I know you haven't."

"You mean it worked?"

"Too well. Victor Hansen is the most brutal killer the world has ever seen. His proficiency in combat is superhuman. He slaughters infantry platoons by himself. If you believe the guards outside that box, he kills men by looking at them. He knows nothing but violence. He believes in it like it's his god. He murders the way most of us breathe, and left to his own devices, he would kill every man, woman, and child on this planet. Van himself put Victor in the box. If he ever gets out, he's never going back in."

"Then why don't we just pump a canister of VX into that stupid box and call it a day?"

"It's complicated. Graveyard has enemies that we may not be able to fight alone, enemies he hates as much as we do. For that, we need him alive."

"What about the other one? If we find him, and re-cruit him, we don't need Victor anymore. Right?"

"You already see where I'm going with this. Sid Hansen was always more stable—snarky, and a little dense, with no respect for authority, but more stable."

"So how are the newspapers going to lead us to him? That's what I don't get."

"Van Hansen is an obsessive prepper. Impossible to catch off guard. For contingency plans he stored caches of weapons all over the country. Now, I don't know the locations, but Victor definitely does. And I'm guessing he saw something in one of these pa-pers, something unusual, something that happened close to one of those locations."

When he finds what he's looking for, it's a curiosi-ty more than anything else, tucked away on the sixth page of yesterday morning's front section: a dubious report of a video store clerk supposedly tearing off a man's arm during a robbery attempt.

"Get Kill Team Two," Walter says.

EXT. MOVIE THEATER – DAY

Lily arrives at the mall after picking up a few things from home: a blue spaghetti strap top, a grey pleated miniskirt, stiletto heels. She's bringing her A-game today, and these are just some of her tools.

She parks outside the Cineregency Cineplex, right next to the brown Chevy pickup truck she recognized on her pass through after school. She's sure it's the same one. There aren't many trucks that rusty still on the road.

She opens her purse and pulls out two things: a roll of masking tape and her iPhone. More tools. She uses her teeth to cut the tape. It only takes a minute for the rest. She keeps moving.

As she walks up the cement steps to the Cineplex, she passes a man in a tracksuit smoking on a bench. He nearly breaks his neck ogling her. She doesn't need to look back to see if he's looking up her skirt from the bottom of the steps. She already knows. They're like sheep.

She enters the lobby and stops to contemplate where to look first. Krohike's manager saw the apparition in a projection room, which is on the second level. She'll need to be sneaky to get up there. That, or she could flirt with one of the ushers a little and see where it gets her. If Krohike is here, she can probably get him to take her upstairs and show her around. Then she would have to ditch him somehow.

It all turns out to be irrelevant. The hollow man is here. He's right in front of her, walking past the concession for the front doors. He looks just like he did the night before—same ratty jeans, same camo hoodie. It even still has some specks of dried blood on it.

"I knew it!" she calls out. She extends her arm to finger him accusingly. "I knew it!"

He stops briefly, wide-eyed like a little boy caught flipping through dirty magazines.

"You smell like popcorn," Lily says.

"I don't know you," the hollow man says, striding on. "I've never seen you before."

"Just like Krohike," she says. He smells like popcorn because of the movie theater.

"Who's Krohike?" he says, slowing for a moment to give her a confused look.

"Some guy I know." She shakes her head dismissively. "Whatever. Point is, you're busted!"

"I don't know you."

He passes her and continues for the door. She follows.

"You were, like, researching your cover or something in here, weren't you? To, like, play a better video store clerk?"

"What?"

"You're like Patrick Bateman. There is no real you—only an entity, something illusory. You simply are not there."

"What the fuck are you talking about?" he says in a bemused tone that surprises her. "I'm leaving now. Go away."

He pushes through the Cineplex doors and begins walking down the stairs to the parking lot. Lily is right behind him.

"I'm coming with you," she says.

"No you're not."

"Try and stop me," she defiantly says.

The hollow man stops and turns in the blink of an eye. Lily squeaks as he snatches her wrist in his right hand. His grip feels unbreakable, like her arm is caught between two boulders.

"I don't have to try," he says, glaring at her with dark intensity.

"Let go of me," Lily says. "I'll scream rape."

"You won't live long enough to scream anything." His crushing grasp tightens. Her hand goes numb.

She narrows her eyes at him. She won't back down. No. She's staring into a black abyss and it's looking back at her, but she won't back down.

"There a problem here?" calls the man in the tracksuit behind them.

"Is there?" Lily whispers to the hollow man.

The death grip on her wrist suddenly goes slack. She feels needles in her fingers and wiggles her hand to shake it off.

She winks back at the man in the track suit. "No problem."

As she turns back, she sees her quarry climbing into the rusted-out pickup. She runs for her car. He's already screeching out of the mall lot as she starts her engine. She tries to follow him, but he drives like *Bullitt*. He swerves past the cars ahead of them, weaves through oncoming traffic, and drifts around a corner.

And then he's gone.

EXT. VIDEO TIME – DUSK

Crime scene tape blows wildly beneath the hurricane winds of a military chopper. Solid black with no markings, the roaring machine sets down in the video store parking lot.

Lonnie is first on the ground. He sees the world through the plastic of his oxygen mask. The blue glowing pilot light of his flamethrower points the way ahead as the others follow him. They call him the Arsonist for all of the obvious reasons. He likes to burn things. He wants to burn Sid Hansen tonight.

The Ghoul is easily two feet taller than any of them, a behemoth thing, clad entirely in black body armor that makes Lonnie's own heavy flame-retardant jump suit seem like a pair of swim trunks. Most men couldn't lift that armor—much less wear it all day. The machete the Ghoul brandishes in his left glove is spiked and serrated in a way that is far more aesthetic than practical. It looks like a horror movie weapon.

"Fresh meat!" the monster bellows. Lonnie has never heard the Ghoul say anything but that and a few other stock phrases, including *"Flesh for my hunger,"* *"I hunger,"* and some slight variations along those lines. He's like one of those talking dolls, except he says really fucked up shit when you pull his string.

The Indian Tracker is exactly what he sounds like. He used to be more practical, but lately he's taken to wearing a feathered headdress and smoking cigars everywhere. It's weird, but it doesn't keep him from doing his job.

Tracker kneels outside the video store and sniffs

the air. Lonnie can barely wait to pick up the trail. He doesn't like the son-of-a-bitch they're tracking. They have a history. Sid Hansen kicked the crap out of him a few years ago, when the kid walked right through Graveyard's security, breathing tear gas like it was a flowery summer scent and demanding to talk to Walter as if clearances were all just a joke. He kicked Lonnie in the testicles so hard that one of them ruptured. For weeks, it hurt so bad to move that he thought he would never walk again.

"Well?" Lonnie asks in his thick cockney accent. "How is it, then?"

Tracker places a hand on the ground. He smells his hand.

"Fresh meat," the Ghoul repeats.

"We know," Lonnie says.

"Blood," Tracker says. "Lots of blood. Two trails end here. Many lead away. Two with blood on them."

"Which one is it, chief?" Lonnie says. "I want the bloody tosser."

"One wore perfume," Tracker says.

He sniffs one more time and scowls.

"Hot Topic perfume," he says.

"We follow the other then," Lonnie says. He turns back to the chopper, yelling at the soldiers waiting inside. "Gear up for airborne assault and maintain visual contact."

"Command said not to engage," Tracker says.

"Command can sod off," Lonnie tells him. "I owe the fucking twat, an' I'm gonna burn 'im alive."

EXT. SHATTERED HOUSE – DUSK

Lily parks the Malibu in front of a house so decrepit she can't believe it still stands. It's surrounded by overgrown weeds, making it hard to see through the dense tree cover. She never would have found the place if not for the pickup parked in the dirt driveway.

She steps out of the car, taking off her sunglasses. She tosses them on the passenger seat next to a laptop computer.

"Fuck."

She looks up at the rotting old frame ahead of her. The windows are boarded up. The roof is collapsing. *It could be worse*, she tells herself.

She steps up to the pickup and reaches into the bed. She tears her iPhone free and peels several large strips of masking tape from it.

She approaches the front door, all the way watching the ground for muddy spots that her heels might sink into. She's relieved when she gets to the cement front porch and hasn't lost her shoes. The door has an empty hole in place of a knob. She can bend down and see right into the house. Above the hole in the door is a hinged metal bar with an open padlock dangling from it. So he padlocks his house. That's ... interesting.

The door flies open, scaring her. She jumps back and shrieks. The hollow man stands in the crooked door frame, glaring down at her with those abyssal black eyes.

"How did you find me?"

"I taped my iPhone to your truck and set it to

email its location to me every two minutes," she brags. "There's an app for that."

"Fuck," he mutters.

"Yeah." She offers him a smug smile. "Pretty cool, huh?"

"Yeah totally cool," he says, returning to his usual frosty disposition. "You know, I can kill you out here and no one will ever know."

Lily rolls her eyes at him. "Whatever."

He raises a curious eyebrow.

"Go ahead. Do it," she says. "I ain't scared."

He sighs and turns, walking back into the house. She follows.

"So like, do you own this place?" Lily asks, panning around the collapsing house.

"No," he says.

"Well, I guess that's good. It kinda looks like a crack den." Lily narrowly avoids stepping through a dark hole in the wavy wooden hallway. She peers into it and sees nothing but black. She convinces herself man was not meant to know what subterranean horrors lurk in those depths, and continues down the hall.

There is no furniture to speak of, except an ancient refrigerator stained brown from decades of smoke damage, and a TV stand with no TV on it. Some copies of *Maxim* and *FHM* and a few other lad magazines sit on top of it. The top one is a *Revolver* with a cover photo of bleached blond faux-punk Taylor Momsen dressed like a stripper, holding some guns.

"Is this what you're into?" Lily asks, pointing at the magazine. "She's totally corporate manufactured, you know."

The hollow man doesn't seem to be listening.

What she notices then makes her jaw drop. It was so absurd and so in-her-face that it somehow didn't register with her immediately. There is a dinner table in the middle of the room covered with guns and ammunition piled to absolutely cartoonish heights. Bandoliers drape over the sides of the table and a few loose bullets roll off the edge from the vibrations of her footfalls. Her mind conjures an image of Ted Nugent leaping into the pile and swimming in it like Scrooge McDuck. Lily doesn't know much about guns, but she knows this is some serious firepower.

"Where did you get all these guns?" she asks.

"Walmart," the hollow man says. "Low prices every day."

He opens up the refrigerator, pulling out a bottle of crisp and refreshing Aquafina® water.

"I think these guns are illegal," Lily says.

"Really? You should call the cops. We'll see who comes out on top in that fight."

He removes the camouflage hoodie he's worn every time she's ever seen him, tossing it on the countertop nearby. Underneath, he has a simple black T-shirt that exposes bulging arms covered in a cross-hatch of old scars from his hands to his elbows.

"Holy shit," Lily says. "What happened to your arms?"

"I followed a strange man home from a movie theater."

"You don't have to be a dick."

"Yeah I do. Why won't you go away? What the hell do you want from me?"

"I need your help."

"I don't do charity work." He gulps down some water from the bottle.

"My stepdaddy used to fuck me," Lily says. It just comes out point blank. The hollow man in front of her spits his mouthful of water on the floor.

"That, uh," he chokes. "That's not my business, really."

"Like, when I didn't want him to."

"Oh. You mean he, uh, he r—"

"No."

"What?"

"That. It wasn't that."

"Then what was it?"

"I just don't say it like that."

"Okay . . ." his fuddled eyes move away from her, down to the floor.

"I need you to kill him."

"What?" His gaze bounces right back up to her in surprise.

"I need you to kill him so he never hurts me again."

The hollow man gives her a grim look. "You have no idea what you're getting yourself into here."

"Yeah, I do," Lily tells him. "I don't have any money, but if you do this for me I can do other things for you."

"Like what?"

"You know. Like, other things . . ." she bites her lip seductively.

"Oh," he says. He still doesn't get it. She can read him that well now.

She puts her hand on his crotch.

"Oh," he says. Now he gets it—and it's amazing to her how dense he is. She chased him all this way dressed like a fucking streetwalker, and he never put any of it together until this second. They're like sheep—all of them.

She unzips his pants and wraps her fingers around his dick. It's already hard as a rock.

"You can fuck me right here," she says. He likes sluts with guns? She can give him sluts with guns.

She tries to hop up onto the kitchen table, but clumsily rolls off when a bunch of bullets avalanche under her butt. She reaches back and waves her hand across the table, scattering ammo and handguns all over the floor.

She pulls up her skirt and hops back up on the space she cleared. She lies back on a bed of shell casings as she slides her black lace thong down her legs.

"Come on," she says. "I want you to fuck me on your big pile of guns."

"I don't have any . . ." he says. Any what? Guts? Balls? He's being a total pussy right now. He probably means condoms.

"It doesn't matter," she says. She wraps her legs around him and pulls him up against her.

He leans to kiss her, but she plants a hand on his face and pushes him away. She doesn't like to kiss any of them. It's not a fairy tale. She doesn't want someone to call her pet names. She doesn't want a fucking romance.

"Don't make love to me," she says, preparing for the coming disappointment. She holds her palm over his mouth. "Fuck me!"

She barely gets the words out before he pins her

hand to the table. His other hand is around her throat like a vise. He's choking her. She can hardly breathe. She has to claw his fingers away. Desperately, she gasps for air.

She lets out a shriek as it happens. He clamps her body down as he stabs her over and over. She didn't expect this at all.

The room seems to dim as her pupils dilate. His hand returns to her throat as she feels her blood rush to where she was wounded. She moans as her insides contract and the world fades away.

It's just a little death.

When her heart stops pounding and she regains some composure, she feels his warm leavings inside. Her legs are coiled so tightly around his torso that her muscles ache as she unwraps herself from him

She needs a cigarette.

INT. MAXIMUM SECURITY FACILITY – DAY

Dr. Danny McElroy slams the heavy steel double door behind him as he scans the room angrily for Sam Siegel. Inside the box, the subject is on the floor, pasty white, slack jawed, vacant eyes looking up at the ceiling without blinking. It's as dead as a body can look before the flies get there.

"How long has he been like that?" McElroy yells.

The guards offer little more than a glance. Most of them are closer to the box than usual—a few even having crossed that stupid line they spray-painted around it some months ago. Superstition is what that is. Most days Danny is amazed these idiots haven't called an exorcist or some other bullshit artist to drive the evil spirits out of the poor bastard in that box.

"I said, how long has he been like that?" he demands again.

Sam Siegel turns from a conversation with another trooper holding an unnecessarily big gun of some kind. McElroy petitioned to have the guards removed twice already, and again to have their weaponry reduced to batons. Both times, his requests were rejected by the warden. These fucking Neanderthals need their big boom sticks to compensate for their own petty insecurities. They dress like they think they're Special Forces commandos, with body armor and helmets. It's enough to make Danny ill.

"Ten hours," Sam says.

"You must be shitting me," McElroy says. "Ten hours and nobody bothered to call for help?"

"We're not in a hurry."

"Open the cage. I'm going in there."

"Nobody's going in the box with him."

"Damn it, Sam. My patient needs medical help."

"You're not going in the box. Nobody goes in the box with him."

"You really want me to go to the warden with this?" McElroy shouts. He can't believe this barbarian. "You want me to tell him an inmate died on your watch and you didn't report it for ten hours?"

"I don't work for the warden," Sam says. "And as far as I'm concerned, that piece of shit can stay right there in that box until there's nothing left but maggots. Then maybe I'll open the door."

"You're a real tough guy, Siegel. You know that? Real tough with your tiny dick and your big guns. Ten of you all standing around, afraid to open a door for a naked dead man."

"Drag him the fuck out of here," Sam says, motioning to the two apes closest to Danny.

"Touch me and I'll sue you into a damn dumpster," Danny says. He smacks a guard's hands away as the grunt reaches for him. "I know my way out."

Danny backs toward the door. Sam and the others watch him tensely. As he reaches the door, most of them return their attention to the box and its mysterious occupant.

The door is already against Danny's shoulder when he notices something important. The control panel for the cage has been left totally unguarded. All of the apes are too busy gawking. The little brass key that dangles from the rotational switch in the middle of the panel only needs to be turned to throw the door open and put all these idiots in their place.

That inmate is dead because of the positively medieval conditions in this place, and Danny plans to blow the lid off the whole thing . . .

Sam Siegel sees him reaching for the key and shouts at him to stop, but the big dumb gorilla is too far away to do anything about it. Danny turns the key and a deep air horn sounds as a spinning red light flashes to alert them the cage door is about to open.

"Close it!" Sam yells. The guards rush Danny and the control panel, but it's too late. The door slides open, quite possibly for the first time since it was built. The overpowering smell of death and decay that wafts out of that cage is enough to knock a man over.

Danny covers his nose as one of the guards tackles him.

"See?" he says, wrestling to escape from under a commando who weighs almost twice as much as he does. "He's dead! I told you! You killed that prisoner, and the world is gonna find out about it, Siegel. You and whatever barbarians you work for!"

He's pinned against the floor, but he can see the open cage door from under the brute holding him down. He sees a flash of pale white. The man in the box bounds off the doorframe the way a monkey would, or some kind of cat—more agile than any human. He has something in his hand—a knife? No. That's impossible. Broken glass? No . . . it's a folded up triangle of newspaper.

Blood sprays the floor as the man from the box stabs the nearest guard in the neck with the newsprint shank. The other sentries in the room react instantaneously. Danny's ears throb with pain as the echo of automatic weapons fire assaults them from all sides.

The man on top of him is off in a split second, shooting at the prisoner from the box like the rest of them. A body falls next to Danny and gore sprays him in the eyes.

"Fuck!" he shouts.

He wipes his eyes in time to see the man from the box pull a combat knife away from one of the guards and slash the man's throat with it. Danny screams. He reaches for a gun on the belt of the dead man next to him. He's never fired a gun before, and fears what might happen if he drops it or shoots one of the guards by accident. He sees something then. The guard has something else on his belt—something he knows well from self-defense courses at the hospital. A Taser.

Danny grabs the Taser and pulls it free from the dead man's belt. He rolls over and sees, to his astonishment, that all of the guards between himself and the cage are already dead. The last of them crumples in a heap as he aims the Taser at the man from the box.

"Don't come any closer!" Danny yells.

The pale, naked, blood-splattered killer in front of him says nothing at all. He looks down at the twitching red dot glowing on his chest. He smiles menacingly as he advances, stepping over a corpse along the way.

"Stay back!" Danny yells, but the killer keeps coming.

He pulls the trigger and closes his eyes. The Taser launches its dart at the prisoner and Danny hears the familiar rapid clicking that means it is working. He opens his eyes.

The man from the box is still coming for him. The Taser wires hang from his chest, swinging as he stomps forward.

Danny pulls the trigger again. He watches as the Taser rattles and the man from the box's chest twitches, as if he might be slightly tickled by the device.

The murderous man from the box towers over him, grinning silently. He leans and takes the Taser from Danny's hands.

"Thanks for the newspapers," the killer says.

Danny tries to run, but he doesn't even get up off the ground before he feels the Taser wires coiled around his neck. They tighten like a noose, then worse. They saw into his flesh. His head feels like it's being crushed under a battle tank and he thinks it might have popped when he sees the steamy red liquid spray the floor.

The last thing he ever sees is the man from the box leaving the room, the Taser dragging along the floor behind him.

INT. SHATTERED HOUSE — NIGHT

"What's your real name?" Lily says. She's crawling around on all fours feeling under his kitchen table for her lost panties.

"You don't need to know," the hollow man answers.

"We just had sex," she reminds him. "What kind of girl do you think I am?" She stops and looks up at him from the floor. He's no expert, but he's pretty sure he knows now exactly what kind of girl she is.

"A promiscuous one." It's nothing to him but a statement of fact.

"Ass." She sticks her tongue out. It's a strange gesture. He'll never quite understand why anyone does that. She finds her underwear in a wad and shakes some shell casings out of it. Nines mostly, a few five-sevens and one seven-sixty-two.

He finds his open bottle of water where he left it, on a rotting old countertop with a stray weed growing up through it. He takes a swig, watching her. She lies back on the floor, stretches her legs high in the air, and pulls those black thong panties up her silky smooth legs. She's a beautiful girl. She looks like the girls in the magazines he looks at.

"How can you even see in here?" Lily says. The sun disappeared while they were fucking, and the house is now almost completely dark.

"I'm good at seeing in the dark," he says. He shrugs.

"Awesome. Can you hand me my purse then?"

He grabs the tiny handbag she left on the counter,

tossing it to her. It smacks into her lap. He had worried it might be a bomb when he saw her set it down, but he smelled no explosives.

"Thanks," she says. "I guess."

Lily opens up the handbag, withdrawing a box of Marlboro cigarettes and a lighter. As she flicks the lighter, he instinctively turns his back on her to avoid ruining his night vision. The smell of smoke fills the room, but he barely notices. He only smells her: the flowers in her perfume, the fruit smell of her hair, the salty wetness of her insides. That smell is on him now—all of them are. The only thing anyone has ever left on him before was blood.

"You want a smoke?"

"No." He never smokes, and never will. That was beaten into him from early on.

"Cool. So let's try this again," she pauses to exhale a lung full of smoke. "Hi. My name is Lilith Elizabeth Hoffman. What's yours?"

"Sid," he says.

"Sid?" she repeats. "Just Sid?"

"Yeah."

"It's kind of a menacing name. Sid. I don't know anyone else named Sid."

"I don't know anyone else named Lilith."

"It's because of the music festival. My real dad was a roadie there."

"You have a real dad, and then another dad?"

"And another dad. My mom is like a total hussy. My actual dad, like, the guy who got her pregnant, was just a one night thing. I never met him. She married this other guy when I was a baby, and I barely remember him. Then after him there was Ted."

"The guy you want me to kill."

"Yeah. How soon can you clip him?"

"Clip him? I'm not clipping anybody. I'm out of that kind of work."

"We made a deal."

"No we didn't. You—"

He stops. He hears something he doesn't like. It's faint, but it's there, in the distance. It sounds like a simple buzzing from here. To anyone else it would be nothing—maybe the sound of a far-off freeway. To him it is an all-too-familiar cadence.

"What is it?" Lily says.

"You don't hear that?" he answers. Of course she doesn't. She's just a girl. She's not what he is.

"No. What are you freaking out about?"

"It's a chopper," he says. "We've got problems."

"Problems? What kind of problems?"

Sid grabs an M4 from the ammo pile and smacks the magazine to make sure it's seated firmly, then snaps back the charging handle to chamber the first round. He straps a KA-BAR knife around his leg.

"What the fuck?" Lily says. "What are you doing?"

He snatches the cigarette out of her mouth. By now, the buzzing has become a thunderous war drum. He throws the cigarette down on the floor and stomps it out under his boot heel.

"Hey!" she says.

"They're coming. Stay down and stay quiet, and you might live through this."

He's telling her a lie—a damned lie.

INT. SHATTERED HOUSE – NIGHT

Lily can see nothing but black. She can't hear much either. The helicopter outside sounds unnervingly close. She feels around in the dark for Sid, for the table, for a way out; anything.

"Sid?" she yells. "Where are you? I can't see!"

Crash! The sound of glass shattering makes her spin instinctively. It was here in the room with her, but she sees nothing. Someone else is here with her. She nearly screams, but she thinks it is best to stay quiet.

Then two loud cracks stab at her ears and a lightning flash illuminates the room. It doesn't last long enough for her to make out anything. Darkness again. Her ears ring like she just walked out of a Cannibal Corpse concert. She can feel her heart pounding.

Smash! Crack! Crash! More feet stomping on the floor here in the room with her. Then more shots. She covers her ears. It's so loud it hurts.

Someone slams into her and she screams. She's sure this is it. This is the moment where she dies. She forces herself up from the floor and wipes her eyes. She's all wet now.

A jet of flame erupts through the back window and sets fire to the ceiling. She can see now, and it's a scene of unadulterated horror.

A soldier in black clothes grabs her shoulder. A foot-long knife juts from his throat and a dark red spray gushes into her face. She is already bathed in blood. It's in her hair and her mouth. She can taste it now. She screams again.

Sid elbows the soldier in the face, knocking him to the floor. He pokes the muzzle of a machine gun into the guy's chest with one hand and holds down the trigger. There's so much blood. In his other hand, he's holding the severed head of another commando. Lily can see some of the exposed spine sticking out from the stump of the neck.

"We have to get out of here," Sid says. "These are Graveyard operators."

"Who?" Lily yells. Her ears are still ringing.

The dead guys on the floor are dressed all in black army clothes with body armor and helmets. Some of them have patches on the shoulder with a big white Jolly Roger, only the skull has fangs like a vampire.

A second jet of flame blasts through another rear window into the kitchen, setting more of the ceiling ablaze.

"I'm having a barbecue!" someone shouts from behind the house. He has some kind of accent, maybe English.

Sid looks back at the window and growls.

"This looks a little undercooked!" Sid yells. "I'm sending it back!"

He hurls the severed head out the window.

A man in a long black coat appears in the window only a second later. His face is obscured behind a thick plastic breathing mask, like a firefighter would wear. He's holding a big gun with a hose attached to a tank strapped to his back. It's a fucking flamethrower.

"There you are, cocksucker!" he says.

Lily screams. Sid grabs her by the shoulder and shoves her face down into the floor as he flips the kitchen table over in front of them, shielding them both from an onslaught of flame. All around them, ammo cooks off and explodes. It sounds like popcorn.

"He's going to kill us!" Lily screams.

"That asshole?" Sid says. "He's a little bitch."

Smash! Behind them, the front door bursts from its hinges and falls to the floor like a piece of timber. A behemoth figure steps through the threshold into the hallway. He must be nearly eight feet tall, with legs like tree trunks. He's covered in black armor. His face is a screaming skull.

"Fresh meat!" he says.

"Now *that* asshole is a different story," Sid says.

Sid levels the machine gun at the monster in the front door and rattles off an entire magazine into the thing. The behemoth doesn't stop, doesn't even slow down. He produces a machete the size of a Viking broadsword from his back. He's coming for them.

"We're trapped!" Lily shrieks. More volcanic death blazes overhead.

"Stay with me!" Sid says. "We're going that way."

He motions to his left, but she has no idea what the fuck he means. There's nothing there but an empty room. It's a dead end. He continues to fire shots into the monster's skull-face, one at a time. It has no effect.

"What way?" Lily yells.

Sid whips the gun around and launches a grenade at the wall. The explosion is deafening. In an instant, the room is filled with acrid black smoke. She's blind again. She's jerked off her feet by her arm and then she's stumbling through the house, just trying to keep up as she's pulled along.

EXT. SHATTERED HOUSE – NIGHT

Sid shoves Lily into the dirt outside and pulls a .45 automatic from his pants. He shoots that fire-spraying bastard in the fucking kneecaps and stomps forward to tear him limb from limb.

"Bollocks," the fallen Arsonist manages to say, lifting his flamethrower to set Sid on fire. He's far too slow. Sid snatches the end of the gun as the Arsonist squeezes down on the trigger, and a jet of flame spews into the air to engulf the helicopter hovering just above the house. The helicopter jerks to the right, then spins wildly out of control. The chopper veers deeper into the woods, the tail circling the rest of the vehicle, a fiery pinwheel of death, before it slams into the trees and explodes in a massive fireball.

The Arsonist screams as Sid feeds him the business end of the flamethrower.

"I hope you like it extra spicy," Sid says. He pulls the trigger and incinerates the Arsonist's face and insides. He never liked that guy.

Sid turns just in time to see a stone tomahawk spiraling toward his head. He catches it. The tomahawk's owner approaches him from the trees. Tracker points at him as he raises another one of the crude weapons.

"I challenge you to the blood duel of the Crow people," Tracker says. Sid has no idea what he's talking about and he doesn't give a fuck.

"Whatever," Sid says. "I don't have time for this."

He fires off a bunch of .45s at Tracker and the Indian leaps behind a tree.

The Ghoul comes around the corner of the house, growling and gibbering about meat. Sid can't fight them all this way. He snatches Lily's hand, dragging her to her feet. He pulls her around the other side of the house while shooting at Tracker. After a few dozen yards she manages to kick her cumbersome shoes off and keep up with him on her own.

"Why do you always run from the skull guy?" Lily says.

"He's bulletproof!" Sid shouts. "Bulletproof guys are a pain in the ass!"

When they turn the corner into the front yard, they see something Sid expected but still finds disappointing now that it's for certain. The old pickup truck is a blazing inferno.

"Shit." Sid looks farther down the dirt driveway to spot Lily's purple Malibu in the dark, somehow unnoticed when the Arsonist set his car aflame.

"We're taking your car," he says.

"I left my keys in my purse!"

Sid smashes the driver's side window. He dives through into the car and shoots out part of the steering column.

Lily runs around the vehicle and jumps in the passenger side, as he begins furiously rubbing bare wires together.

"You can hotwire a car?" she says.

"Easy," he responds.

Sid doesn't need to look up to know the Ghoul is coming. The cars are parked closer to the side of the house they came out on, and so the man simply turned and went the other way to intercept them.

"Uh, Sid," Lily says nervously. "That guy is coming."

"I know."

Sid rubs the wires together again. Nothing. Again.

"He's getting closer," Lily says.

That fucking monster never runs. He's never in a hurry. "I know!"

From the corner of his eye, Sid can see the shape of the armored giant coming for them. That huge machete is out and raised in the air like the blade of a guillotine.

"Sid! Sid!" Lily screams.

The car starts as the machete cuts through the roof. It stops only millimeters from Lily's nose. She screams again, curling lower in the seat.

Sid throws the car into reverse and the sound of screeching tires fills the air. The machete is ripped free of its steel trappings by the monster's grip as the car lurches backward.

INT. LILY'S CAR – NIGHT

Lily feels the bridge of her nose to see if she's bleeding—not that she could tell with the amount of gore already splattered all over her. She looks ahead and sees the car is moving dangerously fast on a gravel drive. She snaps her seatbelt on and braces herself against the dashboard.

"What the fuck was that?" she yells. "Who are those people? Why are they trying to kill you?"

"They'll try to kill you too now," Sid says. "You know too much."

"What? I can't hear anything!" Lily screams. "I think I have permanent tinnitus!"

"Pussy." He shouts his next words. "I said, they'll try to kill you too now! You know too much!"

"I don't know anything!"

"You saw them. That's already too much!"

"I was minding my own business and the next thing I know I'm being hunted by the Cobra Commander's goons!"

"Yeah, you're real innocent. You just had sex with me so I would kill a guy for you!"

"I didn't think this would happen! Why the fuck would anybody think this would happen? Those guys were like a whole team of bad action movie clichés! The only thing missing was the guy who deflects bullets with a sword!"

Sid turns to her, alarmed.

"How do you know about him?"

"What?" Lily's not sure he's following the same conversation she is. "I don't ... I. What?" She sits back in her seat. Her heart races faster than the car; she thinks she's hyperventilating. She breathes into her hands. He can't possibly be implying that there is really a guy who can do that.

Something occurs to her—something maddening. Maybe Kayla was right.

"You really are a vampire!" she says.

"What?" he says.

"You're super strong and you live alone in the woods. I've never seen you eat real food. You're the undead—cursed to drink the blood of the living for all eternity. Oh, God."

"Seriously?"

"Make me like you. Turn me. I'm ready for eternal undeath! Drink!"

For the first time, he laughs for real—not the fake chuckle she heard him force when he was trying to pass himself off as normal. This is a wild, ominous, predator cackle. This is really him.

"You're being ridiculous," he says. "There's no such thing as vampires."

He's right. She did sound ridiculous. She sounded like a stupid little girl.

"Then how do you explain this?" Lily shouts. "How are you so good at killing people?"

"Lots of practice."

EXT. SHATTERED HOUSE - NIGHT

Helen hangs onto a rail in the chopper as it hovers above the treetops. Ahead of her, Walter grabs a line and rappels down to the grass outside the smoking ruins of the old farmhouse. She looks back at Deadeye, the kill team's world-class marksman, and his absurdly large rifle. She asked him about it once. It used to be a Barrett rifle, but he modified it into something else entirely. Everyone just calls it Betsy.

Deadeye winks at her and spits a mouthful of chaw into a coffee can.

"He's pissed," he says.

Helen sighs. She grabs the line and follows the commander down to the ground. The fire that destroyed the house has cooled to a smolder, and the only illumination is from the spotlight on the choppers.

She hits the ground next to a charred cadaver she's pretty sure used to be Lonnie Pitts. She pokes the corpse with her foot. Pitts was a strange man, a sick man maybe, and she won't miss him.

Tracker approaches them from the heavy tree cover surrounding the house. Walter shouts angrily over the helicopter blades.

"What the hell happened here?" Walter says.

"He went north in a car," Tracker says. "He has a girl with him. The Ghoul chased them. All the others are dead."

"You were supposed to wait for me to get here!" Walter rages. His forehead looks like it might burst.

"The Arsonist wouldn't wait," Tracker says, his

stoic demeanor unfazed.

An operator hops off the chopper and runs toward them holding a handheld radio and headphones.

"God damn it, Lonnie!" Walter screams. "How many times did I tell you to keep it in your fucking pants?"

Walter draws a Sig 9 from a shoulder harness under his jacket and fires most of the magazine into the Arsonist's burnt corpse. Helen leaps back and shields herself instinctively. "There! You fucking happy now, you son-of-a-bitch?"

Walter inhales deeply as he puts the gun away. Tracker never blinked the whole time. The operator with the field radio leans away in fear.

"Tracker," Walter orders. "Get on the chopper with Deadeye and find the kid again. He couldn't have gone far." He turns his angry attention to the radio man without speaking any words.

The radio man holds out the handset and Walter snatches it away. He pushes the headphones against the left side of his face and answers with an angry "What!"

He pauses for a moment, listening with his hand pressed against his head. Helen watches as his face, red and enraged, turn pale white.

"What do you mean, he's out?"

EXT. COLORADO – NIGHT

There are two kinds of people in this world: Victor Hansen, and weaklings that must be purged. Victor wants to throw every baby through a jet engine just to hear the sound it makes when it hits the turbines. He wants to put a bullet between the eyes of God. He wants to clog volcanos with bodies. He wants to piss a rain of acid from the top of the tallest building onto a crowd of virgins just to see their meat melt. He wants to collapse the sky itself just to pull survivors from the rubble, offer them a few seconds of false hope, then rip out their intestines and run.

He was made to kill-and he loves it.

For the first time in two years, Victor is free from that plastic fucking box the old man put him in. He feels soft now. He hadn't killed anyone in so long he'd almost forgotten what it felt like. He doesn't want that to ever happen again.

He grips the wheel of the Jeep he stole upon his exit from ADX. There were a few trucks outside he could've hotwired, but he passed on those and instead waited for an occupied vehicle so he could kill the driver. The Jeep's driver was a middle-aged woman with graying hair. Victor crushed her skull under his heel before he took this ruggedly stylish Wrangler Sahara, with its legendary Jeep® brand capability. Now he's in the wind.

They will undoubtedly track him, and the Jeep will make that easier, so he needs to change cars soon. He has plans. First, he needs to get to weapons. The easiest way is to make it to one of the old man's storage lockers. Victor's father was obsessed with contingencies and emergencies. He made the boys memorize hundreds of code words and meeting sites, and stashed heavy military hardware at a host of secret locations across the country. The closest is in Santa Fe. Hopefully, Victor's idiot brother hasn't already looted all the good stuff from that particular locker. Sid is likely still hanging out near the locker in Morston, which is several states away, but there's no way to know if he came through Santa Fe already while Victor was imprisoned.

Assuming he can load up on machine guns and explosives at the Santa Fe locker, Victor's next step is to hit Graveyard right in their dangling gonads when they're not ready for it. They'll expect him to keep running. *Never do what they expect. Deception is key.* Whatever the enemy thinks should be wrong, and whatever the enemy *knows* absolutely *needs* to be wrong.

At the Graveyard building, he'll kill everyone, then blast his way into Walter's vault on the top floor. That vault is filled with all kinds of nifty toys Walter and his predecessor picked up during their secret operations, but most importantly, the thing Victor wants most of all: the Lindemann device. The Lindemann device can change the world into exactly what Victor wants—a place where there is no more room for weakness. Where strength is all that matters, and Victor is the strongest.

Somewhere along the way, he'll find the old man and kill him for what he did.

Before any of that, he will need another car, and the tiny red dots of taillights in the distance ahead signify a perfect opportunity to acquire one. Victor presses harder on the gas, accelerating through the mountain landscape to close in on the vehicle. It grows in his view from tiny specs into a large older-model diesel pickup equipped with a push bar and search lights mounted on a steel frame above the cab. Victor only slows the Jeep when it's inches from the truck's bumper. He honks the horn repeatedly, chuckling quietly to himself as he does so.

A hand emerges through the cab's rear window, flipping Victor a middle finger over the truck bed. The truck veers left and crosses the center line. Victor laughs harder as he pounds on the gas, bringing the Jeep up next to the truck. A man in a down vest and cowboy hat rolls down the window to call Victor a faggot.

Victor stares coldly into the cowboy's eyes and presses his lips together to give him an exaggerated kiss with only the cool Colorado air rushing between them. He never breaks eye contact. That agitates the cowboy further. Victor points at the man, performs the pantomime for sucking a dick, then points to the side of the road. He slows the Jeep and pulls over to the brim. The huge truck pulls to a stop fifty yards ahead of him.

The cowboy emerges from the passenger's side of the vehicle, raving and waving his hands. Victor opens the door and steps from the Jeep, still stark naked from his imprisonment in the box. Two more men come from the truck.

"You picked the wrong truck'a hillbillies to fuck with, ya fuckin—" the cowboy stops as he beholds Victor's startling nudity. He looks back at his friends and laughs. "What the fuck? We got some kind'a freaky faggot here."

The truck's driver laughs with him. "They got all kinds a letters now, Jim-Bob," he says. "L-G-B-T-B-B-Q. I think this one's an F, for faggot."

Victor laughs as he casually meets the cowboy halfway between the cars.

The old man taught him and his brother every martial art known to man, and some others—others that are forbidden, thought lost, or impossible. Victor Hansen is a master of karate, judo, jiujitsu, kung fu, krav maga, savate, aikido, muay thai, pencak silat, escrima, sinanju, and a host of others—even the forbidden ansatsuken of myths and legends.

Victor howls with rage as he drives his fist into the cowboy's chest, crunching through bone and sinew. The cowboy's eyes nearly bulge from his head as Victor's fist breaks through his ribcage. Victor tears the weakling's still-beating heart from his chest and shows it to him. The man tries to scream, but nothing comes out before he collapses.

The driver of the truck pulls a gun, a CZ P09 Duty chambered for 9mm with standard magazine capacity of twenty. He aims the gun right at Victor's eyes with notable stability. This man is an accomplished shooter. Still, it will do him no good.

Victor Hansen cannot be harmed by bullets.

It took Victor a long time to figure out why, because the old man never told them. The old man didn't tell them a lot of things, and undoubtedly there are still secrets to be uncovered, but the bullet question is one he has answered. For years he thought he was simply quite good at dodging them. That eventually became statistically impossible to a ridiculous degree. Then, for some time, he believed a higher power was intervening. He learned the far more mundane truth from a researcher familiar with classified government research projects. The old man equipped his boys with extraterrestrial deflector shields taken from the dead bodies (and some survivors) at a crash site in the forties. Less than ten of the devices are believed to be in human hands, and all of the other known ones are utilized by the inner circle of the New World Order to prevent sniper assassinations.

The driver fires the entire magazine at Victor as the super killer calmly approaches, takes the gun, bashes the man's face in with the butt of it, and circles the truck for the other passenger.

He thinks he'll get creative with that one.

EXT. U-STORE IT - NIGHT

The car stops in front of an outdoor storage unit, one big orange garage door in a row of other big orange garage doors. Sid cuts the engine and jumps out of the car. Lily exits the car on the other side. She hasn't stopped asking him questions since the house.

"So these Graveyard people," she says. "Who are they?"

"They're a private military company that works for the New World Order," Sid says. To Lily, it sounds like a story a hobo would yell from a street corner.

"There's no New World Order," she says. "Guys in tin foil hats made that up."

"No. They're real. I've met them."

He kneels to check a padlock hanging in front of his shins, affixed to the storage unit door.

"So Graveyard is like some kind of top secret army death squad?" Lily asks.

"No," Sid says. "It's more than one squad. There are hundreds of them. They're not part of the United States government. They're a private military company. They're contractors—you know, mercenaries. The Order pays them to do their dirty work. The company is run by a guy named Walter Stedman. He's a complete dick. Those guys at the house were Kill Team Two, his second best team."

A feeling of dread fills Lily's guts.

"If that was his second best team . . ." she says. "What about the best team?"

"You're looking at him."

"You were on Kill Team One?"

"I am Kill Team One."

He searches his pants pockets for something, growing increasingly aggravated as he digs deeper with no result.

"That doesn't make sense," Lily says. "You're one guy."

"Yeah, I know," he says. "The designation makes it confusing."

"And you're, like, seventeen."

"Eighteen," Sid says, as he pulls something tiny from his pocket, wrapped in white cloth. He unravels the cloth, revealing a key to the storage unit.

"How? Are you like genetically engineered? Or a cyborg?"

"No. I'm just a guy."

"Then how do you do the stuff you do?"

"My dad was the last Kill Team One. He trained us."

"Us?"

"Look, you really don't need to know."

"Yeah. Exposition is lame."

He turns the key to release the padlock, which he tosses to the ground at his feet. He slides the garage door open and reveals a big black van parked inside.

"All you need to know is I'm the ultimate super soldier," he says. "I used to work for these guys. I ran away. They've been hunting me ever since."

"This is totally rad."

"It's not rad. I don't want to do it anymore."

"What? But you're, like, super kill-guy! Every guy on the planet wants to be you!"

"That's because they watch those stupid movies you like. They think it's all casinos and gorgeous women. It's not! It fucking sucks!"

"Really?"

"Yeah. I've been doing this since I could walk. It's constant. You never get a break. Somebody's always trying to kill you. Buildings blow up. The car chases never end. This shit tonight was nothing. Exploding helicopters? That's a Monday at the office. Last year I killed a werewolf with a toothbrush. A fucking werewolf! A mythological creature and I was just like, eh, marginally impressed. And the gimmicky minions come out of the woodwork like you wouldn't believe. Let's see . . . there was a guy with rock skin one time. That was fun. Oh. Here's one: a French assassin tried to kill me with a laser gun hidden in her vagina. I really think that messed me up for life, by the way. Who does that?"

"That's gross." It's all she can say. The questions conjured by that last image all overwhelm her at once.

"Yeah. No shit. And I'm tired of it. I want to be like you people! I just want to sit down, eat a submarine sandwich, watch some Netflix and not worry if somebody is going to throw a thermal detonator through my fucking window."

"The action hero just wants to be a regular guy."

"Yes!" Sid pulls open the back door of the van and exposes a pile of guns and bombs even more exhaustive than the one he had in his house. "Now, let's go kill all these fuckers so I can be on my way."

INT. HELICOPTER – NIGHT

Deadeye crouches in the helicopter with his su-permassive rifle at his shoulder. Tracker led them here to the middle of a forest in total butt-fuck no-where and he says this is where they need to be. Deadeye doesn't see shit, but he trusts the man. Tracker has never been wrong before.

"There," Tracker says, pointing through the open chopper door into the night. Miles of trees stretch out between them and the nearest lights of civilization.

Deadeye searches the trees for signs of movement and sees nothing—just leaves and darkness.

"Pilot," Deadeye says. "Get the searchlight on the trees down here."

"No!" Tracker interrupts. "Not in the trees. There." He points again into the distance ahead. That's when Deadeye realizes he's not directing them to the woods. What he's pointing to is much farther away. The Indian's eyes are just that good.

Deadeye raises Betsy and peers through the scope. The tiny blur of lights in the distance comes alive. There's a gas station, a storage park, a cheap motel, and a White Castle drive-thru.

"Where, Tracker?" Deadeye says. The question is absurd. He has a 5000x magnification lens and the Indian still has to tell him where to look? "Where is he?"

"The storage park," Tracker says.

"You sure?" Deadeye asks, backtracking to the storage park and scanning the rows of orange-painted overhead doors from an angle.

"His scent is like the bear rife with the blood of a fresh kill."

"Whatever you say, chief." Deadeye laughs.

He sees a purple Malibu parked in front of one of the doors. It's five clicks away. Nobody has ever made a kill shot with a rifle at that range. Most marksmen would call it impossible.

"We need to get closer," Deadeye says.

"He'll hear the chopper," Tracker says. He waves his hand for them to stop.

Deadeye looks away from the scope for a moment. He spits his chew into his coffee can and looks off into the tiny blur of lights again with his naked eyes. He shakes his head, snickering to himself as he puts his earplugs in.

It's time to make history.

INT. STORAGE UNIT – NIGHT

Lily crouches in the back of the van inside the storage garage. She's holding a canister she identifies as a grenade, but she couldn't say much more about it. Guns and bombs aren't really her thing. Sid rustles through the carpet of munitions at her feet. He's like organizing his guns or something. She has no idea.

"So what is this thing?" Lily asks.

"It's a flashbang grenade," Sid says, glancing at the thing in her hand.

"What does it do?"

"It makes a flash and a bang."

"Hence the name . . ." she nods. It makes sense.

"Yeah."

"So what do you do with it?"

"Don't worry about it," he says, sounding slightly annoyed.

"Fine, jerk." Lily puts the grenade down and plops on the van bumper at his back.

Sid picks up a big black gun and sticks a bullet clip thing in it. Lily thinks she should probably read a book about guns or something if she's going to hang around this guy.

"Listen," he says. "I need you to stay here while I ditch your car. It might throw them off a little."

"You're not going to blow it up or anything?" It might not matter anyway after what the Ghoul did to the roof. It doesn't take much to total a cheap used car.

"No," he sighs. "I'm not going to blow it up or anything."

"Is this safe? What if they show up here?"

"If they show up here, they'll kill you. Hope they don't show up here. I'll be back in four and a half minutes."

He turns and walks toward her car, big gun slung over his shoulder. Four and a half minutes? How could he possibly be that precise?

"'Kay," Lily says. She doesn't like this at all.

Sid steps across the molding line that divides the storage unit from the blacktop parking outside. His foot doesn't make it down on the pavement before he's in the air. Something skids across the concrete at his feet. A rock? Did he drop something? Lily isn't sure.

"Shit," Sid grunts. He drops the gun on the ground behind him.

"What?" Lily says. "What is it?"

He's already in the back of the van with her, digging through piles of equipment. Something like a firecracker sounds in the distance.

"What is it?" she says. "What's wrong?"

Clank! The sharp noise of puncturing metal startles her. She looks up and spots a hole in the side of the van the size of a baseball. She turns and sees another hole behind her, on the opposite side of the van, only inches from her head.

"What did that?" Lily says.

She hears that distant crack again, but by now she understands.

"Sniper," Sid says. "In a chopper five clicks southeast. He's so far the bullets get here before we hear them."

Sid tosses a grenade over his shoulder out into the

parking lot. It hisses and emits thick black smoke from under her car. He throws a few more behind it.

"What are you gonna do?" she says.

Sid reaches under the seat behind her and pulls out something long and cylindrical, olive colored . . .

"Is that a rocket launcher?" Lily squeaks.

Clank! The entire van shakes. Lily squeals. She checks to make sure none of her is missing.

"I need cover fire," he says. He snatches up another big black gun from the floor and presses it into her arms.

"What am I supposed to do with this?" she says.

"Just stick it around the corner and pull the trigger."

"And?"

"That's it. It's not rocket science. You go bang bang. I run out there with a MANPADS and helicopter goes boom. I've done this a bunch of times."

"But . . . but . . ."

The garage is quickly filling with smoke.

"I can't see anything!" Lily says. He's already gone by the time she gets the words out—vanished in the blanket of black smoke that fills the van and all her surroundings. Lily coughs. She can barely breathe.

She stumbles out of the van, dragging the gun Sid handed her. She needs to get out of the smoke. Wait. No. That's a bad idea. The smoke is keeping the guy with the huge gun from seeing her. But it feels like her lungs are on fire.

She drops to the ground, remembering what they taught her in kindergarten about fire safety. It sort of works—a little bit.

Okay, it doesn't really work. It still feels like she's breathing out of a Pontiac Judge's tailpipe. She forces herself to stay. If she leaves, she'll probably catch a bullet through the head. She's smarter than that.

Lily feels for the doorframe and determines that she's in the corner. She'll do what Sid said. She has to trust him. He knows what he's doing, and it's the only way she might get out of this now.

The gun is still in her hands somehow. She dragged it with her without thinking. She pokes it around the corner with one hand, barely able to hold it up straight. The muzzle wobbles crazily.

"Okay, Lily," she says. "You can do this. Girl power."

She turns away from the gun and closes her eyes as she pulls the trigger. The gun rattles in her hands. She tries to hang on, but it jumps and kicks and she can't keep it steady.

Suddenly, she feels a sharp pain and drops the gun. She rolls onto her back and screams. Her blood is on the floor.

INT. HELICOPTER – NIGHT

"Did you get him?" Tracker says, holding his hands over his ears.

Deadeye scans slowly through the gray for signs of life.

"I think so," he answers.

They won't know if he hit his target until the smoke clears. If he did, then it's a world record—another one. Too bad he can't tell anybody about it.

"There!" Tracker points.

"What?!"

Tracker points into the woods now, somewhere below them. Deadeye raises his enormous rifle again to zoom in on the darkness below. He searches for any sign of movement at all.

"Where is he? Where?"

Before Tracker can answer, something flashes down below, an ignition that illuminates a section of trees outside the view of his scope. Deadeye pans left to the source and sees something horrible. It blazes toward him blindingly and he has to look away.

"Oh, shit," Deadeye says.

That's all he has time to say before the helicopter explodes in a white-hot eruption of flame.

INT. STORAGE UNIT – NIGHT

Sid throws down the Stinger SAM on the way back to the storage unit. He enters the garage waving his hands as the smoke thins. This wasn't much of a challenge in his realm. He's shot down moving aircraft with a rifle before. Using the stinger, with its heat-seeking laser targeting system, was practically a joke by comparison—and with a stationary target, too. Any child could do it.

As the smoke clears, Sid sees Lily lying on the floor curled into a fetal position. She's still breathing. Her right arm bleeds from a gash along the outside of her right shoulder. He pokes her with his foot.

"I got shot!" she shrieks.

"Show me," Sid says.

She points to the gash on her arm. Her finger wobbles as she points. She's quaking with fear.

"That?" Sid says. "That doesn't even count."

"What? A fucking bullet went through my arm!"

"Are you kidding? That was a fucking cannon. It would've taken your whole arm off if it hit you."

"Then what the hell did this, asshole?"

"I think maybe just the superheated air around the bullet breezed by your arm."

"Fuck you, superheated air. That's the stupidest thing I've ever heard."

"It's barely a flesh wound. We don't have time for this shit."

He goes around to the front of the van to check for something he hopes he won't find. Luck is not on his side: he finds a gaping hole in the side of the van and leans over to look through. He can see the floor on the other side. It goes straight through the engine block.

"Fuck."

"What?"

"We have to take your car." Sid scoops up a handful of munitions and carries them out to Lily's Malibu.

"My car? Where?" she squeaks, getting up off the floor to follow him.

"You're driving," he says.

He pulls open the back door of the Malibu and dumps an armload of guns in the back seat.

INT. COMM ROOM – DAWN

The comm room at the Graveyard building is a mess. It's large, with six rows of desks all manned by nerdy guys hunched over a bunch of iMacs. The walls are alive with flat-screen monitors displaying maps and live feeds of cable news networks. This place has always reminded Helen of her old job at the NSA, except their computer labs were bigger. She sticks close to Walter in the sea of nerds.

"Where is he?" Walter says. His voice is gruffer than usual. Helen slept a bit in the chopper on the way back, but she knows Walter didn't. His eyes have grown uncharacteristically wild and bleary since last night.

The analyst Walter looms over is named Roger, but everyone calls him Archie because he looks like the comics character. Curly red hair, goofy smile—he even always wears a sweater. It's uncanny.

"We got him on camera hotwiring a jeep outside ADX," Archie says. "Local PD found it flipped over in a creek bed ten miles south."

"He switched cars," Helen says.

"He's coming here," Walter says.

"Why would he come here?"

"It's just how he is. He's not going to go hide in a shed in the woods or get an assumed name and a job at Safeway. He's going to start killing on a very large scale, and he'll start here for two reasons: one, he hates us, and two, we have something he wants."

"What is it, Walter? The box he asked you for?"

Walter ignores her question. Instead, he fires off

another at Archie. "Where are Deadeye and the Indian?"

"There's still nothing from the chopper," Archie says.

"They're all dead," speaks an icy cool voice from behind them.

Yoshida Tanaka waits quietly in the comm room door frame. He is almost like a shadow, clad entirely in sleek black formfitting attire. His silky black hair hangs down the back of his neck. He carries an ancient-looking Japanese sword at his side, which Helen has never seen him without. She wonders at times if he sleeps with the thing.

"How do you know?" Walter asks.

"You set them against not a man, but a demon," the ninja says. "I knew before it happened."

"You don't know, Tanaka," Helen says. "You're in the dark on this just like we are."

"Perhaps you should come visit me in the dark some time," the ninja says. Helen can't decide if it's a come-on or a threat.

"I need all hands on deck for this one," Walter says. "You gonna stick around for the action?"

"What choice do I have?" the ninja says. "We all face doom if he is not stopped."

"What kind of doom?" Helen says.

"The worst kind," Walter says. He smacks the analyst in the shoulder. "Archie, I want a chopper on the roof ready for dust off until I say otherwise."

"Will do," Archie says.

"I need you to come with me," Walter says to Helen.

INT. LILY'S CAR – DAWN

"It looks like a Thai whorehouse in here," Sid says. He's poking at one of the pink fuzzy dice dangling from the rearview mirror. The matching playboy bunny seat covers and floor mats don't help.

"Fuck you! I got shot!" Lily shouts. She's driving, and her hands are wrapped around a pink and purple leopard print steering wheel cover to further prove his point.

"It's not that big a deal," Sid says. He slides a brass blasting cap into a block of C4, and then follows the wire with his fingers from there to the next cap. He inserts that cap into another block and continues. He's been at this for some time.

"No? How many times have you been shot?"

"Not at all."

"What?" Her demeanor suddenly shifts from infuriated to bewildered.

"I've never been shot."

"You don't think that's weird?"

"Why would I?"

"People shoot at you all the time, right? Like, how many hundreds of times?"

"Tens of thousands. Probably millions."

"And nobody ever hit you at all? Not once?"

"No. Not really."

"So, what, are you like Captain Kirk, and everybody else is a red shirt?"

"I don't remember all the shirt colors . . . what are you talking about?"

"Hold up. Have you actually been *in* a Thai

whorehouse?"

Sid says nothing. He's been a lot of places, but he's never been to Thailand. He only knows about it from a magazine article about sex tourism there. He picked it up in a Walmart while stealing provisions for the shack he lives in.

"Oh God," Lily says. "Of course you have. You've probably fucked every hooker on both sides of the Pacific. You probably gave me some rare Indonesian super VD. Now I have to go get checked. If I die from AIDS, I'm gonna punch you."

He hasn't fucked anyone except Lily. The closest he ever got was watching his brother. Victor had a way with women—a way of torturing and mutilating them until their bodies gave out. For a long time Sid thought that was what sex looked like. He was stupid then.

"And where the hell are we going?" Lily says.

Sid finishes with the current strand of C4 bricks and drops it into a backpack. He tosses that pack in the back seat with the others.

"We're going to the Graveyard headquarters building in northern Arizona," Sid says.

"But those are the guys trying to kill us."

"Right."

"So shouldn't we be running away from them?"

"That's exactly what they'll expect."

"So instead of running, you're going to go fight, like, a hundred guys with machine guns, just you and the element of surprise?"

"Don't worry. I have a plan."

INT. GRAVEYARD VAULT – DAWN

The ninth floor of the Graveyard building is so quiet Helen could hear a roach's footsteps on the tile. There is no one on the entire floor except Walter, two elevator guards, and herself. She follows him down the hall toward the vault, a thing of near mythical status and the focal point of the few dozen people worldwide who really know anything.

"I've never brought you up here before," Walter says. "Have I?"

"No." Helen studies the walls and floor, as if expecting to see something magical in them, but they're just walls.

"What have you heard?"

"I don't know, sir. Lots of stories." She's just trying to stay cool. The way people talk about this place, the Holy Grail might be locked away up here.

"You heard the one about the alien bodies?" Walter asks.

"Yes," Helen answers apprehensively, waiting for him to shatter her world into pieces with a forbidden truth that she and thousands of others have sought for their entire lives.

Walter forces a chuckle.

"That one's horse shit," he says, invoking nothing but disappointment from her. "So is Walt Disney's frozen head. It might be somewhere, but not here. What about the water-powered car? You heard that?"

"Yeah. Horse shit?"

He gives her a smirk of lofty swagger.

The vault door is eight feet around and hinged. It

sits at the end of a short hallway off the main corridor. There is a panel on the wall with a camera, a microphone, and a key slot. As far as Helen knows, Walter has the only key in the world that will open this vault door. He wears it on a chain around his neck. She watches as he draws the key from under his shirt and sticks it in the lock.

He speaks his name into the microphone and then faces up at the camera. The door vault slowly begins to open.

"There's stuff in here that nobody ever needs to see," he says. "Some of it could put the whole world at risk. Some of it we just aren't ready for yet."

The inside of the vault is lined with safety deposit boxes; bigger objects sit on the floor or on pedestals. Walter walks into the vault ahead of her.

"Don't touch anything," he says.

Helen follows him and begins eyeballing some of the things that aren't locked up. There's a steel spear propped in the corner that looks about as old as civilization from the rust all along it. Near that is a suit of medieval armor on a stand.

"This is what Victor wants," Walter says. He lifts a large stainless steel briefcase which was propped in the corner and drops it on top of a rolling gurney in the center of the room. Helen turns her attention to the box and looks it over. There are no distinguishing features, other than the three-digit combination locks on either side of the carrying handle.

"What is it?" Helen asks.

"Just an apocalypse in a box," Walter answers.

"Okay then."

"From here until I say so, this is the football. We

need to make sure Victor doesn't get the football. At all costs—all costs—Victor doesn't get the football."

"Got it," Helen confidently responds.

"Say it," Walter demands. "Victor doesn't get the football."

"Victor doesn't get the football."

"Good. Now come with me. And bring that thing with you."

Walter walks from the vault. He stops after a second and looks back. Helen is hesitant to follow.

"Come on," he says.

"Wouldn't it be safer in the vault?" she asks.

"Not if we're all dead. Then he'll have all the time he needs to knock that door down."

INT. LILY'S CAR - DAY

Lily stares over the steering column, out into the bright desert. Sid gathers the bags he packed from the back seat, dragging them out into the dust in a big pile. She doesn't like this. She doesn't like it at all.

"Stay here," he says. "And don't fall asleep."

"You're leaving me out here alone?" Lily says.

"Yeah. What?"

"I've seen way too many horror movies not to be creeped out by this middle of nowhere Route 66 desert shit. I know what happens out here."

"What happens?" He leans into the door frame, looking at her inquisitively.

Dozens of images of screaming final girls fight for the main screen in Lily's head. So does the thought that she wouldn't be the final girl. She would be the slutty friend: the girl who shows her tits ten minutes into the movie and then gets killed first.

"Scary things," she whimpers.

"I promise you," Sid says. "I'm the scariest thing out here."

"Fine. But—"

He's gone.

"Sid?" she calls out. Nothing. He's just gone. He left her here. The passenger door still hangs wide open.

"Great. This is creepy."

She crawls across the passenger seat and looks out into the desert through the open door. She sees nothing but brown soil and a few cacti in the distance.

She reaches for the door handle, pulling the door

closed quietly, then sits back down in the driver's seat. She sighs.

She imagines the mutants from *The Hills Have Eyes* are watching her right now. No matter how hard she tries on her own, the idea won't go away.

Finally she resorts to her iPhone. She flips through the selection of music she keeps stored there, looking for something suitably cheery, and digs for the Beats headphones she knows are under the seat somewhere.

EXT. THE DESERT – DAY

Sid creeps along the desert terrain. He carries with him the half dozen sacks he filled with C4 explosive charges in the car.

He scans the brown dust ahead for anything strange. He's looking for a particular spot he hasn't seen in many years, not since his father first brought him and Victor here for training on this particular contingency plan. That was eight years ago, when he was ten, but he has a perfect memory which was beaten into him by his father's constant and violent insistence that every detail is important in matters of warfare.

His memory does not fail him. He finds the general area he's looking for and stomps on the ground until he hears a hollow clanking beneath his feet.

He reaches down to brush the dirt away, uncovering a trap door that has likely been hidden since his last visit as a child.

He reaches for the wire handle and hoists the door open to expose the darkness beyond. It's go time. He drops the bags first. Then he jumps down into the black.

When the Graveyard building was constructed, decades ago, the old man saw to it that the entire structure could be demolished by taking out a few key support beams in the building's lower levels. He also made sure there were certain discreet ways in and out of the building. Only Sid knows these things now that his brother and the old man are gone.

In the months before he absconded from Graveyard, the company was fighting a particularly nasty war against enemies of the New World Order whom Sid hopes he'll never see again—literal monsters. Those horrific things lured the old man and both boys into an ambush at a diner in Texas that only Sid managed to escape. After Sid made it back to Graveyard alone, Walter made him the new Kill Team One and sent him out on a seemingly endless run of revenge killings. It was practically a genocide—a revengenocide. It was a mission Sid ultimately found tedious and a little bit distasteful. It didn't help that Walter constantly belittled him throughout the operation. After a few weeks, he dropped off the grid and never looked back—not until now.

INT. GRAVEYARD HEADQUARTERS – DAY

Helen waits on the second floor balcony of the Graveyard building's lobby. The balcony overlooks the front doors and their metal detectors, flanked by guards who permit entry into the rest of the building. Behind her are the elevators leading to the upper floors. At her sides are the tactical operators of Bravo team, crouching behind sandbags beneath the balcony railing. Walter insisted on the sandbags. She questioned him, but he just made another comment implying she didn't know what she was dealing with when it came to Victor.

She has three teams of ten operators here. One with her and the other two dug in at the front door. Walter has two more teams upstairs on floor ten. Another three teams are patrolling the building, sweeping for any signs of a breach.

She expected this to be a big joke to most of them, but it isn't that way. Some of the newer guys are dicking around, but the older operators are quiet. They were here the last time. They know, and their solemn demeanor worries her.

Chris Coch, the guy next to her, is one of the quiet ones.

"Hey, Anderson," says Hudson Pulasando, the marksman for Bravo Team. "Don't worry. Me and my squad of ultimate badasses will protect you."

"That's sweet of you, Hudson," she replies. "I still won't touch your shrimp dick."

A few of the operators laugh.

"Don't inflate his ego," says Coch. "Hudson's dick

makes a brine shrimp look like a horse cock."

Walter's voice comes in over Helen's radio. "Anything down there?"

Helen looks over the railing through the lobby's great glass front and sweeps over the desert landscape outside. She does this as more of a formality than anything else. She expects to see nothing. Her expectations are correct.

"Not a peep," Helen says.

As if guided by a greater power, one solely invested in situational irony, the building rattles from the detonation of an explosive charge.

"Then what the fuck was that?" Walter yells over the radio.

"I don't know," Helen says.

"All teams, report!" Walter commands.

Helen listens as they each check in from locations all over the building.

"Delta, we're on six. Nothing up here."

"Guard station," the next one calls. It's one of the operators stationed at the front gate on the outskirts of the perimeter. "All clear out here. Was that in the building?"

"I need answers, people," Walter calls.

"Command, November," radios a voice Helen doesn't know. "We're on sub level two. Lot of smoke down here. We think it came from the shower room."

"Who is this, Ratzinger?" Walter says.

"Uh, negative," calls the November operator. "This is Camisaroja. Ratzinger's on vacation."

The building alarm sounds. This is the first time Helen has heard it go off since she started work here. It's a pulsing industrial honk like she would expect from a battle ship or a nuclear plant. The loud honking is underscored by a woman's droning voice repeating the same message back-to-back.

Warning. Security breach reported in sector fourteen.

"What the fuck is that?" Walter's voice crackles over the radio.

"Command, guard station," radios the front gate operator. He's breathing heavily and shouting. "You got incoming! Ran right through the fence!—ks like a school— incoming."

Helen mashes down the talk button to ask him to repeat the last part, but then she sees it. It's coming for them, bouncing on the dirt on its way to the building. It's a school bus—a big yellow school bus.

"Bring it down!" she screams into the radio.

What follows is a storm of bullets that would kill a hundred men and leave nothing but torn scraps of flesh and cloth, unidentifiable as anything except ruined human meat. The outside teams hit that bus with 240s and M16s and even a Carl Gustav recoilless rifle.

It keeps coming.

"Take it down! Take it down!" Helen yells into the radio.

The fire teams continue to pour machine gun rounds into the front of the bus, but it roars toward them still. Helen knows that to be impossible. No one could survive that. Unless . . .

Now she sees. The bus crosses into the blacktop parking lot outside the building and sideswipes some parked cars. Above the battered and smoking engine compartment, the bullet-riddled windshield is an empty void. No one is driving the bus at all.

The fire teams keep shooting. She's sure the engine is destroyed, but that doesn't matter. It's already too close. It's already speeding too fast. It never intended to stop again.

"Oh no," Helen says, watching the bus impact the front of the building. She dives behind the sandbags as an explosion of flame and steel and broken glass engulfs the lobby. The blast is so loud it feels like her ears aren't covered, even though she knows her palms are pressed tightly against them.

The building stops quaking and Helen looks up over the sandbags, seeing very little through the thick black smoke filling the lobby. The operators on the balcony with her are filthy but okay, except for Roy Hemp, rolling around on the floor grunting with glass shards in his eye. Chris Coch moves to try and help him.

Helen peers down below but barely recognizes anything. The lobby floor is covered in debris. The front doors are simply gone, the front of the building nothing but a gaping hole. Scattered sandbags litter the room. Bodies and pieces of bodies stick out from the gaps in debris.

Then she sees him and almost screams.

Victor saunters into the lobby through the destroyed building front. He wears a pale green duster that brushes the destruction beneath his feet, and he carries an M240B slung over his shoulder. Gone is the rugged beard that obscured his face before. He looks down and sees a soldier with a broken leg, attempting to crawl away from the rubble.

"It looks like there's been some kind of accident

here," he says. "Is there anything I can do to help?"

The injured commando turns up to face Victor. Helen can't identify him from here. He's too covered in blood and dirt. Unable to speak, he coughs up something unintelligible.

Victor shoots him in the face with the 240 Bravo. The automatic fire of the machine gun destroys the soldier's skull, leaving nothing but a puddle of black and red muck attached to his shoulders.

"Take him out!" Helen shouts. She lifts the MP5 at her side and squeezes the trigger to fill Victor with as much of the magazine as she can. The others do the same.

He stands without even blinking, as hundreds of bullets whiz past his frame. A few nick his jacket. None hit him. None of them at all.

It's simply not possible. None of this is possible.

Victor looks up at the balcony with a wide grin.

"Didn't they tell you I'm impervious to bullets?" he says.

From a shoulder holster under his jacket, Victor pulls a pistol nearly the length of his forearm. Even from up on the balcony, Helen recognizes the Desert Eagle, a gun so big most professionals consider it nothing more than a novelty. Victor fires three shots, one-handed. Three of Helen's fire team fall dead.

"It looks like *you* are not," Victor says.

Helen drops behind the sandbag barrier and looks around at her remaining team. Coch is still trying to help Hemp.

"This ain't happening, man," Hudson says. Then he takes a bullet in the back of the head from over the sandbags. Wet and salty gore splatters Helen's face.

INT. GRAVEYARD BUILDING – SUB-SUB-
BASEMENT – DAY

Plaster falls from the bathroom ceiling onto Sid's shoulders. With his left hand, he forces a commando's head into a toilet. With his right, he drives a KA-BAR knife into the commando's skull. The point of the blade pops out through an eyeball.

Sid turns on another commando outside the tiny bathroom stall—a thin blond man in a red polo shirt under a flak jacket. He's trying to call for help.

"Command, November! He's in the—"

Sid jams the KA-BAR into the commando's guts. He twists the blade. The operator hurls up a pint of shimmering red blood, which drools down his chin onto his shirt.

Clank. Sid hears the unmistakable noise of a rifle being dropped to the floor behind him. He turns.

Another commando holds his hands in the air, almost touching the low ceiling of the little locker room. He steps back, only to bump into the row of urinals behind him. He's shaggy for a commando, and a little short. He has dark skin and patches of short facial hair not nearly thick enough to be called a beard.

"I'm out," the shaggy commando says. "Dude, I'm out. They don't pay me enough for this shit."

Sid nods at the man, considering the words. He sounds genuinely terrified.

"You want me to hit you or something, to make it look good?" Sid asks.

"No. Fuck it," the commando says. "I'm done

with this shit. I'll get a job at GameStop."

"Good luck. They always tell me they're not hiring."

"My brother-in-law is a district manager."

"Really? You think you could get me a job there?"

"Are you for real?"

"Yeah. You wouldn't believe how hard it is just to get a stupid day job when the only thing on your resume is . . . you know . . ."

Sid pulls his knife from the chest of the dead commando pinned to the wall behind him. It comes out with a spurt of blood.

"I'll, uh, see what I can do," says the shaggy commando as he backs his way from the bathroom.

"What's your name?"

"Bruce . . ." says the commando, shuffling down the hall.

Sid shrugs. He'll have to check in with Bruce at a later date.

INT. GRAVEYARD BUILDING – TENTH FLOOR
– DAY

Helen falls out of the elevator as the doors slide open. She twists, diving for the opposite corridor wall, reaching for the only thing that might help slow him down—a grenade.

She fumbles with the grenade in her shaking hands, but eventually gets two fingers through the ring connected to the pin and gives a tug to jerk it free. She throws the grenade into the elevator before the doors close again. Then she's on her feet, running down the hallway toward the swarm of black-body-armored operators ahead of her. Walter Stedman is in the middle of the pack, holding a USAS-12 at the ready.

"I take it that means he got past the lobby," Walter says. His voice is full of dry cynicism and his face is grim.

"They're all dead!" Helen screams. "They're all dead!"

"Fuck."

"What?" one of the contractors says.

"She joking?" another one says. It's Sheffield, the Alpha Team commander.

Behind her, the elevator doors are blasted half open by the grenade she tossed. The sound of the car screeching down to the first floor and imploding against the cement bottom of the elevator shaft follows.

"She's not joking," Walter says.

"We have to blow the stairwell," Helen says. "It's

the only way to stop him."

"We have superior numbers in a tunnel fight," Sheffield says. "He's not getting through here alive."

"He's impervious to bullets!" she shrieks.

"What?" Sheffield says. "Did you get hit in the head?"

"I know what I saw! They emptied all their mags at him and he just stood there!" She's leaving out the part where she ran like a scared little bitch. She watched him kill them all, some with a knife, and then she ran. She can still see him grinning at her through the elevator doors as they closed. He was in no hurry to catch her, and that worries her the most. "We have to try to blow him up."

"You're delirious. Somebody knock her out before she demos the whole building."

"Hold off on that, son," Walter says. "I believe her."

"You want to blow up the building?" Sheffield says, his voice filled with uncertain confusion.

"I think he's impervious to bullets."

"That's not possible."

"Anything's possible, son. And Helen Anderson doesn't tell whoppers."

"Then what are we supposed to do? Mount up a fucking cavalry charge?"

"I have an idea," calls a voice behind them. Helen can't see him through the densely packed fire team, but she knows that voice and she almost screams.

Victor is already there.

"You can all die," he says.

INT. GRAVEYARD BUILDING – SUB-SUB-BASEMENT – DAY

Sid steps out of the bathroom, dropping a satchel of C4 against the wall across the hallway. He memorized the floor plan of the sub-sub-basement as part of his training. He knows a major support beam runs through here. He's got five more packs to deliver, and then he can get the fuck out through that tunnel he bombed in the level below.

He is more than a little curious about the noise from above. It sounds like the Battle of Okinawa up there. The combination of sustained small arms fire and explosive detonations makes it almost impossible to hear the shadowy assailant approaching his back . . .

Sid whips around and levels his pistol at the threat: a tall Asian man with flowing black hair and a skin-tight suit with a Japanese sword sheathed at his hip. It's the fucking ninja.

"You?" the ninja says, as if he expected someone else. Sid has met this ninja once before, long ago, and only briefly. He seems to have made an impression.

"I hate ninjas," Sid says. He really does. He hates their inexplicable and contradictory codes of honor, and their dirty illusions, and their disappearing into puffs of smoke, and their weird language with four million different letters that all look like someone had a seizure with a paint brush. Ninjas are just so complicated. They're everything he is not.

"I shall vanquish you, demon!" the ninja says.

With only twenty yards between them, Sid pops off

a shot at the ninja's nose. He spent the extra tenth of a second to aim. He can shoot the wings off a termite at this distance without even looking down the iron sights, but he also likes to be sure.

The ninja draws his sword from the sheath and smacks the bullet out of the air in one fluid motion. It slams into the end of the hallway, far beyond the dark figure that was its target.

"Bullets do no good," Sid says, rolling his eyes. "Shocking."

Sid sighs and brings the M4 up from his back as he holsters the pistol. He does this without ever losing a bead on the ninja's face. Immediately, he squeezes the trigger of the assault rifle, opening fire on the ninja with 5.56 rifle rounds in full-auto rock-and-roll mode. Sid controls the gun in a way most people assume is a thing of fantasy, placing each shot almost exactly where the last one hit, all thirty of them—in eight seconds.

The ninja's sword becomes a silver blur, flashing brightly as it twirls. He bats each and every round out of the air. They skitter across the walls and floor as they continue down the hall to slam into the concrete where the corridor turns. Even Sid is impressed.

"Wow," Sid says. "You are *really* good at that." It's an understatement. This guy might be quicker than him.

"Bullets are like flies to be swatted by those truly in touch with their inner power," the ninja says.

Sid launches a grenade at his face. That's insanity at this range, indoors, with a low ceiling, but nobody lives forever. He doesn't anticipate the ninja letting the grenade blow them both up anyway.

He anticipated correctly. The blade cuts the grenade in half. The halves fall to the floor behind the man's boots without detonating. Thick black powder spills from the broken casing and hangs in the air, slowly settling to the floor around the ninja.

Sid opens the under-slung M203 grenade launcher below the fore rail of his rifle and dumps out the empty casing from the grenade he just fired. He packs another into the barrel and slides it back to the closed position.

The ninja throws a ton of sharp things at him. Kunai, shuriken, needles: ninja shit. He hates ninja shit. Sid ducks under a kunai and sidesteps a bunch of shuriken, deflecting one with the rifle. All of them are tipped with ninja poison for sure. That's another thing he hates about ninjas: they put fucking blowfish toxin on everything they touch.

When the projectiles stop coming, he stands and stares. "You done?"

No answer.

He launches the next grenade at the ninja's stupid fucking face. The blade cuts this one in half, just like the last, but this time something is different. This grenade doesn't simply come apart and tumble to the floor. No. This one bursts in a spray of amber colored liquid that splatters the ninja's face and chest.

"What the—" the ninja starts, but it turns to a choking sputter as he begins clawing at his face.

"Tear gas, retard," Sid says. "That's what you get for flashing all that chop suey shit at me."

Sid drops his rifle magazine on the floor and packs the next one into the receiver. He works the charging handle and raises the rifle to his shoulder, but the ninja explodes into a puff of black smoke before Sid can squeeze the trigger.

He stands for a moment, searching the smoke for any signs of his target before concluding the ninja is really gone.

He shakes his head as he picks up the rest of the satchel charges. "Where do they find these guys?"

The sound of an explosion on one of the levels far above continues into a screeching cacophony that races down to meet him. Thirty yards ahead, beyond where the ninja stood, the elevator doors explode out into the hallway. An eruption of soot fills the entire corridor.

Now he has to know what they're doing up there.

INT. GRAVEYARD BUILDING – TENTH FLOOR
– DAY

Helen watches Victor down the barrel of a gun. She's lying on the floor surrounded by cadavers, again. Victor cut down both fire teams with a machine gun while all of them shot back hundreds of times—only to miss hundreds of times, like something out of a bad nightmare.

There's so much blood on the floor Helen smears a trail through it as she tries to scoot up behind him. She doesn't know how she survived the onslaught of bullets killing everyone around her, but she did, and now she has his back.

Victor holds Walter Stedman up against a wall at the end of the hallway. The Graveyard commander is already riddled with bullets, and he spits blood all over Victor's face.

"Too easy, Walter," Victor says. "I told you I'd kill you all."

"I'm not dead yet, you fucking abortion," Walter says.

Victor cackles madly in Walter's face.

Helen inches ever closer. She's trying not to breathe. During all the shooting, Walter dropped the case on the floor. It rests now only a few feet from Victor's heels, in a lake of blood a quarter inch deep. Helen makes her way for the case, not for the kill. She already learned that shooting at him is futile and fighting him hand-to-hand results in a closed casket funeral for anyone who tries. She's certainly not going to try. Walter had to waive her close quarters combat requirements to hire her on at the company.

She can't kill him, but she can grab that case and run.

"I'm not even going to kill you, Walter," Victor says. "I'm going to leave you here so you can watch me turn all of this into a predator's paradise. No more sympathy. No more charity. No more weakness. A world where none but the strong survive, and the strong thrive. The killers will thrive."

Helen leans forward. She can almost reach the case. Just a little farther.

"It's suicide," Walter says. "You'll murder the world."

Victor shrugs. "Nobody lives forever."

She wraps her fingers around the briefcase handle and lifts. As she pulls it up off the floor, it emits a slimy pop from the suction of the blood pool enveloping it. Uh oh.

Victor turns.

"I knew you were there," he says. He lurches forward so fast she doesn't see him coming. She feels the boot in her chest before anything else and she's face up on the floor. Her chest is on fire. It's a struggle to draw breath.

"I was saving you for later," Victor says. "I want to eat your pretty skin while you watch."

INT. GRAVEYARD BUILDING – TENTH FLOOR – DAY

Sid pokes his head around the stairwell doorway and sees the last thing he ever expected to find here or anywhere else—a dead man, his brother, Victor Hansen.

Victor is dressed in a signature pale green duster just like Sid remembers, and that's half the reason he recognizes him from behind. The other half is the squealing woman he's choking against the wall—practically an accessory for his brother.

They're surrounded by dead Graveyard operators. This was a real battle. Actually . . . no. This was just Victor. Sid can tell by the excessive mutilation of the bodies.

Walter Stedman is here too. Fuck that guy. Things did not end well between them, and there's no question in Sid's mind that Stedman is the one who gave Kill Team Two the order to hunt him down.

"I guess if you can't keep your panties on," Victor says, "we might as well get started now."

"I'm not gonna let you have the box," the woman says. On the floor behind them sits a hefty metal briefcase smeared with blood.

"Walter forgot to tell you something else about me. Besides being impervious to bullets."

Victor draws a foot-long knife from his belt. The blade is wavy like a serpent—another signature of his. He slides the blade between her thighs and presses the tip against her crotch.

"I take whatever box I want," Victor says.

She screams.

Sid shrugs and steps back into the stairwell. Not his problem. Time to—what did that space pirate guy say in the movie Lily showed him? Blow this thing and go home?

"When you scream like that it makes me so hard," Victor says. "Do it again."

Nothing. She refuses to scream. A mistake. With Victor, you give him what he wants or it gets so much worse.

"I like a challenge," Victor says. "Let's see if you scream when I cut your tits off."

Sid stops on his way down the stairs. He has seen this all before, across the ocean in a gallery of horrors, years ago. He did nothing then. There was nothing he could do then, just like there is nothing he can do now. It would be a willful tactical error for him to intervene—a huge mistake. There's just *something* he can't place about this that brings his rage to the forefront.

Even without any new screams in the air, he can hear the memories of hundreds from the past. He can see their faces. The worst is the first one—the one Victor took apart in front of him. She was barely grown. It shouldn't bother him. It's stupid. It's just more bodies on top of the pile. The old man trained him never to look back. An animal never looks back and neither should you, the old man would say.

Keep going, he tells himself. *Keep going. You're going to blow this place up in a few minutes anyway. Everyone up here will be dead. Just walk away. It's what that Han Solo guy would do. Right? Right?*

He turns back up the stairs and walks out into the

hallway. He can't explain why. It's easily the stupidest thing he's ever done. He's just so angry he can't stop himself.

Victor turns to face him instantly, dropping the woman on the floor.

"Sid!" Victor says.

"Victor," Sid says.

"Long time, no see. How is everything?"

"Terrible. Economy sucks. I couldn't keep a job at a video store."

"I heard about that. You could always join up with me. I'm about to crush civilization to dust and usher in an age of constant roving violence."

"How's it pay?"

"In blood and pussy."

"No dental?"

"I liked you better before you found sarcasm."

"I never liked you."

Sid raises the M4. Time to finish this. He taps the trigger for quick single shots. Victor won't eat bullets that easy. He needs to test him. He fires off a shot and misses. Then another. Another.

Victor points a 240 Bravo Sid's direction and Sid responds by holding down the trigger.

Victor's victim dives for the floor between them as the crossfire begins. The walls begin to flake away from flying bullets. Sid roars and Victor laughs like a raving lunatic as they fire off everything they have at each other. Sid can feel bullets whizzing past his skull and shoulders. He should dive for cover, but his hate keeps him here, shooting like mad, fixated on his target with an intensity that excludes all self-preservation. When his rifle runs dry, he pulls two pistols and continues shooting. The pistols click empty the same second Victor's machine gun sucks up the last of its belt.

The two of them remain standing, unharmed.

"You're empty," Sid says.

"That's what the prison shrink told me," Victor says. He drops the Bravo and extends the kris blade Sid's direction.

Sid pulls his KA-BAR from its sheath.

"All right," he says. "Let's do this."

Sid cautiously steps down the hall, his right hand extended with the KA-BAR pointing at his brother. He must not overcommit. His brother is not a slob like the soldiers he fought his way through to get here. He can leave no opening and make no mistake. He has dueled his brother before; he has never won.

They come together and the tempest forms.

Sid jabs. Victor swats it aside and counters. Sid deflects the stab away with his elbow. He slices high, low. His brother dodges.

Victor brings down an overhead stab that Sid needs both hands to catch. He stops the blade only inches from his nose. Steel grinds on steel as he tries to overpower his brother. He cannot. He leaps away.

"You're still weak," Victor says.

"You're still an asshole," Sid answers. He takes a swipe at Victor's head, but hits nothing.

Victor comes back with a flurry of attacks. The knives smack together—*Clack! Clack! Clack!*—as Sid deflects each of the blows.

Victor punches him. He tastes blood as Victor connects with his jaw. He jumps back. No. A mistake. Victor will expect him to disengage.

It's too late. Victor is already there bashing him again. He kicks Sid in the shin as he advances and stabs his kris knife through Sid's arm. It slides between the bones, impaling his right forearm. Sid screams. Victor levers his blade to twist Sid's arm. Sid's knife slips away in a rush of sharp pain, but he catches it in his left hand. He stabs at Victor, but his brother is too quick. Victor grabs Sid's knife and kicks him in the chest. The kris knife, gripped firmly in Victor's hand, breaks free in an eruption of blood as Sid sails backward into the woman on the floor. She collapses underneath him.

"Pathetic," Victor says. He stands with both knives in his hands, shaking his head in disappointment. "This isn't even a challenge."

Sid rises as Victor tosses both knives to the floor behind him. Sid swings at his brother with his right fist, blood dripping from the open gash. Victor catches his arm and proceeds to pummel him with punches and kicks. Victor bars Sid's sliced arm and swings him against a wall with a hard thud that ignites a burning pain in his shoulder.

"Fuck!" Sid screams.

Victor rolls his eyes. The woman attacks him.

INT. GRAVEYARD BUILDING - DAY

Victor knows that bitch is behind him. He knows she picked up his knife from the floor. He is always aware. Never let your guard down, the old man always told them. Victor never lets his guard down.

He turns and catches the knife blade in his left hand, inches from his throat. The woman appears shocked. He squeezes down on the blade and his blood oozes from his clenching fist. He does this only for show. He wants her frightened. He wants her terrified. Her eyes widen and she changes tactics.

To Victor, the tiny, involuntary movements she makes are like flashing neon signs declaring what she is about to do. She shifts her weight to her other foot. The muscles in her neck tense up on the left side even before she lifts her arm. He sees these things instinctively, and marvels at her incompetence as he snatches her punching arm with his free hand.

Victor head butts the dumb cunt in her stupid face for what she did. She deserves it. He's careful not to damage her too much. He wants her whole for the fun he'll have with her later.

She tries to kick him. That he simply ignores. She's no kung fu master. She's even an embarrassment compared to the other useless faggots he murdered here. Her kicks feel like a rolled up newspaper smacking against his legs.

"I'm going to have fun fucking you raw," Victor says.

"It'll never happen," comes a raspy voice from over his shoulder. It's Walter Stedman. "Not with your spaghetti noodle dick."

Victor turns and sees Walter, barely standing, bleeding from four bullet wounds, challenging him. Spaghetti dick? How dare he? Victor does NOT have a spaghetti dick. His dick is a fearsome weapon and Walter Stedman is a pathetic old man who does paperwork and gives orders—not a real warrior.

He laughs at Walter.

"Come on, Victor." Walter says. "I'll show you what a real man has hanging and then maybe I'll let you suck it."

Victor takes his knife away from Helen and drops her to the floor again. His fun has been interrupted too many times today. There will be more deaths to atone for this.

Walter has his own knife, a Gerber Mark II dagger.

Walter lunges at him, careless, angry, slow. Victor catches him in the guts with the kris blade and Walter's eyes widen. It was a laughable attempt, unless he had some other motive . . .

Walter raises his hand to show Victor the grenade he is holding. The spring loaded handle flips away and tumbles to the floor.

"Run," Walter says. He's talking to that stupid cunt.

Victor tears the grenade from Walter's hand and throws it down the hallway. It clanks against the corner at the end of the hall and then lands amidst a pile of bodies fifteen meters away. Victor uses Walter as a human shield as the grenade explodes and shrapnel peppers the hallway.

Victor drops the old dead fool when this is done. His brother is gone. That woman is gone. The case is gone. Victor grunts in anger.

INT. LILY'S CAR - DAY

Lily's headphones block out all sound except that pumping through her iPhone speakers. She sings along to Beyonce Knowles' epic megahit "Single Ladies (Put a Ring on It)." Available now from Columbia Records.

"Wuh. Uh. Oh. Oh. Oh. Oh. Wuh—"

The passenger door swings violently open.

"AAAAAaaaaaahhhhh!" Lily screams. "Don't kill me!"

It's Sid. He's lugging a big stainless steel briefcase with him. He dumps it on the floor mat and falls into the seat next to her.

"You had on headphones?" he scolds.

"You said stay awake," she screeches back. "I was up all night driving!"

"Drive! Go!"

"Where are we going?"

"It doesn't matter! We need to get the fuck out of here! Go!"

Lily turns the ignition and shifts the car out of park. As she nudges down on the gas and the car begins to lumber forward through the dirt on the way back to the Interstate, she notices Sid is bleeding profusely from his arm. It drips onto the seat covers and smears the dash and window—everything he touches is gore stained.

"You're bleeding everywhere!" she says. As if it matters anymore; the car already needs a new roof and a steam clean. Her hair is crusty with spilled blood and her skin is covered in a red film. She looks like one of the models at a horror convention, or do the models at a horror convention look like her? Is this life imitating art imitating life imitating—

"You need to drive faster!" Sid roars in her face.

"Okay!" she yells back. "Which way do you want me to go?"

Sid reaches under his seat and snatches something that looks like an RC car remote from underneath. Lily has seen enough Bruce Willis movies to recognize what it is: a remote detonator.

"What are you doing with that?" she says.

He slides out the aluminum antenna and presses the trigger. Lily sees a smoke plume stretch into the sky in the far off distance.

"Holy shit! What did you do?" she says, unintentionally slowing the car as she gawks at the explosion on the horizon.

"I blew up the building," he says.

"Why?"

"To establish rapid dominance! You need to go *faster!*" He's screaming into her ear now.

"What? Which way?"

"Away from that!" He points out her window and she sees it: a black semi, just the truck with no trailer, rolling toward them down the interstate with the massive cloud of explosion dust in the distance beyond.

The tires latch to the blacktop as she pulls onto the highway from the desert soil.

"You need to go—"

"I *know!*" Lily shouts. "*Faster!*"

She stomps the gas pedal to the floorboard and the car lurches forward, pushing her back against her seat.

Sid climbs over her shoulder into the back seat and picks up a handgun from the floor. He shoots into the rear windshield. The gun going off in the car with the windows up feels about as comfortable as putting a firecracker in an open tin can and holding it up to her ear. The windshield cracks into a spider web of a thousand strands, but doesn't break.

"Hey!" Lily attempts to interject as Sid kicks the winhield entirely out of the car. It flaps away in the wind before crashing to the street behind them. The semi crushes it under eight of its sixteen wheels.

He's already shooting at the semi through the gaping back of the car. It's not nearly as loud this way.

A rapid succession of plinking sounds alerts her to something frightening. A glance in the rearview mirror confirmed her fears.

"Is he shooting at us?" Lily yells.

"Yes!" Sid continues shooting at the semi.

"Who is that?"

"My brother!"

"I'm glad I'm an only child!"

Sid shoots at the semi more, but it shows no sign of slowing.

"Why don't you, like, throw a bomb at it or something?" Lily says.

"I know how to blow up a truck!" Sid shouts.

"Then why are you shooting at it?"

"Do you want to switch seats? Huh?"

"No . . ."

"That's what I thought."

He throws a grenade out the back of the car.

"That's what I told you to do!" Lily whines.

"Shut up!" Sid says.

Behind them, the grenade vanishes under the grill of the semi and then explodes in a sharp crack. Acrid black smoke pours from under the truck as it surfs on hot sparks, fishtailing and swerving back and forth across the yellow line.

It finally flips and rolls behind them, then vanishes behind a curtain of dust and smoke.

"Holy shit! Holy shit!" Lily exclaims. "I just lived a Jim Cameron movie. This is awesome."

"Don't stop," Sid says. He climbs over her shoulder again and flops into the passenger seat. His arm dribbles more red onto her lap as he goes over the seat.

"Your arm," she says. "It's still bleeding!"

"Shoulder's dislocated, too," Sid says. He grabs his bloody right wrist with his left hand and . . .

"What are you doing?" Lily asks.

He slams his shoulder against the passenger door until it emits a loud crack. He growls like an animal.

"Ew!" Lily squeals.

"We need to hide the car somewhere," Sid says. "And I need to stitch this up."

EXT. GRAVEYARD BUILDING – PARKING LOT
– DAY

Helen heaves to push a car door open past what-ever obstacle is keeping it closed. She manages about six inches of clearance before the door won't budge anymore, and gives up. The inside of the car is covered in thick dirt and other debris. She can't see anything out there.

She was lucky, though. She was already climbing into the car when she heard the blast. Otherwise she would be buried in that shit, crushed to death or bleeding out or asphyxiating in there.

She closes her eyes and squeezes through the little bit of clearance she has, groaning the whole way. She finally pushes her hips past the crack in the door and stretches out onto the roof of her Hummer. The front end has been smashed in by a boulder of concrete and rebar. The Graveyard building is nothing but a pile of rubble three stories high.

"Motherfucker," she says.

"The demons did this."

She yelps, startled as someone speaks from behind her. It's the ninja. He stands atop a steel I-beam lying at an angle across some nearby cars. A long piece of torn cloth is tied around his head, covering his eyes.

"Your eyes," Helen says.

"Will heal. For now, the flow of chakra around me is the only sight I need."

He steps toward her, but trips on a piece of rebar. He topples onto the roof of the Hummer next to her.

"That seems to be working real well," she says.

Standing up on the roof, she offers the ninja a hand.

The ninja hisses quietly as he pushes himself to his feet without her help. As he regains his feet, he lashes out with his sword in a single swing that lasts only a nanosecond. The blade is sheathed again before she realizes what happened.

Helen isn't sure what she just saw. For a second, she thinks he waved his hand at her, or sneezed. Then the bottom of her flak jacket falls to the ground, sliced in half. The blade didn't cut the tank top she has on underneath it.

"Touché," she says.

"We now face a grave threat. The demons have reunited to bring hell to Earth once again."

"I don't think so. Sid ran away with the case. He tried to kill Victor."

"He burned my eyes and destroyed the compound!"

"He saved my life."

"Perhaps you were confused. You are but a woman."

"Fuck you, Tanaka. I went head to head with death incarnate in there, while you were what? Beating your face against a hive of killer bees? You can either be constructive or you can shut the fuck up and I'll leave you here."

The ninja emits a growling sigh that Helen can only describe as very Japanese.

"We must find Sid Hansen," Tanaka says.

"That's more like it," Helen says.

INT. LILY'S CAR - DAY

A neon sign reads OFFICE in blue letters. Beside the word is a glowing red arrow pointing down and to the left. It hangs in a window next to a brown steel door held open by a wedge on the linoleum floor beyond the door frame. Sid observes these things from the passenger seat of Lily's car, parked in the blacktop lot outside this shoddy building.

He has a mysterious box that the most dangerous people in the world will kill to obtain. He has a madman hunting him. There is no ammunition remaining, and Lily wants a motel room. Sid doesn't like any of this at all.

"You can't use a credit card," he says. "They'll know right away."

"How long do I have to stay off the grid?" Lily asks. Sid hangs on the phrase she uses, like she thinks she's an operator now.

"Depends. I took out everybody that can I.D. you, except the Ghoul."

"The Ghoul?"

"The bulletproof guy in the skull mask."

"Oh. That guy. Where do you think he went?"

"No idea."

"Well, we need a place to stay where we can get cleaned up."

"I don't like motel rooms. There's only one way in and out. It's like asking to be cornered."

That is true, but she still may be onto something. If Sid can find a way to get her a room without using a credit card or identification, then he could leave her there for as long as it takes him to finish this business with his brother and Graveyard. Of course, she'd have to be smart enough not to give up her cover while she stays there. Sid isn't so sure about that part.

Lily turns the rearview mirror to look at herself. She brushes her blood-spattered hair back and begins tying it behind her head with a scrunchie she retrieves from the console.

"What are you doing?" Sid says.

"I'm going to get us a room." Lily reaches into her bra and pushes up her breasts.

"You're covered in commando gibs. You can't let anyone see you like this."

"I got this, dude," she says, exiting the car. "You just have to trust me."

He watches as she tiptoes up to the motel office barefoot through the parking lot. She rolls her skirt up along the way, to make it shorter, and pulls it lower to expose her hips. Then she vanishes beyond the door beneath the neon check-in sign.

He waits five minutes.

Then ten.

He's about to walk into the office and kill everyone he sees, when she emerges again, smiling at him. She dangles a key on the end of a ring with a big plastic room number tag attached.

Unbelievable.

"How the fuck did you do that?" he asks, as she opens the door and sits down in the driver's seat.

"Never underestimate the power of pussy, Mr. Kill Team," she says.

"You're covered in blood."

"I said I just came from a GWAR show."

"A what?"

"It's a metal band. I dated this guy who—just don't worry about it."

"Okay. What were you going to do if it was a girl at the check-in desk?"

She raises an eyebrow. "It *was* a girl at the check-in desk."

A deluge of visuals pours into Sid's mind as he fills in the blanks. It is unexpectedly intriguing.

"Did you figure out what the MacGuffin is yet?" Lily asks. The metal case he recovered from the Graveyard building still sits on the floor under his feet.

"Why do you keep calling it that?"

"Cause that's what it is. It's a MacGuffin."

"What the hell is that?"

"It's a plot device in movies and stuff, like the diamonds from *Snatch* or the briefcase from *Pulp Fiction*."

"I don't follow."

"It's just a thing that everybody wants. You don't even really have to know what it is, but all the characters will do anything to get it."

"Walter Stedman died to make sure my brother didn't get it."

"That's classic MacGuffin," Lily says. She feigns choking. "You. Must. Cough. Make sure the MacGuffin never falls. Cough. Into the wrong hands . . ."

She's joking, but Sid doesn't laugh. This thing is trouble.

"Let's go get cleaned off," Lily says. "You go first. You smell like a bleu cheese factory's dumpster."

EXT. DESERT - DAY

Who watches the watchmen? The question has fascinated Helen for most of her life. She has been a watchman for most of it now. She was literally a watchman for a large department store in high school. Then she worked in the Ombudsman's office at Yale. Then she went to work at the IRS. Then on to the NSA. At all of those places, the watchmen needed watching. At (almost) all of those places, the watchmen were being watched. At Graveyard, no one watches them. Most people don't believe they're real. And therein lies another problem.

Quis custodiet ipsos custodes? is the original Latin phrase about the watchmen. It had nothing to do with politics or dictators in its original usage. It was about keeping a cheating wife in line. Translated literally, it is *Who will guard the guards themselves?* The question is more applicable when stated that way. It turns out the answer is no one. No one is watching Graveyard and no one's guarding them, either.

There were no emergency crews back at the building. No National Guard. No FEMA. Not even a fire truck showed up. If there is a contingency plan for what happens when somebody blows up the secret base of the invisible black ops commandos that don't exist, Helen does not know what it is.

The two of them picked through what rubble they could lift, salvaging very little. She found a shotgun inside a smashed-in locker with another flak jacket. They met up with the guys from the gate station and a few operators who were on a sub level when the building imploded. No one had a car. The parking lot was buried in an avalanche of concrete, glass, and steel. The chopper on the roof went down somewhere in the dust cloud. There was another on the airfield behind the building, but no one knew how to fly it. Helen and Tanaka didn't have time to stand around waiting for help that might never come, so they started walking.

It took them an hour to reach the interstate.

"This truck brought a shipment of ammo crates to the back dock this morning," Helen says. She puts her hand on the shredded rear tire of the semi, which rests on its side near the brim of the road. They've found it flipped and abandoned out here. She initially hopes they can turn it over somehow, maybe with a jack—who knows. In any case, the truck is useless now.

"He travels east," Tanaka says. The ninja stands closer to the road, observing the wilderness around them—with what, Helen can't say. His eyes don't seem to work.

"It looks like Sid shook him. These tires are shredded. Probably a grenade."

"Here," Tanaka calls from the dirt ahead, closer to the road. He moves like a cat. He's there one minute and gone the next. It's getting on her nerves.

Helen hustles ahead to catch up. She's disgusted by what she sees when she closes in. Lying in the dirt, at the tips of the ninja's tabi, lies a soiled and bloody cadaver. The truck driver, she suspects at first, but then she gets closer. It's a teenage boy, maybe a college kid, with some flip flops and a rock band T-shirt.

"The truck driver?" Tanaka says. The ninja is stone faced as always.

"No," Helen answers. She grimaces. "Victor must have taken another car."

Helen kneels down and turns the body to check for I.D. She doesn't know what good it will do. Graveyard's analysts are probably all dead, and the FBI isn't likely to help her. Even if they do, Victor isn't likely to keep the car more than a few hours.

"There is a car approaching," Tanaka says.

"Seriously?" Helen says, surprised.

Helen is amazed by everything the ninja does. She has to strain her eyes to see the tiny speck moving toward them along the road. Tanaka knew somehow before it even came over the horizon.

"Here," she says, tossing her shotgun down in the dirt. "Help me move this body away from the road."

Helen grabs the body under the arms and lifts. The head dangles like a nylon stocking filled with lead and drags along the ground as she tugs the body away from the street. Tanaka picks up the legs and helps.

They dump the cadaver far enough from the road that it won't easily be spotted, and Helen drops her flak jacket in the dirt.

"Now hide behind . . ." Helen fruitlessly searches the open, gray landscape for somewhere the ninja can hide. ". . . something?"

The ninja is already gone. Exactly where he went is a mystery, but she doesn't care. Helen walks back to the street and waves her hands in the air to flag down the car coming her way. It's a small red sedan—a Chevy Impala, she sees as it comes closer.

The car slows to a stop and the driver's side window slides down with the whir of an electric motor. The man inside is middle-aged and serious looking, even in a sweaty maroon tank top. He wears black horn-rimmed glasses that dwarf his gaunt face.

"You have an accident out here?" he says, tipping his head back to the wrecked semi.

"I'm a federal agent, sir," Helen says, leaning down to the window. "I'm gonna need to commandeer this vehicle."

"Are you a cop? You have a badge?" the driver says, incredulously.

"This is my badge," Helen says. She draws a 9mm M&P Shield from her pants and points it in the window. "Now step out of the car."

The driver flinches at the sight of the gun. He blinks several times, as if uncertain what to do, then opens the door, stepping out to the pavement. As he exits the vehicle and stands up in front of her, Helen realizes she has a problem.

The driver is over seven feet tall.

He looks down, almost straight down, at her as he closes the door and leaves nothing between them.

"Oh," is all Helen says, eyeing the huge figure.

He bats the pistol from her hand with a slap, and the gun tumbles to the dirt beside them.

"Help!" Helen yelps.

The ninja appears at her side instantly. He waves his hand in front of the hulking motorist and speaks calmly. The motorist stops advancing on them.

"Your mind has become clouded," the ninja says, waving his hand between them. "You are very confused about why you are here."

"I'm really confused about why I'm here," the motorist says. He gazes off into the desert without focus.

Helen picks up her pistol from the ground at her feet and then goes to retrieve her shotgun and flak jacket. "You're going to have to teach me to do that."

INT. MOTEL ROOM – NIGHT

Sid grinds a stake as he sits on a fluffy upholstered chair in the corner. He's fashioned his makeshift weapon from a broken bedpost and a sharp rock he found. It is far inferior to the KA-BAR knife he lost in the Graveyard building, but for now it will do.

The motel room has a bed, table, nightstand, TV, and the chair Sid is sitting in. It's a palace by his standards. Though he did, for a time, live in a cave where he subsisted on the cooked flesh of his enemies, so his standards are not high.

Sid showered, wrapped his arm in toilet paper, and walked to a Kroger store down the street, where he stole a bottle of rubbing alcohol, a pack of surgical sutures, some clothes for both of them, and a bucket of chicken. He came back to the room, stitched his arm, and ate some of the chicken. He did this all while Lily was taking a bath. He is nearly finished carving the edge of his stake as she emerges.

"You're making weapons," she says. "Why am I not surprised? Do you ever stop?"

"You can never stop," he says. "I told you that's the worst part of it."

"I think it's exciting."

"You'll learn."

He glances up from his carving and sees she is wearing nothing but a towel wrapped around her hair. She's still dripping on the carpet.

"You're naked," Sid says, realizing he has never seen her naked before. Even when they had sex, she kept her clothes on.

"Yeah," she answers. "Are you in the Taliban or something?"

"No."

"You sure you don't want me to put on a burqa?"

He doesn't answer the question. He's not sure he even understood it. He can't remember what he was doing a few seconds ago. She could have toweled herself off in the bathroom. Why didn't she?

She smiles at him over her shoulder and removes the towel from her head. Her shimmering, wet, raven hair dangles loosely beyond her shoulder blades, dripping onto her heart-shaped butt. She drops the towel on the floor in a way that raises his suspicion. No one is that clumsy.

"Oops," she says. Her legs remain straight as she arches her back and bends at her hips to reach all the way down to the floor, salaciously exposing all of her lower intimate parts to him. She retrieves the towel and begins drying her wet hair.

He studies her body as she turns to face him. Her skin is smooth and milky white, shaven clean all over. Her taut breasts are tipped with tiny pink nipples that seem to belie the little girl underneath all the black dye and tattoos. One of them seems to be placed curiously like a warning at the gate.

"Why wasteland?" Sid says. It's a playful question. He means nothing by it, except to tease her maybe. "What does it mean?"

Lily narrows her azure eyes at him. Not the reaction he expected.

"It's personal," she says, as she finishes toweling herself dry. She flips the nearby light switch and the room goes dark. She remains there for a moment in the darkness. If she thinks he can't see her, she's wrong. He has the night vision of a cat. He watches her hands at first. Hands don't lie. He sees where they go, and then he sees the fleeting look of sadness on her face. She shakes it away in an instant, but he saw.

She flops down on the bed, and there they are, alone in the dark.

"Sid," she says. "How many people have you killed?"

"It's personal," he says, as he pulls his shirt over his head, throwing it to the floor at his feet. He can't wait to feel her bare skin against his.

"I see what you did there," she says. She laughs.

"Yeah?"

"How about we play a game?" she suggests, giggling. "I'll answer a question for you and then you answer a question for me. We'll take turns. Sound like fun?"

"Okay," Sid responds rapidly. "I go first. Tell me about the wasteland."

"Except that." Lily shakes her head. "That one is off limits. And I go first."

"I don't like the way you play this game," he says, standing up and setting the wooden stake on the nightstand between them. He sits down on the bed next to her and begins taking his shoes off.

"How many people have you killed?" she asks.

He thinks about it for a moment to tabulate an answer.

"Uh, four something," he says, dumping his shoes on the floor next to the bed.

"Does it ever bother you?" she asks, staring up at the ceiling.

"You're cheating." Sid lies back on the bed and removes his pants. They fall next to him, on top of the shoes. "It's my turn."

"Fair enough." Lily rolls over to face away from him and sighs. "Go."

"How many men have you fucked?"

"Twenty-six," she answers, without even a second to think about it. She had the number ready, as if it's one she keeps in her mind all the time.

"Holy shit!" Sid exclaims.

"What?" Lily squeaks.

"That's just a really high number."

"You killed four hundred people!" She punches him in the shoulder.

"Four thousand," Sid corrects her. Four hundred kills? When he was a toddler, maybe.

"What?" Lily howls. "How did you have time for anything else?"

"I didn't." He shrugs. "What's your excuse?"

Lily rolls her eyes, sighing. She pulls up the edge of the comforter underneath them.

"It's my turn," she says, curling up at the top of the bed and then slithering under the comforter to get away from him. "Ass."

"No it isn't," Sid says. He frowns, annoyed at the featureless lump off flowery fabric next to him. "I just answered two in a row."

"You did?"

"Yeah." He pulls back the comforter on his side of the bed and crawls underneath to join her in the cold blackness of fresh sheets. "You asked me 'What?' and 'How did you have time for anything else?' and now you asked me what questions you asked me and I answered that, too."

"Fuck. You're too good at this."

"I'll call it even if you answer a really good one for me."

He scoots in close to her. She's warm. Her soft neck buzzes against the tip of his nose like it's electric. He puts his bandaged arm over her. The feel of her flesh against his is intoxicating.

"Yeah?" she says. "I bet I know what that's gonna be."

"Then answer it," he says. He didn't care about the answer before. It was just something stupid, but the more she resists, the more he has to know.

"It means exactly what it says," she says.

"That's not an answer."

"What is it with you men that you're all so dense you need it spelled out?"

"That's a question."

"I can't have babies because of what happened with Ted. I just thought wasteland was a metal thing to put there because of it."

"Metal?"

"Yeah. Like death metal. Self-destruction. Nihilism. We're all slowly dying. That kind of thing. This other one is a quote from a serial killer." Lily brushes her fingers across the script that reads 'Death comes with the territory. See you in Disneyland.' "How come nobody ever asks about that?"

"There's just something attention-grabbing about the other one. I think it's the location . . ."

His hand glides along her flesh and across the wasteland. He places a finger between her moist lips.

"You're doing it wrong," Lily says. She takes him

by the wrist and places his hand on her hip.

"You wanna show me the right way to do it?" he says, moving his hand back to her feminine parts.

"Are you gonna kill Ted for me?"

"Seriously?" He can't believe she's still on about that. After everything that happened, he didn't even remember she asked him to kill somebody.

"Seriously." She slaps him away again. "We made a deal."

"I told you, I'm not killing anybody so you'll have sex with me."

"Then I'm not having sex with you."

Sid turns over and lies on his back. His erection rages like a bound attack dog. He seethes with frustration. She knew this would happen. She came out of the bathroom naked and wet, rubbing herself dry, making his blood boil over. She planncd this. She's playing him.

He turns over and places his arm around her again. He cups her breast in his hand and pulls her close to him forcefully. He whispers into her ear.

"You know, I really don't need your permission," he says.

"Excuse me?" she says. She turns over and faces him. Her nose rubs against his whiskers. "No means no, asshole."

He glares at her with his killing eyes. She glares right back at him.

Lily will fight him. She's not the kind who lies back and cries woefully as she's taken. He would have to beat her, or choke her, or break some of her fingers. Unconscious or otherwise, she would comply then.

He can't do that to her.

He growls, turning away.

"Of course . . ." she says. He feels her fingers close around his epic anger boner. "If you do what I ask, yes could mean yes."

"Fine," he says, begrudgingly. "I'll do it."

"I knew you'd come around," she says.

"All right." He puts his arms around her again. He places one hand at the small of her back and draws her close to him. "Let's do this."

"Hold your horses," she says. She braces against his face with her elbow to push him away. "Not until you do the job."

"You've got to be kidding me."

"Nope. I want you to bring me his head first."

"Where is he?" Sid starts to reach for his shoes. "I'll go do it now."

"He's in prison in New York State. He gets out in two months."

"You're fucking torturing me here," Sid says. He drops the shoes and falls back down next to her again.

"Chill out," she says. She plants her hands on his chest, pushing him down against the bed as she climbs on top of him. "I'm going to do something to help you relax, but first I'm going to show you how to touch me the right way."

She comes through on both promises.

INT. VIDEO TIME – NIGHT

Amy waves goodbye to Glenn from Xtreme Clean. There's a guy with a dirty job right there. She couldn't do what he does. Mopping up dried blood and other bits would wear on her nerves. She couldn't even watch him clean the floor. She stayed in the stockroom, studying for tomorrow's econ exam, the whole time he was there.

She'd done an okay job of avoiding the disgusting mess for the last two days. It was hard, considering most of it had been in the front doorway, but she'd managed all right. The police took the bodies, of course, but the gore all over the front counter and tile walkway was the store owner's problem. Marty, the owner, paid Xtreme Clean to power wash it all away.

Amy hears someone tug at the door behind her and the bells chime as it opens. She forgot to lock the door behind the cleaning crew.

"We're closed," she says, before turning to see who walked in.

The man standing in front of her has dark hair and icy blue eyes. His cheekbones are bruised, his forehead lined with straight line scabs from recent cuts, and his thick green duster is scuffed at one shoulder and elbow. He smiles at her warmly "Oh, I'm sorry. I didn't know. But I'm not here for a videotape. I'm looking for someone. Maybe you can point me in the right direction?"

"Maybe."

"I'm looking for the other girl who works here," he says. "The dark-haired one."

"Who's asking?"

"I'm an old friend. We go way back, she and I."

"And do you have a name, old friend that goes way back?"

He doesn't answer. He smiles and backs away from the counter. He looks down at the shimmering tile beneath his feet.

"I heard about what happened," he says. "It looks like they did a wonderful job cleaning up the mess."

"Yeah," Amy says. "We got some real pros in here."

"It would be a shame if they had to come back and clean up another one so soon."

EXT. GAS STATION - DAY

Sid exits through the automatic sliding doors of a gas station food mart carrying three bottles of water, two sandwiches wrapped in clear plastic, and a Styrofoam cup of black coffee. He is greeted by the sight of Lily sitting on the trunk of her battered car, her legs crossed next to a faded Joy Division bumper sticker. Her face is half hidden behind a thick-framed pair of black sunglasses. She releases a stream of grey smoke from her mouth with a dry vacancy of expression that implies to Sid she hates the air itself and wants to fill it all up with her exhaust.

"Why do you do that?" he says, setting the sandwiches down on the trunk next to her.

"Do what?" she snarks back.

"Smoke cigarettes. They're poison."

"They can't be worse than those gas station sandwiches."

"I'm pretty sure they're worse."

Lily extends an open box of cigarettes toward his nose. She presses one of the rolled paper cylinders from the package with her thumb. "Wanna find out?"

"No." Sid hands her the coffee and she takes it with an acidic grin.

"You're such a tight-ass."

"I am not a tight-ass."

"Why did you pick this gas station to stop at?"

"It's a brick structure with a rear exit to a forested area and a large number of sight blocking stickers in the front window to obscure against sniper fire, as well as a steel dumpster which could provide hard cover against large caliber firearms. The adjacent highway is also heavily trafficked, making it unlikely that anyone trying to be discreet would—"

"Hang on, I can't hear you over all the puckering of your tight ass, tight-ass. If you weren't a total murder machine I think you'd be an English professor or something."

"I don't make tactical errors."

"I don't make tactical errors," Lily says in a mocking imitation of his gruff voice. "You never just do anything just because? Even if it's bad for you?"

"Like what?"

"Booze? Gambling? MMORPGs? Smokes?" She holds out the cigarettes again. "Come on. You know you want to." She looks at him seductively over the rims of those shades. Sid studies the white box with its gold trim. Angry and official-looking block letters near the bottom of the package issue a warning to him from the surgeon general.

Sid considers her proposition. The old man would say no. Hell, the old man would break her hand for annoying him, but listening to the old man is what made Sid into the aberrant super killer he is, with little hope of ever fitting into the normal world. Listening to somebody normal like Lily might help him round things out a bit.

He takes one of the cigarettes and presses it between his lips. Lily has a lighter out faster than a cobra's bite and she's igniting the paper. She tells him to inhale. He does. It reminds him somewhat of the clouded fumes the old man made them breathe in the makeshift gas house he built in the pine barrens where Sid used to live.

"I'm not getting anything from this," he says, exhaling a cloud of smoke.

"You have to give it a minute. Sheesh."

Sid drags on the cigarette again and waits for something to happen. "This is stupid."

"You're stupid," Lily says. She slugs his shoulder. Her wrist is bent and her fist all wrong. All the power comes from the whipping of her forearm instead of her shoulder.

"You punch like a bitch," Sid says.

"I *am* a bitch. A bad bitch."

"That's not an excuse. Come here." Sid snatches her wrist and tugs her down from the car despite her protestations. He takes her coffee, setting it on the trunk. He pulls her right hand between them and molds her fingers into an acceptable fist. "Tuck your fingers in. Thumb goes on the outside. No, not pointing out like that. Keep it against your fingers. Wrist straight. Clench tight. Good." He plants her fist against her cheek bone, then grabs her shoulder and turns her whole body just a few degrees to his left.

He steps back and reads her body. He nods and holds up his hand. "Now punch," he says. She swings at his raised palm, snapping her elbow, her arm moving in more of a hammering motion than a rear hand straight punch. It's pathetic. "Raise your elbow and throw your shoulder forward, rotating your body as you punch. Again." She does most of what he says. She's slower now, and awkward. "You're telegraphing."

"What does that even mean?"

"Don't wind up. Your fist should move straight from where it starts to where you're striking." She lowers her fists and he flicks her face.

"Ow!"

"Don't drop your guard. Again."

She does. It's terrible, but less terrible. He shows her how his fists rotate as he punches. After a few dozen tries, she can finally do something that's half-way presentable.

"Is this good?" Lily says, punching his hand again.

She's still telegraphing, and her shoulder doesn't come up high enough to guard her face from the side. The old man would have beaten Sid for such a feeble effort, but this is a crash course and will have to do for now.

"It's okay," he says.

"How was that cigarette?" she asks, plucking the remaining nub of cigarette filter from his mouth and flicking it to the blacktop.

Sid shrugs. "Pointless. And poison."

"That's half the fun," Lily says. "Tight-ass." She weaves her head around and he can tell she's rolling her eyes at him behind those black shades. "So what's the plan for today?"

"We need weapons."

INT. GARY'S GUN SHOW – DAY

Lily walks into the gun show and flips up her sunglasses. She rests them on top of her head as she scans the crowd for a perfect mark. She's wearing some jeans Sid stole for her and the spaghetti strap top she's worn for the last two days. She had to run it through the motel laundry machine three times to feel okay about wearing it again.

She spots her man after a minute: older, chubby, alone except for a little Pomeranian. He sits on a metal folding chair behind a collapsible Rubbermaid table covered in guns and gun parts. The little dog yaps as she approaches.

"Hi," she says.

The sloppy hick raises his head, surprised.

"Sparky, shut up," he yells at the dog. "There something I can help you with, honey?"

"I think so," Lily says. She brushes back her hair. "I need a really big barrel for my lower receiver."

"I think I can help with that," says the gun trader. "How's your lower look?"

"Oh, it's stripped right now." She leans over the table so he can see all the way down the front of her shirt. "Wanna see?"

"Uh," the gun trader says. She has him hopelessly mesmerized. "Sure."

Behind him, Lily sees Sid swipe some parts from a crate on the floor.

She snatches something from her purse: another five-finger-discount from a big box retailer. She sets the item down on the table. It's an AR-15 lower receiver.

EXT. PARKING LOT - DAY

In the parking lot outside the huge convention center hosting Gary's Gun Show, Sid stands behind Lily's car. An assortment of gun parts lays spread across the trunk top.

"Did I do good?" she says, as she approaches from the convention center.

"Yeah," he answers.

"I told you a man can't resist looking at a pair of tits."

"I need the part you have in your purse."

She pulls it out and plops it down on the trunk.

"So what does that thing do?"

"It's like the main part of the gun. All the other parts get connected to it."

She watches as Sid snaps tiny metal springs and pins into the receiver. Then he puts a much larger spring into a plastic tube, screwing that into a threaded loop. He keeps attaching parts without taking his eyes off her. It takes him less than thirty seconds to build a whole rifle.

"You're really good at that," she says.

He smiles.

"Wanna go back to the motel and I'll show you what else I'm good at?" He smacks her butt.

"Look at you. So cocky so fast." She puts her hands on his belt.

"I'm a quick learner." He really is.

Lily's iPhone vibrates against her hip. She pulls it from her waistband and glances at the display. Amy, probably calling about the store. Lily rubs the slider to ignore.

"Do you think they're looking for us?" she asks.

"Looking for you?" Sid says. "Probably not. Me? They're always looking for me."

The iPhone buzzes again. Amy calling. What the fuck? Lily slides the phone to answer.

"Hello?" she says.

Amy's quivering voice whimpers through the speaker.

"Lily. He's hurt—" she chokes into a scream. "He's hurting me!"

"What? Who?"

No one answers.

"Amy!" Lily shrieks.

"Hello, Lily." The voice coming over the speaker is vicious, nearly inhuman with rage. It reminds her of a lawnmower running. "I'm going to make this very simple. Tell my brother to bring the case to the video store by midnight, or I'll gut this cunt and strangle her with what I pull out."

Lily's heart races.

"Lily, please!" Amy cries. "He—" the scream that follows is the unmistakable product of him breaking some part of her.

The phone cuts out.

```
INT. LILY'S CAR - DAY
```

The steel case sits on the back seat, silently taunting them. Lily looks at it between the seat backs, her face pressed up against Sid's shoulder.

"That thing could be a god damned suitcase nuke for all we know," Sid says. "We can't let him have it."

"I'm not saying let him have it," Lily shoots back. "I'm saying we just dangle it at him and then you kill him."

"Yeah. No thanks," Sid scoffs. "That sounds like a real good way to end up dead."

"What happened to the guy who ended, like, fifty commandos and blew up a building yesterday? You kill the bad guys and save the girl. That's what you do."

"That's not what I do at all. I don't think you've been paying attention."

"I'll suck your cock if you do it."

"Before or after Victor eviscerates me and incinerates my carcass with grenades?"

"What's his deal anyway?"

"He's a super soldier like me."

"Yeah, I know that, but he's not like you, really."

"He's stronger, faster, smarter. He's better in every way. Always was. The scars on my arms? He gave me almost all of them."

"But I mean something else. Like, what makes him tick? What does he believe in? What does he want?"

"I don't think he believes in anything he can't hold in his hand. I know exactly what he wants. He wants to murder everyone he can. He has a rage, a bloodlust you can't possibly understand. In Afghanistan, I watched him rape and dismember a girl because she took some bottled water from a supply depot. She couldn't have been older than fourteen. You know what that looks like?"

Lily is silent. She doesn't know what she could ever say to that.

"I did nothing," he says. "There was nothing I *could* do. I just walked away. I don't think she even took the water. He just wanted to do his thing."

Lily watches quietly as his brow crunches into a look of frustration.

"You hate him," Lily says.

He looks up at her and his face is one of quiet realization, as if it's something he never considered himself before she told him.

"You didn't want to walk away," she says. "You wanted to stop him. It bothers you."

"It doesn't bother me," he aggressively denies.

"Oh no," Lily sneers. "Nothing ever bothers you."

"Nothing." His insistence is so strong it only serves to disprove him. He protests too much.

"Yeah? Why didn't you just leave me behind before? You know, instead of fighting an army of soldier guys and blowing up that building? That would have made more sense."

"Because . . ."

"I'm still weighing you down. You should just put a bullet in my brain and get it over with. Go back off the grid. I mean, if you really don't care."

"I don't think . . ."

"You know, I watched you brutally murder a whole

squad of guys you apparently used to work with, blow up a building like it was nothing, pimp-slap a dude with his own arm you ripped off, shoot down two helicopters, and through all of that you were ice cold, like Ben Stein—well, bad example maybe—like Walter White."

"Who?"

"But you're still haunted by this girl from the desert with the bottled water."

"It's really more of a mountain climate."

"Whatever. You haven't forgotten her. You don't even want to talk about it now. You're changing the subject."

"No I'm not."

"And you've gone well out of your way to stop those commando guys from shooting me to pieces, when it really wasn't your problem."

"I needed to do all of this. You just came along for the ride."

"Bullshit. You have a soft spot for pretty girls."

"Fuck you!"

"You totally do! You have a soft chewy center. You're a Tootsie Pop!"

"I will smack the shit out of you if you don't shut the fuck up right now."

"Like you did last night when I told you no means no?" Lily grins. Honestly, she was shocked when he didn't wrap his killer hands around her neck and have his way with her violently in that motel room. She was half hoping he would.

"I'm not soft!" he barks.

"I don't think I even have to argue with you about this anymore. You're going to start the car and go back to Morston and look in that video store no matter what I say, because you're thinking about what he's doing to Amy and you can't stand it."

"You're wrong."

"Am I? Am I really?" Lily rotates in her seat so her whole body is facing him. She narrows her eyes and glares at him—through him. He glares back with angry intensity, but she doesn't let up. After only a second of silence she sees the slightest shift in his gaze away from her. His eyes dart right back to meet hers, but that microsecond lapse is enough to confirm everything she just surmised.

They continue to glare at each other in silence for another full minute before he rubs the frayed wires together to start the ignition.

INT. VIDEO TIME – NIGHT

Sid enters the video store, leading the way with a .45 automatic in each hand and a rifle slung across his back. Lily tags along behind him. This after an hour of scoping the place with binoculars and seeing no signs of life.

He crouches behind the front counter.

"Get down," he says.

She drops down next to him.

"You really do the two gun thing?" Lily asks.

"Everybody does that," Sid says.

"Really?"

"Yeah. They're called handguns. You have two hands. Two is better than one. It's not that complicated."

He jumps out from behind the counter and sweeps his gun sights across the store. Lily watches as his ice cold face turns to a cringe and he lowers both guns.

"What is it?" she says.

"Go back to the car," he barks.

"What is it?"

Lily stands up and marches toward him.

"You don't want to see this," he warns. He's too late though. She already sees.

Amy's half-naked corpse stares up at them with wide vacant eyes from the floor of the family aisle. What he did to her—Lily has to look away.

She buries her face in Sid's chest.

"She was supposed to be a kindergarten teacher!" she cries.

It doesn't make any sense, what she said, but it's

somehow okay not to make sense right now.

Sid stands like a monument with his guns in his hands and, she's sure, an uncertain grimace looking down on her. She suddenly feels feverishly hot and her stomach churns.

"I—I think I'm going to—"

She dashes for the back of the store. Sid yells something after her about not being safe, but she doesn't care. She bashes open the door to the stockroom as she dry heaves. She runs for the tiny bathroom and practically falls through the door.

She drops in front of the toilet, pulling back her hair to vomit. She hasn't eaten and there isn't much to come up, but she needs to get out what she can. When it's over, she sits on the dusty floor next to the toilet and cries.

Lily only saw for a second, but she can't make the image go away. Every time she blinks she sees it. She sees the eyes, the blood, what was wrapped around her neck . . .

She cries. All she can do is cry.

It takes her a moment to notice her phone ringing. She pulls it from her bra and looks at the screen. **MOM** flashes on the display. Probably wondering where she is. She taps the answer button. She needs her mother right now.

"Mom?"

"Are you ready to die, Lily?" It's the chainsaw growl of Victor's voice.

Lily screams. Not this. Not her mother.

"Oh God," she shrieks. "You murdered Amy!"

His laugh is a gruff fleeting thing that ends almost as soon as it begins.

"I got bored with her," he says. "Next it's Mommy's turn."

"Oh no," Lily cries. "Please don't."

"That's what your friend said. She said it over and over—for a very long time."

"She didn't do anything to you!"

Victor cackles like a madman. "No, she didn't. Now I have a new deal for you, baby girl. The Galleria. Noon. By the main entrance. Tell my brother nothing. He's too much of a nuisance."

"I can't. I can't."

"But you have to. How else do you think this ends? He couldn't help that bimbo in the video store. He can't help your mother, and he can't help you. Bring me the case, and you can live. If you're not there, I'll pour bleach down Mommy's throat and then I'll come for you. I'll find you, and when I finish twisting and carving your body, you'll choose death over the living hell I leave you in."

Lily's mother screams into the phone. It disconnects.

The power clicks off in the whole video store. Lily is plunged into darkness. She waits for the stockroom flood lights to come on, then remembers she never replaced the batteries even after Amy asked her three times. She didn't think it was important. It's not like the power goes out that often.

She wonders then why the power went out now. There isn't a thunderstorm outside or anything. Something is wrong.

She stumbles back into the stockroom. She takes three careful steps into the room before she hears it: the rise and fall of breathing; quiet, but not in her head. Is there someone in here with her?

"Sid?" she says. No response.

She knows she'll never make it through the jungle of broken movie displays on the floor back here without tripping and injuring herself. Duh. Her iPhone has a backlight. She pushes the power and spins it around to illuminate the way ahead.

Something shuffles on the floor. There's someone in the room with her.

Quickly, she turns around. The light of the phone display illuminates something black and moving, fabric. A curtain? A shirt?

A screaming skull.

The hulking monster swings a machete at Lily. She ducks, feeling the blade buzz the top of her head. It sticks in a shelving unit beside her.

"Flesh for my hunger!" bellows the Ghoul.

Lily fills her lungs to scream, but the monster lashes out and snatches her throat. She feels her feet leave the ground as he hoists her into the air with one hand. She can't breathe. Her legs flail wildly. She grabs his arm and tries to push herself free from his grasp, but she can't.

The monster bashes her against the wall, rattling her brain. Her back throbs like she's been stabbed. She punches the Ghoul in his rubber skull face, but it's like punching King Kong. He doesn't even flinch.

He clamps his other hand down around her throat and squeezes. She feels her eyes bulge like they're about to burst from her head. The room, already black, somehow becomes darker. Her legs are like rubber. She can't move them anymore. She reaches out for anything she can.

"Meat," he says. She hears it muffled, as if through a pillow or a wall. *Not like this. Not like this.* It rolls through her dying brain as she begins to slip away. *Not like this.* Not blind with agony, struggling to move her dead limbs. Her body feels broken, maybe severed from her head.

"Cut!" someone says.

The world becomes a black and white blur. The stockroom gains a stillness that should be impossible for objects that were never in motion.

"You were great, kiddo," says the voice. It's nasal, with a slight lisp. She knows it from somewhere. "I think we got it."

She lifts her head from the cold concrete floor and is blinded by a powerful light. Lily lifts a hand to block out the burning beam shining in her eyes. Beyond that is a face, someone in a collapsible cloth chair. He has a receding hair line, nubby little teeth, pointed nose, enormous Hapsburg jaw—it's Quentin Tarantino.

"And that's a wrap, everybody," he says.

"What do you mean?" Lily asks.

"It means it's over." He shrugs. "Now we go to post."

"What about me?"

"You? You're done."

"You mean I'm dead . . ."

"Yeah."

"I don't want to be dead."

"It's not really up to me. I have to be true to the characters—true to the story."

"Why?" she cries. "Why like this?"

"Because it's fun!"

"It wasn't fun for me!"

"Well, I gotta hand it to you, kiddo. Strangulation is hard. I never quite buy it in anything. That's why I strangled Diane Kruger myself on *Inglourious Basterds*."

"You're not really Quentin Tarantino, are you?"

"You know exactly what I am. I'm not really into the Ingmar Bergman look anymore. *Bill and Ted's Bogus Journey* spoiled it. Would you prefer more of a Neil Gaiman interpretation?"

"No. You can't have me."

"Aw, kiddo, you know what you are. You're not the final girl. You're the slutty friend. You said it yourself."

"No, it's not true! I didn't know. That's not what I think!"

"You're not doing anything to drive the plot. This story doesn't need you."

"Please! I'm not worthless! I don't think that anymore!"

"Hey while you're here, you mind if I give you a foot massage?"

Lily gasps to life. She's on the floor in the stockroom, facedown. She pushes against it and forces her wobbling legs straight. She trips on some signage in the dark and falls again, but she doesn't care. She tumbles over a pile of steel peg hooks and pulls open the door to the store.

She runs, screaming, panting, crying from the back. The front room is lit by the lights of the strip mall parking lot and Sid is a black shadow silhouetted against the store windows ahead of her. She shrieks at him as she passes.

"Run!" she screams. "Run!"

Sid gives her a confused glance and then turns to see the Ghoul standing framed by the stockroom doorway.

The monster howls as he pulls the yellow DeWALT® power drill, which is perfect for projects at home or professional construction, from his left eye socket, tossing it aside. An eyeball comes with it.

The Ghoul snatches Sid up off the ground and bowls him into Lily. He smashes into her legs, and the two tumble to the ground.

Sid rolls to his feet and unshoulders the rifle. He levels it at the Ghoul and unloads a magazine into the monster. The Ghoul seems only slightly annoyed.

"Why do I still carry this thing?" Sid says, tossing the gun to the ground and pulling a KA-BAR knife. He shakes his head, then charges full bore at the Ghoul, roaring and bearing his teeth. He leaps into the air and drives his knife into the monster's face, burying the blade deep in the creature's brain.

The monster reels a step, then another, dazed, before falling to the floor at Sid's feet. Sid looks down at it for a moment, then kicks it.

He turns and walks back to Lily.

"You okay?" he asks, pulling her up from the carpet.

"He has my mom!" Lily screams. "He has her! He's going to kill her just like Amy!"

"Hey," Sid scolds her. "You need to stay calm."

He takes her hands in his, but she rips them away and swats hysterically at him as he tries to grab them again.

"Why didn't you save her?!" she screams.

"There was nothing I could—"

Lily punches him in the chest. It's bullshit. It's all bullshit. He could've saved her if he was faster, if he didn't argue with her.

"No! That's not how it works!" she shrieks. "You were supposed to save the girl!"

"This isn't a movie, Lily," Sid says. "People die."

"You're still alive! Amy's dead! Is my mom next? You're just gonna let him kill her?"

The KA-BAR knife clanks to the ground behind them. Lily turns and screams.

The Ghoul stands again, having plucked the knife from his head.

"Aw, what the fuck?" Sid laments. "I stuck a knife in his brain!"

Sid kicks the Ghoul in the testicles. It has no effect.

"That's different," he says. Then the Ghoul sledgehammers him right through a wire shelving display of movies labeled EMPLOYEE FAVORITES. The rack collapses on top of him.

He doesn't get back up.

The Ghoul turns to Lily. She screams as those outstretched gauntlets come for her again—moving to crush her throat until she passes into void. She won't die like that. Not like that.

She runs down the drive aisle through the center of the store and takes a turn into Action. She hears the Ghoul stomping after her. The monster hurries now, moving faster than she would have guessed he could. Her heart races with fear. He'll catch her. He'll choke her again.

Lily turns a corner and tiptoes into Horror. She crouches on the floor and listens to locate the thing.

The rising and falling rasps of his breathing intensify as he closes in. She comes up with an idea. Reaching above her shoulder, she quietly plucks a copy of *Friday the 13th* from the shelf. She tosses it up and over into the next aisle. It comes down on the floor with a loud clatter.

She hears the monster spin to examine the fallen cassette tape. This is her chance. She needs to go for the front door.

Summoning all her courage, she makes a break for it. Sprinting as fast as she can down the center aisle, she makes for the door. She closes in fast, refusing to look back. All she can do is drive forward. She raises her hand to slam down the release lever to open the locked door.

She trips. No. Something trips her.

"No!" she screams, tumbling to the floor. She smacks, shoulder first, into the carpet. Her feet are somehow entangled. She's being dragged.

She raises her head to see the Ghoul, standing in the center aisle, winding a thick black cord around his arm to reel her in. Her feet are wrapped in some kind of weighted bolas. She claws the carpet desperately as the Ghoul drags her closer. He raises Sid's big black knife over her. She shrieks and closes her eyes, waiting to feel the sensation of cold steel driven through her body.

It never comes.

She opens her eyes to see the Ghoul balancing the knife in his giant hand, looking it over as though it isn't worthy somehow. He dumps it on the floor be-hind him and draws a huge rusty hacksaw from a sheath on his back. She struggles free of the cables, but he steps on her pelvis and flattens her against the floor. He must weigh six-hundred pounds. She thinks her hips might crack under him.

"No! No!" she cries. Tears stream down her face as the monster places the teeth of the saw against her exposed midriff.

She screams so loud her lungs burn and her throat gives out.

Something blocky and black smashes down over the Ghoul's head. Glass shatters. He's wearing the store TV like a space helmet. The beast gurgles as a sizzling electric shock violently rattles him to the floor.

Sid stands behind the fallen monster. He reaches out and pulls Lily to her feet.

"Fuck you!" she curses, violently kicking at the monster's ribs until she falls into Sid's arms. She presses her face against his chest as she catches her breath. "He was gonna saw me in half."

"You gonna be okay?" he says.

"Yeah," she answers. "I, um, I dropped my cell phone in the back . . ."

"I'll get it."

"Okay." Lily glimpses Amy's motionless foot around the corner of the counter. She closes her eyes. She can't be here with the body any longer. "I'll, um, I'll be in the car."

INT. VIDEO TIME - NIGHT

Lily's iPhone is on the floor underneath a fallen pile of acrylic sign holders. Most of them are broken and jagged. Either the Ghoul stepped on them or Lily fell on them. The girl should be dead. Her eyes were filled with blood and her neck was wrapped in a purple collar of bruising. She got lucky.

Sid picks up the iPhone and flicks the display on. Somehow, it is not broken. He turns and heads for the front of the store.

As he nears the front counter, he notices something amiss. The Ghoul's body is gone.

The monster hisses from behind him, stepping out of the action movie aisle.

"Meat!" it says.

Sid rolls his eyes.

"I don't even care anymore," Sid says. He flips the monster his middle finger and continues on his way.

"Meat?" the Ghoul says.

Sid walks out of the video store. He stuffs the iPhone in his pants pocket, walking around toward the rear of the building.

The Ghoul stomps along behind him.

"Meat! Meat!" the monster repeats.

Suddenly, blinding headlights illuminate them both. Sid squints in the face of the burning brights as an engine revs loudly.

Lily's purple Malibu lurches forward, squealing tires and trailing smoke through the blacktop. Sid steps out of the way and the car zooms past him, crashing into the massive monster on his tail.

The Ghoul wraps around the front bumper, dragged halfway under the car as it roars toward the brick wall next to the video store front.

Crunch! The front end of the car smashes into the wall. The hood curls upward as groaning metal twists around the monster's chest. Smoke pours from the engine compartment as the beast bellows with fury and pounds his fists on the hood.

Lily steps out of the car.

"Did I get him?"

Sid shrugs. "More or less."

"What the fuck *is* that thing?" Lily says.

Sid leaps onto the hood of the car in front of the Ghoul. The monster lashes out, reaching to grab him with flailing fingers. Sid's hand shoots out and snatches the rubber mask, pulling it away with a quick jerk.

The face underneath is a raw and bloody mess of ground burger. Pointed shark-like teeth form a wide Glasgow smile, and black muck squirts from his gaping eye socket.

"It looks like what would happen if the *Cloverfield* monster made a baby with Freddie Kruger," Lily says.

It really is something awful. Sid never saw the Ghoul's actual face before, but it suddenly makes perfect sense why they keep a mask on him all the time.

Sid opens the rear driver's side door and reaches into the back seat. He drags the MacGuffin out and passes it to Lily.

"Take this and go stand over there," he says.

"Why?" she asks, stepping cautiously away from him. "What're you going to do?"

"I'm gonna blow up the car."

He levels a pistol at the gas tank.

"Sid," she says. "That won't work. They proved on *Mythbusters* that—"

Boom! The car explodes when he shoots the gas tank. He glimpses Lily shielding her eyes as the blast sweeps her hair back.

"Okay, then . . ." she says.

Sid watches as the Ghoul burns. Flames tickle the sky and the air stinks of melting rubber. The monster's screams fill his ears for some time before they finally die away, and the flailing slows to nothing.

"The cops will be here soon," Sid says. "I need to know everything he said to you."

He turns. Lily is no longer there.

Amy's car lights up and the engine starts. He watches curiously as the car backs out of the space.

"Hey!" Sid says. "Where are you going?"

The car switches into drive. Sid runs toward it.

"Stop!" he yells. "Don't do it! He'll kill you!"

He watches as Lily peels out of the parking lot in Amy's car and zooms off into the dark.

"Stupid girl," he says. "Fuck."

Cha-chink. A shotgun pumps behind him. Sid turns to face the ninja and Helen Anderson. She holds the shotgun. The ninja's hand is at his sword hilt.

"What do you two want?" Sid says. He isn't scared. This is just more annoying bullshit to pile on with the rest.

"Where's she taking the case, Kill Team?" Helen says.

"Fuck if I know."

INT. LILY'S HOUSE – NIGHT

The front door splinters off its hinges and flops to the floor with a loud thud that echoes through the house. The ninja's talent for kicking doors down is impressive. It fell straight to the floor like the hinges were made from butter. The bloody scrawled WhORE faces up at them.

Sid enters first, expecting nothing, but ready for anything. He swings his rifle around to cover the corners. The house is a mess. Someone was here before them.

"Lily?" Helen calls. Sid doesn't like her shouting out. It gives away their position.

Sid moves farther down the hallway into the kitchen. A table lies on its side and a bowl of cereal has spilled on the floor next to it. Someone has sliced jagged lines down the walls and punched through them in places.

"It looks like the Manson family was here," Helen says. She pokes her boot toe at a shattered mass market print of Marilyn Monroe lying on the floor.

"Victor was here," Sid says. He expected more blood. He sees only some speckles on the kitchen counter, probably from a knocked-out tooth or, more likely, a broken nose; he doesn't see any loose teeth nearby.

"The girl is not here," the ninja says. He leaps down the last few stairs but makes no sound as his feet reach the ground level.

"She's scared," Sid says. "She's desperate. She's playing right into his hands. I don't know how we're going to get ahead of him."

"What about Ivan?" Helen asks. "If we can contact him somehow . . ."

"My old man?" Sid says. He sets his rifle down on the counter top and opens the refrigerator door. He's hungry. No reason not to take a look.

"Is he actually your father?" Helen asks. She puts the shotgun down on the arm of a reclining chair.

Sid opens the refrigerator and gasps at what he sees.

"What is it?" Helen yelps. She picks up the shotgun almost as soon as she set it down. The ninja reaches for his sword.

"Steak," Sid says. He pulls a Tupperware container of dark brown steaks from the refrigerator.

"Oh my God," Helen says, holdings a hand to her chest. "I thought . . . I thought there was a woman in the refrigerator."

"What?" Sid tears the lid off the Tupperware container and plucks a juicy steak from inside. He rips into it with his teeth. "Why would there be a woman in the refrigerator?" he asks through a mouthful of steak.

"It's just a thing—I don't know—never mind," Helen says. "That steak is cold."

Sid glares at her as he chews steak vigorously. It tastes different than he is used to, probably because it was cooked. Cooked steak is a whole new discovery. The old man always threw it to him raw.

"And of course, you don't care," Helen says. She puts the shotgun back down.

Sid holds out the container of steaks to offer some to Tanaka, but the ninja turns him down.

"I will never understand you Americans and your beef," the ninja says.

"So, is he actually your father?" Helen asks again, picking up the conversation from before the alarming discovery of red meat.

"Yeah," Sid says, tearing into the steak again. He's already eaten two thirds of it. "Why?"

"I just thought you were made in a lab or something," Helen says.

"Why does everybody always say that?" Sid complains. He continues to speak through a mouthful of steak. He doesn't care if the others can understand him. "Oh, he's really good at killing guys. He must be a genetically engineered cyborg animal man." Sid rolls his eyes. Lily accused him of being a vampire. Ridiculous.

"Oh, I don't know. Maybe because you tear people apart with your bare hands!"

Sid shrugs. "I'm a master of ansatsuken."

"Ankenwhatnow?"

Tanaka answers her question. "The forbidden art of the assassinating fist. A terrible fighting form that was long thought lost."

"Well, whatever," Helen says. "We need your old man. If we can reach him—"

"He's dead," Sid cuts her off, reaching for the next steak.

"What?" Helen says. "How?"

"Last time I saw him, a swarm of man-eating reptilians were piled on top of him." He chomps another steak in half. "There's no way even *he* made it out of that alive."

"You are mistaken," Tanaka says. "Ivan still

lives."

"That can't be right," Sid says.

"I rescued him myself. I have seen him."

"It doesn't matter anyway. There isn't enough time."

"You can't call him?"

"You don't just call my dad. It's not like he carries around the hottest new iPhone in his pocket. There are no photographs of him, no fingerprints, no voice recordings. That's not an accident. There are smoke signals we can use to alert him, but they take days."

"No one finds the ghost," Tanaka says. "The ghost finds you."

"The ninja knows the score," Sid agrees. "We're on our own here."

"So what now, then?" Helen says. "We just wait for Victor to get his hands on whatever is in that case?"

"I thought you knew what was in the case," says Sid.

"No. I think it's some kind of biological weapon."

"I figured it was a suitcase nuke."

"Tanaka, what *is* that thing?"

They both turn to the ninja for an explanation. The waspy Asian man shakes his head slowly.

"All right," Helen says. "So how do we find Lily before he does?"

"I have an idea, but it's kind of shaky," Sid says.

INT. MERLE'S TRUCK STOP - NIGHT

The Devil's Horsemen sit around a table in the corner of Merle's 24-Hour Truck Stop finishing up their 4 AM breakfast as Bald Sack hands out photographs of a twelve-year-old Lily to all of them. The Lily in the photo lacks all of her grim tattoos, but is provocatively dressed for such a young girl. Duck Dick whistles at the photograph.

"When we get to Morston," Bald Sack says. "We're gonna fan out. Cover all the spots we think the bitch might go."

"You didn't tell me she was a serious piece of ass," Duck Dick says, leering at the photograph again.

"That's a twelve-year-old girl you're looking at, chomo," says Gill.

"What's wrong with that?" says Sweet Tits, putting her dental bridge back in to fill the gap between her top front teeth. "I was twelve my first time."

"Duck's a fuckin' chomo is what's wrong with that." Gill snickers. Gill loves to put down Duck Dick whenever he can. The guy is just such a little bitch it's fun to see him cry about it. It was Gill who came up with Duck's nickname on account of him looking like a duck's nasty tentacle dick. It was Gill who tattooed the half-ass anarchy A all across the left side of Duck's face while the shitbird was passed out from booze and dope. *That tattoo could use a touch-up,* Gill thinks as he looks across the table to Duck's flapping gums.

"I ain't no fuckin' chomo," Duck Dick barks, pounding the table. "She's at least seventeen now.

That's legal."

"Eighteen is legal, dumb ass," Sweet Tits sneers. "Everybody knows that."

"Actually," Poochie interjects. "In most states, sixteen is legal. There's only a few where it's eighteen."

"But he's lookin' at the picture. She's twelve in the picture. He's a chomo."

"How old was that hooker you nailed in Mexico City? Fourteen?"

"Thirteen, but that's legal in Mexico."

"He's right," Poochie says. "Age of consent's twelve there."

"So shithead can stick it to an elementary school girl and that's A-okay, but I have a light fantasy about a woman damn near voting age and I'm the chomo?"

"I don't write the laws. All I know is I catch you even lookin' at my daughter, I'll take your little chomo balls."

"Your daughter's twenty-two," Sweet Tits says. "That don't even make sense."

"I think it's a real interesting statement about the Jungian duality of man," Poochie says.

"Fingers is dead, you fucks!" Bald Sack shouts. "And since when do Satanic bikers give one single fuck about the age of consent anyway? Let's get down to it."

"Who is this little skeez anyway?" Lawrence asks. He's the newest member of the club.

"She's Ted Smalls's stepdaughter from back in the day," Gill explains. "He was puttin' it to her and the dumb slut got knocked up. So instead of handling it any proper way, she tried to fix it herself. Fucked it all to hell and back. Landed herself in intensive care.

Everybody found out."

"So it's her fault Ted's inside."

Gill nods. "Yep. Now Bobby Reynolds from over in Norwich, he's got a cousin joined up with the National Guard and he told Bobby he thought he saw Ted's ex-wife at a titty bar over in Morston by the base. So Fingers and the probie rode out there looking for her, and you know the rest."

"We fan out," Bald Sack says with fire in his eyes. "Poochie's gonna cover that titty bar. Sweet's asking around the schools. Me and Lawrence are going to that video store. Gill runs interference. Duck Dick, you cover the mall."

"The mall?" Duck Dick whines. "Why the mall?"

"She's a teenager. Teenagers go to malls."

"Not anymore. Malls are out."

"Where do kids go then?"

"Thrift stores, coffee shops, gentrified urban slums, extremely woke microbreweries, fast casual restaurants with responsibly raised ingredients . . ."

"Quit fuckin' with me, Duck," Sack growls. "I ain't in the mood. You cover the mall."

The group's waitress glides up to the edge of their table and glances around the collection of rugged faces before asking, "So, you ready for the check?"

Bald Sack springs from his seat and punches the waitress right in the chin with a haymaker that jerks her face sideways, sending her sprawling across another party's plates of bacon and eggs.

"Let's ride!" Sack howls. "Hail Satan!"

"Hail Satan!" the others howl after him as they all dash from the truck stop in an angry swarm.

EXT. PARKING LOT - NIGHT

The yellow glow of the Planet Fitness sign casts a buttery tint to the moonless darkness all around. Helen used to go to a gym like this when she was with NSA. There's a comforting familiarity about it. She'll take anything she can get to calm her nerves right now.

She's waiting next to a blue Lexus, leaning against the driver's side door with her elbow on the window. She shed her flak jacket to look a bit more innocuous, though anyone looking close will notice the dried blood stains on her shirt and the split in her blue jeans from Victor's knife.

The police cruiser that rolls into the parking lot has its low beams on. That's good. The last thing she needs is some overzealous asshole cop flashing the emergency lights for this. The car comes to a stop and the door opens. The driver steps out, but he has a flashlight pointed at her face and looks like a shadow with a big cap.

"You lock yourself out?" the cop calls in a husky male voice.

"Yeah," she says. "This is so embarrassing. I didn't think I should call nine-one-one, but it's dark and this isn't the best neighborhood, and I didn't know what to do."

The cop lowers his flashlight. He has a classic bushy cop mustache riding his upper lip. He smiles at her.

"Don't you worry, honey," he says. "That's what we're here for."

Sid bashes the cop in the back of the head with his elbow. The guy's face bounces off the hood of the cruiser before whipping back, and the whole of him folds like an according onto the blacktop.

"How do you do that?" Helen says. "Just knock him out? Just like that?"

Sid shrugs. "It's something you have to practice."

He picks the police officer up from the ground and throws him over his shoulder. Helen sits down in the driver's seat and searches for a lever to pop the trunk.

A hand rattles the wire grating behind her head.

"Ah!" Helen shrieks in surprise. It's the ninja, already sitting on the bench seat in back. "Jesus Christ, Tanaka!"

"It's that knob there," the ninja says. He points at a lever under the steering column. She pulls it and hears the trunk snap open behind them.

Sid dumps the cop inside and then comes around to the passenger door. He opens it, dropping the cop's utility belt on the floor in front of the seat.

"So we have a police cruiser," Helen says, as he sits down next to her. "Now what?"

"We can chain this cop up at Lily's house," Sid says. "Then we cruise. Eventually, Victor's going to make a scene. It's just what he does. When it comes through on the radio, we go there and hope for the best."

"This sounds really shaky."

"I told you."

INT. GALLERIA - DAY

Lily arrives at the Morston Galleria ten minutes early for her twelve noon meeting with Victor Hansen.

As she pushes her way through the doors from the vestibule, she glances at the laminated paper sign stuck to the glass door just in front of her eyes.

NOTICE: NO FIREARMS OR WEAPONS ALLOWED ON THIS PROPERTY

She sighs with relief. Victor can't bring any guns in here, at least.

She screams in her own mind. *That sign isn't going to stop him! Dammit, Lily, you stupid slut! What are you doing here?*

Stick to the plan. Stick to the plan.

The plan is simple: She has to seduce Victor. He won't kill her if she's fucking him. That makes sense, right? How can he kill her if she's fucking him? Then she'll just give him the stupid box and ask him to let her mom go. He'll do it. He has to do it. Men are like sheep, right?

As she walks through the mall, hauling the steel case alongside, she notices a sales guy in front of PacSun ogling her. Still got it, she thinks, and she smiles at him. Then she sees a woman at the counter in Zales Jewelers staring at her, too.

A small boy near a hot pretzel stand, drinking a crisp, smooth, refreshing Pepsi® beverage, looks up at Lily and grips his mother's hand.

"Mommy," he whimpers, tugging for attention.

What the fuck? Lily doesn't understand.

She walks a little farther down the mall corridor

and draws the attention of a leering letch with a faded green anarchy A tattooed on his left cheekbone. This one stares at her like he's watching a dog play a piano, and even begins to follow along behind her as she passes him.

Seeing a sign for restrooms just ahead, Lily ducks into the ladies' room. She walks along the wet tile to where the sinks are and gasps when she sees her reflection staring back at her from the mirrors above. Her neck is a collar of bruised flesh. Her eyes are bright crimson all around her blue irises. She looks like a walking corpse.

She drops the case where she stands and covers her mouth with both hands. Oh, God. Sid said werewolves are real; what about zombies? She doesn't know what to expect anymore. What if that monster did something to her? Infected her with some kind of contagion? What if she really died back there? She feels her chest to make sure her heart is still beating and she's almost surprised when it is.

She gags and jerks forward to retch in the sink, but nothing comes up. She dry heaves again before catching her breath. In the movies, people vomit blood before they succumb to the zombie plague. Is that what's happening? She looks in the sink and sees nothing. No blood.

She takes a deep breath. She's alive. She's not a fucking zombie. That's a thing of fiction. This is not fiction. This is reality.

She splashes water in her face, in an attempt to wash the blood from her eyes, but it does nothing. It's so gross. Her neck aches when she touches it. Lancome Paris doesn't have enough concealer to cover all of the bruising. Victor isn't going to want her like this.

Victor isn't going to want her like this?

Suddenly, the madness of her plan becomes clear. Her mother is already dead. Soon, Lily herself will be dead, and thanks to her, a madman will have some kind of super bomb and then thousands or millions of others will be dead, too. This was a mistake. This was a terrible mistake.

"Lily?" It's a girl's voice behind her. "Lily Hoffman?"

It's Jenny Brunswick. Lily almost screams. The last thing she needs right now is to run into this petty rich bitch. Jenny wears a pink flower print cocktail dress and faux expensive heels. Her shiny golden hair looks like it was fixed by Scarlett Johansson's entire style team. Diamonds sparkle around her neck and that stupid purity ring gleams on her left hand.

"God," Jenny says. "I knew you were a whore, but what are you doing now? Meth?"

Lily says nothing. She can barely restrain herself from tackling the dumb bimbo.

"Did you like the present me and the girls left for you?" Jenny says.

"What are you talking about?" Lily's left eyebrow spasms upward with insane curiosity.

"I think you know," Jenny laughs. She moos at Lily like a cow. "Moo. Moo."

Lily has a moment of stark clarity in which she realizes what Jenny is hinting. "It was you," Lily says. "You left that animal head on my front porch! You wrote on my door!"

Rage. Blinding rage. The world turns blood red as she lunges forward. Lily leaps onto Jenny like a tiger, toppling the blond bitch off her fake Manolo Blahnik heels. Lily straddles her body and punches Jenny in the mouth. She keeps her wrist straight, fist clenched tight, elbow high, throws her shoulder forward. Jenny whines loudly for her to stop. Lily hits her again and again. The whining quickly turns to screaming for help, then to screaming in pain, then to choking, as the girl struggles to breathe through all the blood running down her throat.

When Lily regains control of herself, Jenny's face is an unrecognizable mass of hematoma. She whimpers through split lips and a broken nose for Lily to stop.

"And I fucked your boyfriend, bitch," Lily says. Then she winds up one last punch and bludgeons Jenny into unconsciousness on the bathroom floor.

She picks up the case and walks away. She doesn't feel the throbbing pain in her hand until she is back out in the mall corridor. She must have hit Jenny so hard she broke her own knuckles. That's something Sid didn't tell her would happen.

She keeps moving despite the pain. She needs to get to a phone. They should have one at the mall's main service desk.

Farther down the corridor, she sees why Jenny was so dressed up. At the juncture where the corridors meet, over the water fountain in front of Macy's, sits a temporary stage and runway. Rows of metal folding chairs flank the runway on either side, and several hundred people mingle there in the seats and hovering around them.

They're having a fashion show.

Fuck, Lily thinks. She reaches the service desk, a round kiosk surrounding a middle-aged woman who seems engrossed in a Danielle Steel novel. Lily thumps her elbows down on the kiosk, prompting the mall administrator to look up from her paperback and re-gard Lily with an uneasy semblance.

"Hi," Lily says. "Do you have a phone here I could use? It's an emergency."

"Do you need an ambulance?" the administrator says. "You don't look okay, honey."

"No. I just need to use your phone."

"Well, all right." The administrator pushes a boxy looking hardline telephone across the kiosk, turning it to face Lily. "Dial nine to get out."

Lily picks up the handset with her good hand and tucks it between her ear and shoulder as she dials. She hears the familiar ringing through the line.

"Please just answer," she whispers into the micro-phone.

"Where are you?" Sid hisses over the phone. He sounds angry, but she doesn't care. She's never been so glad to hear his raspy death grunt voice.

"I fucked up," Lily says. "I'm at the Galleria, where the movie theater is. I need you. I—"

And then she sees him.

His combat boots impact the tile in slow motion, each footfall accompanied by pounding orchestral notes. His pale green duster trails behind the boots. His pasty yet muscular chest flashes between the la-pels of the duster, exposing only the middle four letters of a big black word tattooed across it: PEGO. His terri-ble grin stretches from ear to ear, exposing the teeth of a predator. The gun slung over his shoulder looks like it could level a city. His piercing blue gaze meets hers.

She screams.

"He's here! He's here!" she shrieks before she drops the phone.

Victor rips the pin from a hand grenade with his teeth, throwing it, left handed, into the middle of the crowd around the fashion show.

Lily has her back turned when she hears the blast, but she knows a dozen people just died. The machine gun drowns out everything else in the mall: the Muzak, her own frantic panting, and hundreds of terrified screams.

INT. GALLERIA – DAY

The glass doors leading into the mall are cluttered with advertisements and notices of mall hours and directives not to smoke or bring weapons, but all of them are outshone by the bright orange word FACISTS painted across the doors. It is spelled incorrectly, and lengthy orange fingers extend downward where the paint ran from overuse.

Sid pushes his way through the doors and into a hellish nightmare. Further down the hall, a flimsy portable stage is surrounded by a carpet of bodies so thick that no full square of the aqua-gray tile can be seen beneath it. Ahead of him, a mall cop approaches. The man has buzzed hair and thick sporting glasses banded to his head. The radio on his white uniform shirt crackles with the shouting of emergency personnel over an ambiance of wailing death.

"You can't go this way, sir," the mall cop says, before his face twists into surprised confusion at the sight of Sid's assault rifle and other weapons. He is equipped with two handguns, a combat knife, and a ballistic vest with three M67 frag grenades latched to its MOLLE webbing.

"The fuck I can't," Sid says.

The mall cop reaches to tackle him, but before Sid can put a KA-BAR in his throat, the hapless security guard is knocked from his feet by a blur of force that is the ninja's flying dragon kick. The ninja's boot heel connects with the mall cop's chin, sending the poor bastard head over feet, rolling like a tumbleweed down the hallway.

"Mall cops." Sid shakes his head.

"We must move quickly," Tanaka says.

Sid nods.

"You take the bottom floor," Sid says as the two of them dash forward toward the dead and dying. "I'll take the upstairs."

He hasn't seen a bloodbath like this since Afghanistan, when Kill Team Three tried to take him out with a Vulcan cannon in a crowded cafe. He steps over most of the bodies, but has to walk on some. One squeals under his foot, a man with tattoos covering his arms. A torso in a black, flower patterned dress claws her way from the mass of corpses down the corridor, leaking a bloody trail from the jagged dangling mess where her lower half once was.

A tall girl with diamond jewelry comes around the corner in front of him, carrying some very impractical shoes and wiping blood from her broken nose. She appears disoriented.

"Which way to the escalator?" he barks at the girl.

She points as she sniffles, then collapses in his wake. Sid charges onward.

INT. GALLERIA — DAY

The vicious growling of the pale horse fills the mall corridors. Lily hears him calling her out from in front of the store.

"I saw you go in one of these stores, Lily," Victor shouts. "Come on, Lily. Come out to play."

She sits on the floor inside a place called Sports-Collect-A-Mania, next to a large display of baseball player bobbleheads. The store is lit with obnoxious florescent lights and furnished with cream-colored metal shelving.

The MacGuffin remains in her grip, which has turned to iron since she began running from death incarnate. She can't be sure if that's an extension of her newfound resolution to die before giving it up, or simply because her broken hand is so swollen it will no longer open.

She ducked in here when she realized she was never going to outrun him while lugging the MacGuffin. She probably couldn't outrun him without it either. So far, her hiding place has proven effective.

"There's a problem with your strategy here, darling," Victor shouts.

He fishes something from the backpack hanging from his left shoulder, and throws it into the adjacent store.

Lily watches him through little space between two bobblehead boxes. She's deep in the sports store, and he's all the way out in the corridor, seemingly unable to determine which shop she entered. He's too smart to go into any one looking for her and risk her slipping past him. Instead, he stands outside, waiting. She's trapped.

He throws another object into the Forever 21 across the hall.

"Your problem is that the case is bombproof," Victor says. "*You* are not."

Lily's eyes widen as she realizes what he's doing.

"So," Victor continues. "You can come out and give me the case, or I can blast all these stores to ribbons and drag it out of the splatter that used to be you."

A loud smack startles her, as something lands on the tile only a few feet away. It's a bomb.

"The choice is yours," he says. "You have thirty seconds until I push the button."

She has to make a break for it.

Lily shifts to her knees and toes. She peers out through the bobbleheads again. Victor remains in the same spot. He's holding a detonator exactly like the one Sid used to blow up the Graveyard building.

Lily searches the room for anything she could use to hurt him. If she's going to die, she's going to die fighting. What kind of weapon would be in a sports collectible store? A hunting knife, maybe? A golf club? No. She practically smacks herself when she sees it. She tiptoes over to the cash register a few feet away and plucks an aluminum baseball bat from a display stand behind the counter.

Wielding the bat in her good hand and lugging the MacGuffin in the other, Lily sneaks as quietly as she can to the front of the store.

She ducks behind a table covered in baseball cards sealed in plastic containers. She doesn't see Victor anymore. He might have gone in one of the other stores. Now is her chance.

Lily stands and dashes for the mall corridor. The nearest exit is only a few hundred feet to her—

Smack! A fist bashes into her chest so hard that her legs come out from under her and she falls flat against her back. Her lungs shrink three sizes and she clutches her sternum.

Victor snatches her up, setting her on her feet with all the effort of a child picking up a Barbie doll. Still wheezing and unable to breathe, Lily takes a desperate swing at him with the bat. He catches the bat and tears it from her grip with minimal effort. His boot heel crunches into her ribs and knocks her flying into a Pepsi® machine in the middle of the mall corridor.

Then he's up against her.

"I like you," he says. "Very feisty."

"Someone help!" Lily screams.

"Your mom is a real smooth ride," Victor says, as his left hand invades Lily's panties. "But I can't wait to try the newer model."

"What did you do to her?" Lily cries.

"Oh. Shush. Shush." He puts his finger to her mouth. "I only made a few modifications."

"Please don't hurt her anymore. If you let her go, I—I won't fight," she says. She feels the words coming out of her mouth, but she's not really there. It's just an involuntary thing her body is doing to keep her alive. She pets his crotch with her unbroken hand. "I can give it to you real good."

Victor unleashes a rabid cackle.

"There's nothing you can give me that I wouldn't rather take." He licks her face from chin to forehead.

His breath stinks like hot road kill.

Lily spits blood in his face.

He grins.

"Hey," he says. "What's that behind your ear?"

Victor withdraws his left hand from her underwear and reaches behind her ear. Lily's stomach drops. Her heart pounds. She's certain the punchline to this stupid joke will be her bloody death.

"It's—" he whips his hand around in front of her nose. The object he grasps is a severed finger. It is wearing one of her mother's rings.

Lily starts to scream, but Victor forces the finger into her gaping mouth.

"Eat it, cunt! Eat it, and a part of Mommy will be with you forever!"

"Face me, demon!" calls someone Lily did not know was a part of the conversation.

Victor turns his attention to the unknown challenger and Lily spits out her mother's severed finger, gagging as it leaves her lips.

Her white knight is a tall Asian man with flowing black hair and a sword hanging at his side. His eyes are wrapped in a long bandana, the ends of which dangle past his shoulders. A ninja? A blind fucking ninja? No. It's some kind of hallucination . . .

"The ninja!" Victor growls excitedly.

Okay. It really is a ninja.

Victor lowers Lily to the floor, turning back to her briefly. "You be a good girl and wait here," he says, before spinning to face the ninja. Lily attempts to crawl away, but her body moves like a poorly orchestrated marionette. Her chest throbs and burns. Breathing is a struggle. Her hand, now a purple fixture permanently molded around the grip of the MacGuffin, sends shooting pains up her arm as she tries to push herself to her feet. She shrieks as it gives way and she falls against the floor.

Behind her, Victor shoots at the ninja with a little machine gun. Lily watches as the ninja deflects the bullets like he's in *The Matrix* or something. *What the fuck?*

She tries again to stand, going to her knees first using her other hand. Moving from a prone position makes her core feel like it might snap. She looks back again.

Victor charges the ninja, swinging the metal bat he took from her. The ninja whips his sword, taking the end off of the bat. Victor lunges, attempting to stab the ninja with the sharply shaven lip of the bat. The ninja twirls his blade, slicing the bat into perfect cylindrical sections, like a weenie thrown through a jet engine.

"Holy fuck," Lily says. The ninja might win this thing.

She doesn't want to stick around to find out. She forces herself up. Fortunately, her legs are relatively undamaged and able to support her once she stands. She limps forward as fast as she can press herself, moving for the closest way out of this nightmare.

INT. GALLERIA – SECOND FLOOR – DAY

The upper mall corridor overlooks the first floor all the way around. Sid hears the sound of a 9mm MAC-10 submachine gun up ahead and he knows he is going the right direction. He also knows he's on the wrong floor.

He runs along the corridor, looking over the railing down to the floor below. As he closes in on the sounds, he sees flashes of gunfire.

The ninja, sword drawn, does battle with Sid's brother. Beyond them, he sees Lily running away with the case. Sid hangs his M4 over the railing and squeezes off a few shots at Victor. His brother glances up and rolls his eyes.

Victor pulls his foot-long kris knife, using it to catch the ninja's sword midstroke. He pulls another identical knife and stabs at the ninja's chest. Tanaka leaps away, avoiding the attack.

Victor holds his knives outstretched, like a snake's fangs, as he circles the ninja. Sid fires again at his brother, and again hits nothing but the mall floor.

He needs to find a way down to the first floor, fast. It's possible the two of them could beat his brother if they gang up on him. Alone, however, the ninja is fighting a losing battle. Sid can tell from here Victor isn't even trying.

He slaps another magazine into the feed on the M4, and is immediately distracted by someone yelling at him. He turns to see, not just one person, but a small crowd of mall patrons; a woman in a business suit, an older man with a Denver Broncos cap covering his white hair, a boy with green hair who must hold up his pants by the crotch as he runs, and a short chubby woman with skin-tight black pants and a white T-shirt. They are led by a huge man with a bushy caterpillar mustache and an unusually skinny mall cop.

"Take out the gunman!" yells the huge man with the mustache as he lumbers across the corridor toward Sid. He is six foot nine, by Sid's measurement— a measurement that is seldom wrong, and he has muscle packed on like a professional bodybuilder.

"What the fuck?" Sid says, raising a bewildered eyebrow to this ragtag collection of misfits assailing him. These people picked the wrong fight. He has three seconds as they approach, more than enough time to double tap the whole group. He zeroes the rifle on the big man's forehead, but then stops. It just seems . . . unnecessary.

He shoulders the M4 as Mustache lunges for him. He grabs the huge man, one hand around his throat and the other crunching down on his testicles, and hurls him over the railing behind him. Mustache falls thirty feet down, slamming into the floor below. Blood splatters from his face into an explosive crimson pattern on the white marble.

That may have been overkill—just a bit.

The chubby woman turns heel and runs without further thought. Business suit woman takes a low cross in the guts that crumples her up like a paper wad. She falls to her knees and vomits up something thick and soupy. Saggy pants comes in with a flimsy haymaker. Sid tucks his chin and takes the punch with the rock-hard top of his head. He feels knuckles break against it with a satisfying crunch. Then he steps on the waistband of the punk's pants and pushes them down around his ankles. He shoves the kid back at the business suit woman, as she's still keeled over and throwing up on the floor. She ends up with her face in the kid's fallen pants, vomiting into the crotch as he trips and goes down on top of her.

Sid motions for the Broncos fan and the mall cop to come forward. The mall cop responds by pepper spraying him in the face. Sid doesn't blink. Pepper spray is like a refreshing splash of cool spring water on a hot day. He wipes it from his face as the Broncos fan comes at him. Sid weaves under a punch and smears the spray into the old man's eyes. Then he flips the old fogey with a simple o-goshi judo throw.

Sid turns his attention to the mall cop. He glares at the lanky bastard and slowly crooks his head to the side. He studies the man. He takes in his shiny metal badge and his crisp white uniform. He sees his pathetic three-hair goatee and his quivering mouth. He looks in those glossy grey eyes and sees nothing but fear reflecting back.

"Die!" Sid grunts. It is the first word that comes to mind—one he knows well. It was the second word he ever spoke (after "kill").

The mall cop loudly shits his pants, then sits down on the floor and begins to cry.

INT. GALLERIA - FIRST FLOOR - DAY

A shrill scream comes from a husky man as he falls from the floor above and smacks into the marble far behind the ninja. It is a curious thing, but ultimately irrelevant. The ninja doesn't even glance back.

Victor has fought this stupid ninja before. He has beaten this stupid ninja before. He will beat this stupid ninja again. However, this time, only he will live to tell the tale.

He spins his lead knife: his grip is tight, but not too tight. His enemy hesitates. Fear is on Victor's side.

Anticipation explodes into action. The ninja strikes first, leaping forward with an overhead swipe that Victor sidesteps and catches between his knives. Tanaka one-hands his sword as he parries Victor's left knife with the other. Victor kicks the ninja and again they separate.

This time, Victor takes the initiative. He strikes with both knives. Tanaka deflects one, but Victor changes direction and slices the ninja's arm with the other. The ninja does not flinch. This is a true warrior. He brings his sword around in a swipe that nearly shears off Victor's legs. Victor jumps the blade, of course, and knees Tanaka in the jaw. He drives both knives down at the sides of the man's neck, but as they reach their target, they pierce nothing but a thick black smoke. Victor is blinded by the cloud wrapped around him.

Before he can dive away, a sword comes at him through the black. He barely avoids it, the razor edge coming within a millimeter of his nose. He stabs into the smoke around him as he weaves under the out-stretched blade and leaps from the cover of smoke.

He tosses one knife aside as he hits the floor near the MAC-10 he dropped earlier; the ninja's dark form is emerging from the cloud. Victor picks up the MAC-10 and squeezes the trigger. The blade becomes a flashing blur as it swats away the bullets. The solution to this problem is one Victor should've figured out much earlier.

He lunges for the ninja with his wavy knife. He dodges the sword as he attacks, stabbing forward like mad, waiting for his chance. Finally the ninja meets his knife with the sword blade, but Victor muscles forward, forcing the ninja to push back, tying up the sword. Victor points the MAC-10 at the ninja's chest and empties the rest of the magazine into his enemy's guts. Blood sprays from a dozen wounds and splatters Victor's chest.

The ninja falls.

Victor reloads the gun to fire another magazine in-to the carcass. He isn't finished. Winning is one thing, but he prefers to completely obliterate anyone who stands in his way. He smacks the magazine into the MAC-10 and is interrupted by shots fired at his head.

He spins to greet his brother. Shooting at him with an assault rifle, Sid stands in front of a dimly lit store-front only thirty yards away. It is adorned with palm trees and an outcropped stucco roof, which Sid must've jumped to from upstairs to get down here so quickly.

"Haven't you learned that shooting at me is a

pointless waste of time, Sid?" Victor says. He holds his arms outstretched, welcoming the bullets he feels buzzing past his face.

"It might be, but it feels good," Sid hollers back.

Victor responds by throwing a grenade at his brother. Sid catches it and pitches it into Hollister. It's one of the stores Victor threw a satchel charge into earlier.

"Oh my," Victor says. He turns and runs.

"Go ahead and run!" Sid yells. "You can't fight me, puss—"

Boom! Hollister explodes into an inferno that envelops Sid and brings most of the second floor down on top of him.

EXT. MALL PARKING – DAY

Lily hears an explosion inside the mall. She doesn't look back; she just presses forward, lugging the MacGuffin along in her ruined hand.

A police cruiser screeches to a stop in front of her. A woman in a tank top and body armor leans over to yell at her through the passenger side window.

"Get in!" she says, pushing the passenger door open.

"Who the fuck are you?" Lily says, stopping next to the car.

"Just get in!"

This is not okay. Lily doesn't know who the fuck this bitch is. She's not a cop—that's almost for sure. She glances back at the mall. An image of raw terror presents itself.

Victor saunters through the mall exit, brandishing his remote detonator in the air like a barbarian's sword in a Frank Frazetta painting. He opens his mouth to wag his tongue at her as he pulls the trigger down. The mall blows up behind him. The glass doors burst into shards and a wave of flame consumes the corridors inside.

Victor does not look back at the explosion.

Lily gets in the car. As she plunks down in the passenger seat, she thinks she may not be able to stand up again. She pulls the door closed and the car is already moving—not forward, but backward.

"What are you doing?" Lily yells to the woman in the driver's seat.

"I'm gonna run the fucker down," she yells back.

The car whips around until Victor is square in the middle of the windshield ahead of them. He beckons them forward. Lily clutches the oh-shit grip with her good hand and screams as the car burns into a start and zooms toward him.

Victor stands his ground as they close in on him. The engine noise grows into a roar as the car picks up speed. Victor leans forward, baring his teeth.

"Die, you son of a bitch!" the driver growls.

Lily squeezes the grip harder as she anticipates a blood-soaked two hundred pound nightmare smashing through the windshield and into her face.

Victor vaults the car. Lily glimpses the bottoms of his feet as he goes over the windshield and out of sight.

"What?" Lily shrieks.

The driver cuts the wheel and mashes the brake down. The car fishtails around completely to make another pass.

"I'm gonna get the fucker!" she shouts.

Victor leaps on the hood of the car. He balls his fist in front of them, smashing it through the glass.

Helen mashes down on the gas, but Victor grabs the wheel and the cruiser crashes into a parked car.

Victor still clutches the wheel through the broken glass. He pulls back, straining and screaming as he rips the windshield from the front of the car and tosses it to the pavement next to them. The big glass panel hits the ground with a loud crack.

"Fuck!" Lily screams, fighting with the door.

"Die! Die! Die!" the driver yells, pointing a shotgun through the broken out windshield. Victor snatches it away and punches her in the jaw.

Lily opens the door and stumbles from the car. Her feet barely make it to the blacktop before he's on top of her. He shoves her against the frame of the police cruiser, pinning her there.

"I'll get what I want," Victor says. "I always get what I want."

He pries the MacGuffin from Lily's broken hand. It feels like a hundred nails being hammered into her knuckles from every direction at once. Lily groans, simply trying not to black out.

"Hey, shitbird!" shouts a voice Lily doesn't know, from what sounds like a few dozen feet away. She snaps her attention to the source of the shouting and Victor does too, providing a brief respite from whatever torture he has planned for her next.

On the blacktop over Victor's shoulder stand six leather-clad figures with skin weathered by years of sun bleaching and picker's sores. They appear wild and greasy, with broken teeth and faces crunched crooked.

It's Ted's biker gang.

"I'm talkin' to you, shitbird!" says the largest of the crew. He has a gun in his hand and a mane of gray that conceals all but the top half of his face. He points at Victor. "That bitch is mine!"

Victor shifts his eyes back to Lily. "You know these people?" he says.

"It's a long story," she says.

Victor whips a handgun out of his duster and fires off a thunderous string of shots, spilling the biker gang's brains all over the parking lot behind him. After all six of them lie dead, Victor discards the empty gun to the ground.

"Well that was pointless," he says.

"Yeah," Lily agrees.

"Now, cunt," Victor whispers in her ear. "Scream."

Victor squeezes down on her swollen hand. She feels the bones in her fingers snapping. She can even hear them, but she doesn't scream. She sinks her teeth into his neck, biting down as hard as she can. His putrid blood fills her mouth and runs down her chin.

Victor pushes her head against the passenger window of the cruiser, tearing her teeth from him in the process. She spits his blood in his face and he laughs. She tries to scream, but all that comes out is a shrill cry as she dribbles gore on herself.

"You have no idea how much that turns me on," he says. He puts a hand on top of her head and forces her down, pressing his chest against her face, smothering her in his meaty abs. She can't scream. She can't move. She can't breathe. The bold script on his bare chest fills her bloody vision. RAPEGOD.

"What does it say?" he yells, pushing her back from his chest. She gasps for air. She chokes on blood. "What does it say!"

Lily is about to tell him, but then sees something both terrible and exciting.

From the inferno that used to be the mall exit, Sid emerges. Smeared with soot and blood, fresh char marks burned onto his left arm over all the old scars, he marches forward like a hound of hell.

"Victor!" Sid shouts, his big black knife outstretched to point at the bastard. His eyes bulge with rage.

Victor releases her from his unshakable grip, whipping around to face his brother. Lily slides to the ground, her head flopping to the pavement next to the cruiser. She can't run anymore. She can't even stand on her own. She slides under the wrecked police car. It's a good enough place to crawl away and die.

EXT. GALLERIA - DAY

The rage is all-consuming now. Sid has been shot at, stabbed, burned and blown up by his brother—mostly today. But somehow, none of it makes him angrier than seeing Victor hurt Lily. Before, the possibility of his brother playing with her—doing the things he does—seemed like a far-off idea, an abstract occurrence enacted by imaginary characters. Now it is very real and right in front of him.

"I'm gonna rip your guts out!" Sid yells.

Victor grins at him as Lily pushes herself underneath the car at his feet. The pale bastard holds the MacGuffin in his left hand.

"I've already got what I want," Victor says. Then he turns and dashes around the car, disappearing into the grid of parked vehicles beyond the cruiser. It is uncharacteristic of his brother to run from a fight—and to leave living witnesses. Victor must know he's winning by taking that case with him.

Sid follows him into the rows of cars.

This place is a death trap. His brother could pounce from around any corner, or even from the top of a taller vehicle. Sid slows his pace as he goes, but not too slow. He can't afford to lose Victor now.

He whips around the corner of a tall SUV and a hysterical woman comes dashing right for him, breathing heavily and dripping with tears and drool. He ducks out of the way.

Victor pops around a corner and fires at him with the MAC-10. Sid jumps for cover. Five shots bury themselves in the body of the SUV and another one smashes through the rear window. Sid leaps back around the corner, but sees no sign of his brother.

"Too slow!" Victor taunts from somewhere in the parking grid.

He hears something from up ahead. Sid steps out into the open aisle just in time to see a body being hurled his way. He steps aside, and the limp form of an older man in ratty clothes flops down beside him on the blacktop, the head twisted backward to face up at him even as the body is facedown.

Folding doors creak closed and a diesel engine growls as a wall of yellow steel in front of him begins to move. His brother is stealing a school bus. Muffled screaming and the pounding of tiny hands on the windows alert Sid that it is occupied.

He draws his KA-BAR knife and stabs it into the side paneling near the rear right corner of the bus. He hangs on to the knife as the bus chugs forward through the parking lot. Sid finds another hold by punching out a back window and gripping the frame. He needs to get to the front of the bus.

Sid yanks the KA-BAR from the side panel and reaches for the roof. He drives it down through the top of the bus and pulls himself up.

INT. SCHOOL BUS – DAY

Victor pushes down on the accelerator, shredding the bus's tires out into the street. He swerves into traffic and smashes into a small sedan along the way. The hulking bus spins the tiny car about-face as Victor cackles. The children's screams fill his ears. This is really living.

A glance in the mirror above him, reflecting the inside of the bus, reveals two dozen children he guesses to be about age five tumbling over seat backs and sliding down the aisle between. One of them clutches the metal leg of a green vinyl bus seat to avoid being thrown. Behind the children, he sees the unmistakable pointed black blade of a USMC KA-BAR knife sticking out of the ceiling. He has unwanted company.

He can't shoot Sid, but he could possibly shake him from the bus. Victor reaches back and points a MAC-10 at the rear corner of the bus. He opens fire. The children scream louder.

EXT. SCHOOL BUS – DAY

Bullets punch through the metal bus frame all around Sid as he pulls his way forward along the roof. He curses, shifting to his side to make himself a slimmer target, but the bus swerves sharply to the left. Sid loses his footing and goes over the side, dangling from the top of the bus with only his knife to hold onto. A white tractor trailer rumbles along at his back, a giant Frito-Lay® emblem plastered across its side.

"Fuck this," Sid says, pulling himself back up to the roof of the bus. More bullets punch through the roof around him as he draws the KA-BAR out, stabbing it three feet closer to the fore of the bus. He drags himself forward. Then again. Ahead of him is the emergency escape hatch mounted on top of the bus. He drives forward another few feet and then reaches out and grabs the hatch. He pulls himself up over it and tears at the door. It doesn't open from the outside. He roars with frustration.

Sid drives the KA-BAR into the hatch to lever it open. It pops up with surprising ease, but stops after just a few inches. He puts his fingers in the gap and rips the door from the skinny metal rods holding it in place. He throws the hatch behind him. It skitters overboard and crashes into the road behind the bus as he leaps down the hatch.

His brother is waiting for him at the front of the bus. Victor stands with his back turned to the windshield. No one is driving, and he doesn't seem to care. He pulls back on a handle behind him to open the doors.

"I love these things!" Victor shouts. "They even

come with cruise control!" Then he leaps through the open doors at the front of the bus and out into traffic. Sid sees him catch the side of the Frito-Lay® tractor trailer in the right lane next to them.

"Seriously?" Sid says. He charges to the front of the bus, past a gaggle of screeching children, and over one child lying in the aisle between the seats. He can see the bus careening over the yellow line in the road, inching its way into the path of oncoming traffic and certain doom.

He jumps into the driver's seat and jerks the wheel back to the right. An oncoming dump truck takes the left rearview mirror off the bus with a sharp metallic clank. Sid mashes down on the brake and children sail forward in their seats. The one on the aisle floor slides to the front and comes to rest at his feet.

The bus comes to a complete stop on an overpass overlooking the freeway. Sid steps over the child on the floor and stomps down the stairs to exit. Outside, he puts his hand up to stop the next car in the right lane. His plan is to hijack that vehicle to continue the chase. Then he notices something.

The truck his brother jumped on doesn't continue along the same road. It turns right onto a freeway ramp. The ramp loops around to connect with the freeway and then leads back under the overpass Sid is standing on. Victor didn't count on that.

Sid crouches behind the concrete barrier as he waits for the big white semi to come around. He hears the blare of sirens nearing his position as he lines up the jump.

"Hey! Buddy!" a man yells from behind him. Sid glances back to see a tall man in a gray T-shirt yelling at him from a stopped car. "Stop!"

Sid doesn't care.

He jumps over the barrier.

The roof of the trailer sinks in a few inches under his feet as he slams into it, rolling backward down to the aft end. He lashes out with the KA-BAR to keep himself from flying off the back end. As the knife sticks, it's nearly ripped from his iron grasp by the momentum of the truck as it barrels down the freeway. He strains to hold on, but he does. A second later, he stands.

Victor is already there to greet him. He drops the suitcase at his side.

Sid pulls his KA-BAR from the roof at his feet.

"This is a terrible idea," he yells over the noise. The spinning tires all around them howl along the freeway. The wind ripping across him makes it hard to hear much of anything.

"I love terrible ideas," Victor shouts back. He flashes his wavy knife at Sid, and the fight is on.

Victor begins with a series of forward jabs that Sid bobs around. He parries the last and returns with a riposte that rattles Victor's grasp on his weapon.

"You're angry," his brother grunts.

"I'm tired of your shit," Sid says.

"I'm tired of your whining."

"I'm gonna keep on whining after you're dead."

Sid flips his blade in hand and lunges at Victor with a downward stab. Victor catches his wrist while returning his own identical attack. Sid catches Victor's forearm with his left hand. The two of them struggle for the upper hand, knife points inches from open eyes.

Victor kicks Sid away. Sid slashes at his leg as he tumbles backward.

"You son of a bitch," Victor says. He refuses to inspect his bleeding shin, but Sid can see it oozing down his black pants leg already.

"She's your mommy too," Sid growls back.

"You never knew her." Victor comes at him, slashing and thrusting. Sid can barely keep up with the onslaught of razor steel. He has to back up—the last resort. In matters of close combat, it is always better to move laterally.

Victor takes advantage and advances. There's no footing left on the truck. Sid tries to sidestep, but Victor steps to the same side. He lunges at Sid again. Sid goes over the edge of the trailer.

He reaches out and snatches the undercarriage before he goes under a set of monstrous spinning tires. The freeway blacktop buzzes past the top of his head. He looks up to see Victor, gloating down on him over the edge. He won't be able to climb back up to the top with his brother waiting there to stab him.

He has another plan.

Sid winks up at Victor as he slides his KA-BAR back in its sheath and draws a COLT .45. He points it at the tires next to his head and blows them both out. Victor frowns. Sid blows out two sets of tires and starts on the third before the squealing brakes engage and the force of the halting truck swings him forward. He hangs on.

The truck squeals left and right as it slows, coming to a stop haphazardly across both lanes of the freeway. Sid drops down to the pavement, looking up for Victor but seeing nothing. He leaps to his feet, expecting his brother to be on top of him already. Still nothing.

The driver's door opens and two thick brown boots set down on the pavement. He's a tall man in a leather vest with a long gray beard and shiny bald head.

"Who the fuck are you?" the truck driver yells, raging toward Sid. The driver's muscular arms pump with anger. "What the fuck are you doing on my rig?" He points with black fingerless gloves.

"I don't have time for this," Sid says, shaking his head.

"The fuck you do! You're gonna pay for all of—"

Sid cracks the truck driver in the jaw with a flying knee that lifts the man off his feet and sprawls him out on the blacktop. He leaves the driver heaped on the street and looks back up at the truck.

Still no sign of Victor. If he hasn't pounced yet, then he's gone somewhere. Victor wouldn't sit there on top of the truck. He'd keep moving.

Sid glances up and down the freeway. Behind them, the cars are already lining up behind the jack-knifed truck. He sees no sign of Victor ahead or in the grassy median that separates them from traffic bound the other way. On the other side of the truck is a tall sound-wall that would've blocked Victor in. Unless . . .

"Fuck," Sid says. He jumps up onto the bumper, then leaps for the edge of the trailer top. He pulls himself up to the top, where he can see clearly over the sound wall. He spots Victor on the other side, hauling the case through a grassy field and headed toward a large supermarket.

Sid leaps over to the sound wall, dropping to the grass fifteen feet below. He follows his brother.

EXT. GALLERIA PARKING LOT - DAY

Helen awakes behind the steering wheel of the police cruiser. She sees two cars in front of her and reaches for the door. She sees two handles. She has to try twice to get the real one. She pushes her way out the door and the parking lot spins around her as she tries to stay upright. It stops after a moment and she is able to remove her hand from the roof of the cruiser and walk without bracing herself.

The parking lot looks like a warzone. The police have arrived in force and are cordoning off the mall. She can see cops in tactical gear walking the perimeter with rifles.

She walks around the back of the car and finds Lily sitting on the blacktop against the front wheel of the cruiser. Lily's head rests back against the car and she gazes off to something millions of miles away in the sky.

"Lily?" Helen says. "Where did they go? Where's the case?"

"You mean the MacGuffin?" the girl answers. "Doesn't matter. It's just a box."

Helen kneels down to her level.

"Lily," Helen says. She takes the girl's head in her hands. "Look at me. Look at me. Where did Victor go?"

"It doesn't matter. As long as Sid kills the bad guy in an act of spectacular overkill and I remain inviolate to bestow him with sex as a reward then the tropes are satisfied."

"People are dying!" Helen shouts. She slaps Lily across her bloodshot eyes.

"It's gonna be okay," Lily says. "Those aren't even ancillary characters." The ditsy little bitch has lost her god damned mind. "I don't even think this is my story. It's his."

INT. SUPERMARKET - DAY

Sid enters the supermarket through the automatic sliding glass doors at the front of the building. He scans the store for Victor and sees nothing. In front of him is a woman who must weigh six hundred pounds, billowing over the seat of a motorized scooter. She looks at Sid and screams.

He wonders why for a split second, before he remembers he's covered in blood and holding a combat knife.

"Shut up!" he barks. "Which way did he go?"

"Aaaaaahhhhhhhh!" the scooterbeast continues to scream.

A hand grenade sails over a shelving unit and lands at the scooterbeast's feet, on the deck of the powered scooter. Sid runs and dives over a bunker displaying bananas.

Boom! It rains scooter lady in the grocery store.

Sid jumps from behind the banana display and runs down the main grocery aisle. He takes a corner around the shelving unit where the grenade originated and looks down the cereal aisle. He sees Victor running away from him. A woman pushing a shopping cart widens her eyes at Sid and steps back. A man in jogging clothes tries to get out of his way as Sid shifts direction and steps back into his way, then steps the other way and ends up in his path again. Sid goes through him with a flying kick. He surfs the limp jogger for a few feet on the slippery wax floor before he continues running.

Sid reaches the end of the cereal aisle and sees

Victor running through the meat department toward the deli. Victor leaps over the counter and disappears.

Twack! Sid dodges a flying butcher knife which bites into the corner of the refrigeration unit next to his head. It penetrates the metal refrigerator door frame and sticks there. He keeps moving.

Sid hops over the deli counter in pursuit of his brother and sees the flimsy plastic door at the rear of the deli flapping back his direction. He kicks his way through the door and enters the stockroom.

The supermarket stockroom is a dingy place with dirty floors and yellow stained walls. The hallway Sid has entered is long and lined with shelving stacked to the thirty-foot ceiling. He checks both ways; to his left, there is nothing but vacant hallway. To his right, a forklift comes right for him.

Sid narrowly avoids a forklift arm in the face, jumping up between the arms and planting his feet on the fork as the truck rolls on down the corridor. He draws his .45, reaching over the motor and steering wheel to touch the muzzle of the gun to Victor's nose. He squeezes the trigger. His brother dodges left. He shoots again. His brother dodges right. Victor throws a switch on the panel in front of him and the fork begins to rocket up, elevating Sid high above the cab. He shoots at the steel forklift roof to no avail.

Sid jumps down to the forklift roof, then to the floor behind the lift. He unloads the rest of the pistol magazine into the engine compartment and the truck grinds to a smoking halt.

They are now in the supermarket's loading dock, an open concrete room with four ramps leading down to huge sliding overhead doors. One of the doors is opened to the inside of a trailer filled with canned goods. A towering metal frame supporting six levels of wooden shelves packed with inventory skids nearly reaches the ceiling. In front of that sits a big green industrial cardboard baler.

Victor hops from the broken forklift.

"I was having fun with that," he says. He leaves the suitcase in the cab.

"I know," Sid replies. He tosses the empty .45 aside.

The knives are out again.

"I love all this knife fighting," Victor says. "Makes me feel like a kid again."

"It turns out that's not normal at all," Sid says.

Sid stabs viciously at Victor. Victor dodges, bobs, weaves, parries. He counters and stabs Sid in the wounded arm. Sid jumps back. Blood splatters the concrete floor.

"Normal is weak," Victor says. He circles Sid, his knife pointed at him and dripping blood. "You're weak."

Victor slashes at Sid. Sid ducks away, but Victor kicks him in the face. Sid falls backward against the bank of lockers along the wall.

He only has a millisecond to react as he sees the wavy blade driving down at him. Sid rolls to his left and the kris knife stabs into the lockers. He attacks while Victor's knife is entrapped by sheet metal.

Victor catches Sid's attack and diverts the KA-BAR. He traps Sid's hand, driving the knife into the lockers beside his own. Sid rolls away as Victor stomps at him.

Sid reaches to the workbench nearby and snatches

up a framing hammer from a loose collection of tools. Victor picks up a claw hammer from the same workbench. In the span of a second they've transitioned from stabbing to bludgeoning. It's not any less disturbing.

"You can't win this," Victor says. "I'm better than you at everything."

The hammers clash between them, Sid swinging and Victor blocking his blow with the handle of his weapon. Victor turns the claw hammer and yanks back, ripping Sid's hammer from his grip.

"I'm better with knives. I'm better with hammers," Victor says. He throws both hammers to the ground and puts up his fists. "I'm just better."

He throws a jab, which Sid counters into a Wing Chun trap. Victor escalates with a counter to the trap. Sid breaks free with a flying knee at Victor's face, but Victor sidesteps and punches him in the balls. Sid crumples into a heap on the floor.

"The flying knee?" Victor taunts. "Are you joking? Hi-*ya*! I saw that coming a week ago."

Sid picks himself up from the floor. His guts ache like somebody jack-hammered them. Still, he persists. In his mind, his options instantly branch into a tree of possibilities that seems ironclad. Start with a heavy stomp kick because it's not a jab. Victor will be ready for a jab. If Victor sidesteps, throw elbows. If he traps, scoop kick. Anything else, clinch and throw. He already has contingencies for all of those possible responses too. From elbows: if Victor blocks, go to the Bukti Negara leg takedown. If he backs off, flying knees. From the scoop kick: if Victor doesn't let go of his foot, transition to the BJJ triangle. If he lets go, disengage.

He launches himself forward with the raging stomp kick that initiates all of the options mapped out in his head. Victor sidesteps. Sid throws elbows. Victor blocks. Sid goes to the Bukti Negara takedown by snaking his shin behind Victor's knee and pushing on the maniac's chest. Victor turns his knee against Sid's and slips under his arms to get behind him. He elbows Sid in the back of the head and then delivers a two-palmed karate strike to Sid's spine that sends him sprawling back to the floor.

"Let's see," Victor supposes aloud as Sid rolls over on the floor. His back feels like it might crack in half if he stands up. "You came at me with a stomp kick because you knew I would trap some ignorant jab. You never jab. And let me guess, if I backed off from the elbows you would have tried the flying knees again? You're so predictable."

Sid grips a shelving unit nearby and uses it to climb back to his feet. He hobbles forward trying to formulate some kind of new plan—a desperation play that Victor won't see coming. He's too beaten for quick footwork. Maybe a multistage Wing Chun engagement would get him somewhere. He could go for his brother's eyes. "I'm gonna kill you so har—"

He doesn't finish the sentence because Victor shoots across the space between them and slams the heel of his boot into Sid's chest with the dreaded ansatsuken shadow kick, forbidden for centuries, and known only to a handful of masters. The world seems to turn sideways as Sid sails from his feet into a tall stack of boxes. He crunches into the boxes, denting them, and causing the now crooked stack to topple on top of him. That kick would have gone through him if he weren't wearing body armor. He doesn't know how many of his ribs are broken, but it is at least half. He spits blood onto some corrugated cardboard with a logo for Mondo Force® Energy Drink. *Use the force to quench your thirst!*

"I never understood you," Victor says. "I mean, you're a weakling by my standards, but to the rest of them you're walking death."

Sid isn't listening. He's too busy looking at the stupid drink logo and deriding himself in internal monologue. He never stood a chance. He made all the best moves. He made every decision for tactical advantage. But Victor is always three steps ahead of him. Now the last thing he'll ever see is this stupid energy drink box.

"You could've taken anything you wanted," Victor says. "You could fill cities with the mounted skulls of your enemies while you have their squealing women as often as you like, but you have some stupid quality that keeps you from that. I don't know what it is. You'd be better off without it."

Use the force to quench your thirst! Sid's smeared blood covers most of the second clause. He props himself up on an elbow. His chest burns like a gasoline fire and he rolls over into a spilled pile of Marlboro cartons, Gold Pack, just like the ones Lily smokes for no good reason.

Because sometimes you just have to do something that doesn't make any sense.

Victor plucks both of their knives from the lockers on the other side of the storage room. "You know, I think I'll use your bones to decorate my armor."

Sid pulls an M67 frag grenade from his ballistic vest. He still has three of the little round explosives. He yanks the pin from the grenade and holds it up in front of him.

"The old dead man's switch routine?" Victor says. "Walter already tried that." Sid throws the grenade across the loading dock. Victor lurches aside to avoid being struck by the flying ball of metal. "What the fuck?" Victor says, as the grenade skitters along the concrete behind him. Victor dashes for the nearest hard cover—the big green steel cardboard baler. "What are you doing? You'll kill us both, you suicidal dipshit!"

Sid doesn't have a reason.

He pulls the other two grenades and throws them haphazardly in random directions without even looking to see where they go as he rolls out of the pile of boxes and behind a skid of soup cans.

For a few seconds, the loading dock is Armageddon. The first grenade pops, sending shrapnel into the walls and ceilings, shredding an old computer, stabbing at the storage lockers and cardboard baler. Sid doesn't see what the others do. He only hears the blasts and sees the room rattle around him. A light fixture crashes from the ceiling, bursting with a shower of sparks on the floor right next to his head. Canned soup explodes in a salty shower all over Sid. A huge shelving unit collapses, sending thousands of pounds of boxed dinners, cereal and dog food avalanching down to the floor. Acrid smoke fills the already dim loading dock, making it harder to see and even harder to breathe.

Sid checks to make sure his legs are still attached

and he doesn't have any new perforations. He struggles to his feet, waving smoke away as the florescent bulbs flicker on the high ceiling. Uncertain at first if he should stay and look for Victor, or just run while he can, his decision is assisted by the rabid cursing of his brother somewhere in the avalanche of ruined garbage.

When Sid started throwing grenades like a blind idiot, Victor dove into the closest hard metal object for cover: the cardboard baler. It was the right move—a very tactical decision, but neither of them could have counted on the collapsing shelving unit, or the pallet of fifty-pound solar salt sacks that would rain down from above, stacking on top of the baler and pinning its sliding gate closed.

Victor Hansen is trapped in the massive crushing machine.

"Let me out of here, you fuck!" Victor shouts, punching the bright green grating in front of him. "You should be dead!"

Sid stumbles around the baler looking for the control box as Victor curses at machine gun volume only inches from his face.

"You're gonna leave me in here?" Victor says. "Put me back in a cell, you pathetic cunt?"

Sid finds the control box on the other side of the hulking machine, covered by a bent sack of salt that is leaking its dusty contents into the piled food items around them. He climbs on top of a mound of dog food bags and groans as he tosses the salt aside. His arms feel like wet noodles stuck with pins. The control panel has two buttons; a red one and a black one. Sid pushes the red one.

The baler kicks into a cycle and the huge metal ram begins to press forward toward Victor.

"You can't smash me!" Victor screams. "I'm a god damned demon!"

The ram comes closer, leaving less and less space inside the baler as it goes. Sid crawls down from the food avalanche and pulls his KA-BAR from the lockers.

"I will haunt you from the depths of hell!" Victor rages. "I will come for your babies in the night! I'll kill you! I'll kill you!"

Sid retrieves the suitcase from the driver's seat in the forklift. He looks back as the baler crushes down on Victor. The curses turn to incoherent screams, then to the snap-crackle-pop of crunching bones.

Sid turns and walks from the loading dock.

INT. SUPERMARKET - DAY

Sid steps out into the supermarket and finds himself staring down the barrels of ten assault rifles carried by a squad of commandos wearing ski masks.

He sighs. It never ends.

Then a dark figure emerges from behind a tall display of bold and zesty Doritos®. Sid recognizes him right away—the thick frame, mess of greasy, ratty hair, the long black and gray beard of a wild man. He leans on a teak cane, the head of which is a fanged skull. He glares at Sid through eyes as black as his own.

"So it's true," Sid says. "You're not dead."

"You have the case?" the old man asks. His voice is like gravel and his accent carries a hint of eastern Europe.

"Right here," Sid says, holding up the box for all to see.

"Good," the old man says. "Hand it over."

Sid sets the case down on the floor in front of him and a commando steps forward to claim it.

"And Victor?" the old man asks.

"He suffered a crushing defeat," Sid replies. He winks.

The commando delivers the case to the old man, who sets it on top of a cooler stocked with ice cold Pepsi® colas. Live bolder. Live louder—with Pepsi®. He spins the tumblers to the correct combination and pops the lid open. He looks inside and nods approvingly.

"Anybody ever gonna tell me what's in that

thing?" Sid says.

The old man turns the case around to display its contents. To Sid, the machine inside looks like an incoherent mess of copper pipettes, crystals, and colored wires.

"It's called the Riftmaker. The Nazis constructed it to open a dimensional gateway through which their reptilian master race could return to this universe."

That doesn't make any sense at all. "Why did Victor want it, then?"

"Because it never worked. They tested it once and it ripped a gash in reality that thousands of nightmare things poured through from a hundred other universes. The Luftwaffe spent weeks carpet-bombing the island where they held the experiment."

"If Victor set that off on the mainland . . ."

"Endless war with innumerable alien things across the globe."

"He would've loved it."

The old man closes the case and scrambles the tumblers. He sets it down beside his feet.

"What made you run?" the old man says. "Why?"

"You wouldn't understand," Sid says.

"Try me."

Sid leans against a cooler next to the dock room door and picks up a pack of cold bacon. He presses it to his jaw. It feels good.

"I was in Chicago on orders from Walter," Sid says. "Blackout. Two adults and two children. Something about it messed me up. It wasn't killing them. It was something else—the way they were. The things in their house. They were different than me. *Everyone* was different than me. I started wandering down the street. So I'm in downtown Chicago, seeing all these things I don't understand, because they aren't for killing, and I see the only thing that looks familiar to me: a poster of some guys with guns in front of a movie theater. And I realize I've never seen a movie before, so I want to find out what this is all about—find out what normal people do. And I go up to the ticket guy and he says I'm not allowed in because the movie was rated R."

The old man nods slowly. After a moment he prods Sid for more.

"And?" "And?" Sid says. "What do you mean? That doesn't click for you at all? I actually murdered thousands of people before I was old enough to see fictional murder. I found out I spent my entire childhood doing the thing that nobody's supposed to do! Ever! That wouldn't mess with your head just a little bit?"

"No," the old man says. He's telling the truth. Sid knows he is. The old man has a heart of the blackest black.

"Fuck," Sid says. He tosses the bacon package back in the refrigeration bunker. "Well, let's do this. Are these all the goons you brought?"

"Sid," the old man says. "I have ten soldiers with automatic rifles. You have a knife."

"All right. I'll even the odds." Sid drops his knife. "That better?"

The old man motions to one of his commandos. The masked soldier nods and removes his ski mask. As he lowers his hand, Sid sees something he does not at first understand. He doesn't immediately recognize the person behind the mask—and yet he does.

It's him. That is to say, the person under the mask is *also* him. He is another Sid Hansen. This other one is younger and lacks the multitude of scars on his arms, but is otherwise identical.

"You have an army of me?" Sid shouts. "What the fuck?"

The old man nods. "You're no longer a threat to us."

"No shit," Sid says. "Now I'm just a threat to . . . myself. Fuck. This is the biggest mind fuck. You are, hands down, the world's worst dad."

"We don't need you anymore," the old man says. "I can see to it that you aren't bothered."

"Bullshit."

"Not bullshit."

"I don't have to stay off the grid anymore?"

"Get out of here, Sid. Just stay out of trouble."

"Done," Sid says. He sheaths his knife and limps past the army of clones. "This is fucking great. I'm getting a place with central air."

EXT. GALLERIA PARKING LOT – DAY

Lily sits on the end of an ambulance. The Galleria parking lot is teeming with EMTs and police. There are more flashing lights than solid ones. Lily watches as some of them wheel a bloodied figure out on a stretcher. She can't tell if it is a man or a woman, but she searches intently for movement. She doesn't look away until she sees a finger twitch—or so she thinks.

People wander the lot shouting the names of the missing. A man in a brown coat stops, in shock, near the cruiser and calls out to Lily.

"Katie?" he says.

Lily looks him in the eyes and he moves on, realizing she is not the person he's looking for.

"Victor's dead," Sid says. He appears like a ghost, as he so often does. Lily wants to rush up and throw her arms around him, but she's too broken to move.

He reaches down for Lily's hand. He plucks her up off the ground and she leans against the car.

"These people are all dead because of me," she says.

"Victor killed them," Sid says. "And he would've killed a lot more if you didn't help stop him."

"I don't know . . ."

"And you never will," he says. "Come with me."

Sid drags her forward and she limps alongside him. Her legs are not as fatigued anymore, but the rest of her is still a mess. She needs him to lean on.

"Where are we going?"

"I saw something over here," Sid says.

He leads her deeper into the lot, through a half

dozen rows of cars, until they come to the back of a tall black van—a van like the one in the storage unit where the helicopter shot at them.

Sid pulls open the door.

In the back of the van, bound with duct tape and gagged with a rope, is Lily's mother. She's clad only in her underwear and bleeding from the frayed ends of two fingerless knuckles. She lifts her head and Lily dives into the van, despite her injuries. She wraps her arms around her mother and the Hoffman women cry together.

INT. CABIN – DAY

The Fountainhead was the favorite book of a younger Helen—a simpler Helen. It's still a good book, probably even a great book, but she finds more fault with it as she gets older. The end seems less and less believable each time through. She's not so certain anymore Roark could win that trial with just an inspiring speech. And Dominique bounces around from husband to husband like the leading lady on one of those terrible teen soap operas. She marries the first guy because she hates him—rationale that is questionable at best. Then the husband essentially sells her to her next husband as part of a business contract. It made more sense when Helen was fifteen. Still, the first edition Matt found for her is very impressive. The pages don't stink like smoke, and the binding is pristine. A book like this sells at auction for the cost of a brand new sports car. Matt found it in a thrift shop for a dollar.

She puts the book down and kicks her cowboy boots up on the coffee table in front of the davenport. The forest stretches as far as she can see, beyond the bay window. The cabin is one of the larger ones in the area, and used to be a hunting lodge in the eighties, before Matt's parents bought it. Country line dancing is in order for tonight at Bobby Lee's Old Time Saloon in town. She's already started drinking. By the time they make it to the bar, she'll have a good buzz. She'll get tipsy there. Then they'll come back to the cabin and try again to make a baby. That's the plan anyway. There's nothing to stop them now that her career in shadow politics is over.

The aftermath was ugly.

Officially, the massacre at the Galleria was carried out by a solitary Islamic radical who killed himself when confronted by police. The FBI gave him a name, a face, and even produced a body. Where they came up with that character, Helen has no idea. She wasn't involved. It wouldn't have been hard, though. They could've pulled any detainee from a dozen different places around the world, stuck a Glock in his mouth, and made up any story they wanted. Most people believe it. Some people don't. There are already websites springing up to discuss the paranoid theories. So far, none of the ones Helen has seen are close to what really happened.

Marines touched down at the Graveyard building from Yuma not long after she and Tanaka left. They worked to pull survivors out of the rubble and secure any dangerous ordnance found in the wreckage. The vault, found largely undamaged near the top of the ruin, was transported to another site held by Graveyard's parent corporation. Helen doesn't know where that is.

Walter Stedman was buried at Arlington National Cemetery and given a twenty-one gun salute. Helen was there with Lieutenant Ratzinger and Frank Overton, two guys she realized were probably too accustomed to funerals. She was uneasy when she saw Matt talking to them there, and fitting in a little too well.

They never found any sign of Yoshida Tanaka. Whether that means he made it out of the Galleria or was incinerated in the exploding shopping mall is anyone's guess. She had asked Sid what he thought after the fact, and he just shrugged and said, "Fucking ninjas."

The sound of the front door slamming in the other room lifts her heavy eyelids, and she rises from the couch. Matt enters, sweating from his evening jog. Her husband is a beefy specimen, broad shouldered and big armed. He's built like a tank. Bar creeps never hassle her when they go out together. It's half the reason she married him.

"Hey babe," Matt says, holding up a big manila shipping envelope. "This was on the porch when I got back."

"What is it?" Helen says, standing to meet him at the kitchen counter.

"I don't know. It just has your name written on it."

As she steps up to the counter, Matt's eyes scan down her skin-tight jeans and the plaid shirt she tied off above her belly. He smiles, dropping the envelope on the counter.

"Damn, cowgirl," he says. "Maybe we can just stay in tonight." He puts his hands on her hips.

"You smell like an old gym bag," she says. "Go take a shower."

"Look into my eyes," Matt says, in his Bela Lugosi voice, pressing his fingers to his temples and gazing at her eerily. This is an old joke of his, but it seems so much darker since she saw Tanaka do the real thing and make it work.

"Whatever," she laughs, shoving him away. "We're going line dancing, and you're gonna like it."

"Do I have to wear a cowboy hat?" Matt says as he

walks from the room.

"Yes," Helen shouts after him.

She picks up the envelope from the counter and turns it over. Her name is written across the front in thick black marker, and it's sealed in multiple wrappings of clear packing tape. The envelope bulges in the center. Something rectangular is inside. It didn't go through the mail, Helen realizes as she pulls a kitchen knife from a drawer beside her. Someone must've left it on the porch for her. There is a very short list of people who even know about this place, and fewer would know she is here now.

She cuts the packing tape along one edge and turns it sideways to pour the contents onto the counter. Two things fall out. One is a cheap cellphone with a small display and a simple nine-number keypad—perfect for someone to use briefly, then throw away because they don't want to be traced. The other thing is a plain white business card that slides out and falls flat on the counter facedown. She flips it over and sighs.

There is nothing printed on the card but a fanged skull and crossbones—the Graveyard emblem.

INT. GAMESTOP - DAY

Sid wears a lanyard around his neck with a plastic name tag that says DUTCH. It's an assumed identity, one he stole from someone who won't be missed.

Working at Gamestop is pretty simple. Sid has to show up on time and wear his name tag. Sometimes he has to file video games in alphabetical order. People hand him money. Then he hands them video games. Then they leave. They don't pay him much, but nobody shoots at him and there are no werewolf attacks or killer prostitutes trying to seduce him, either.

There was one incident where he eviscerated a shoplifter and Bruce had to explain how that was not permitted—a concept that eludes him still, but he is still learning to blend in.

"You know," Bruce says, from his place on the counter, a video game controller in his hands. "It's amazing to me how bad you are at this."

He's talking about *Call of Honor: Modern Battlefield*, a thing Sid will never understand in any capacity. The idea that people would create a digital simulation of warfare is not that strange to him: war games have been part of his life as long as he can remember, and everywhere he goes it appears that people dedicate copious amounts of their time to enacting fantasy violence. The part that annoys him is that they get it so wrong.

"That's what I'm trying to tell you," Sid says. "This is nothing like the real thing."

"I can see that. You're oh and twenty-two. That

guy is tea bagging you."

"The concept of hard cover is completely wrong in this. They don't get it at all. Drywall doesn't stop 5.56. I shoot through it all the time. I shot a guy through a floor a few months back with a 9mm just on the sound of his footsteps. Why can't I do that? And I can only shoot the direction I'm looking? And my aim is terrible. And this stupid controller thing doesn't feel anything like shooting a rifle. I have no grappling ability at all. Why can't I tackle that guy and take his gun away?"

"It's not *Star Trek*," Bruce laughs. "This isn't the holodeck."

"I don't know what that is, but this game is dumb."

"You coming back to my place tonight? We're grilling out."

"I can't. I have some business to take care of."

INT. THE BLACK OMEN – NIGHT

"Remember to tip the ladies if you sit up front," rumbles Max, the DJ. His words tend to blend together in long chains of subwoofer bass tones that no one can understand. "Now everybody put your hands together. Coming up on the middle stage it's . . . *Chastity*."

He fades up the music she picked: Slayer's "Psychopathy Red." It matches her Slayer string bikini; solid black with anarchy symbols over her cans and the band's logo across her butt.

Lily starts off running up to the stage past a few tables of regulars. Those guys always sit in the back and she can name most of them: Sweatpants Steve, Cross-eye Larry, Reggie—just Reggie, Normal Kevin. The girls call him that because he's inexplicably normal for a strip club regular. Lily thinks that actually makes him the weirdest one of them all. He's probably a serial killer.

She skips up the stairs to the stage and leaps onto the pole. She starts off climbing right to the top and grabbing hold of the wheel attached to the ceiling above. She goes round a few times on that before she wraps her legs around the pole and takes it for a spin.

Prude bitches talk about pole dancing like it's easy. It's not. Lily works at it every day, and she's good. She's very good.

Despite that, the boys don't pay to see gymnastics. She suspends herself upside down, her legs wrapped around the pole, and dive-bombs the stage floor. Her nose stops a few inches from the floor and then she gives them what they pay for.

She scans the upside-down faces along the tip rail below her: three frat boys and a young married couple. The frat boys are all entranced by her tits. The married couple seems less interested. That's disappointing. Married couples buy lap dances. Frat boys don't. She needs to escalate this situation.

She drops down to the stage with the beginning of her second song: VHS or BETA's "Night on Fire." She crawls to Mr. Married Couple on all fours, aims her heels at him and drops her bikini bottom to her knees. She rolls over to her back, putting her legs in the air to kick the panties away and show him everything. He's interested now. The missus leans over and whispers in his ear.

The frat boys don't like losing her attention. The middle one stands a neatly folded five dollar bill on the stage. Lily crawls over. She lies down in front of them and begins doing something that is illegal in a strip club in this state. They like it. So do the marrieds. The wife puts a ten dollar bill on the edge of the stage, face up.

Lily tumbles over their way. She looks back at the frat boys and shrugs. She gives the couple the same show she was giving the boys. The husband is enthralled. The wife strokes his leg. He's pretty jacked, and she's a pretty thing. Lily likes where this might be headed.

The frat boys put ten dollars on the stage. Lily glances their direction and Mr. Married has already put down another ten in front of her. She shrugs at the frat boys. One of them brandishes a crinkled twenty dollar bill in the air and smacks it down on the stage, smiling.

Thump! The stage rattles and Lily turns, startled, to her left. Beside her sits a red and white plastic Igloo cooler. Behind it, Sid sits down in one of the chairs next to the stage.

Big Dave, the bouncer, is already at Sid's side.

"The stage ain't for your beer, chief!" Dave yells. "Time to take your cooler and get out!"

Sid doesn't even acknowledge the bouncer's presence.

"It's okay, Dave," Lily says. "He's with me."

Dave gives her a look of uncertainty before he backs off.

Lily's song ends and she collects her tips and her bikini from the floor before she hops down next to Sid. She picks up the cooler and smirks at him as Max announces the next dancer.

"Is this what I think it is?" she asks.

"You told me it doesn't matter what's in the box," he says.

"This time it does," she says.

He doesn't answer her question.

"Come on." She takes him by the hand. He bounces up from his seat and follows her as she guides him through the club, wearing nothing but her heels.

"Where are we going?" he asks.

"You'll see." She retrieves her clutch from behind the bar on the way. She walks Sid over to Chuck, the other bouncer, sitting in a steel folding chair outside a glass block entryway with wavy neon lights above. A sign over his head reads VIP LOUNGE.

"I need an hour, Chuck," Lily says. She counts out

three hundred dollars for him, which he places in a till in his lap.

"All yours, boss," he says.

"And Chuck," Lily says. She puts a twenty dollar bill in his hand. "I heard about the problems with the camera in there."

"Yeah," he nods. "It's gonna take at least an hour to fix it."

"Damn," she says.

The VIP room is lit entirely with black lights. Lily sets the Igloo cooler down on the only table, in front of the black leather sectional taking up the far corner from the door.

She positions herself between the cooler and the camera mounted in the corner of the room, opposite the sectional, just in case Chuck forgot to turn it off. Sid places his arms around her.

"Hey!" she objects. "No touching the ladies!"

She shoves him down on the sectional. "Sit on your hands."

He follows directions. She sees him snickering at her too.

She looks back at the cooler and hesitates opening it. Maybe she should just take his word. Maybe that's enough.

Then she realizes it is not. She doesn't just need to know. She *wants* to see. She thirsts for it.

She pulls the handle atop the cooler, rotating the lid down to expose the contents. She should cry or scream, and she might have before, but not now. Something in her has changed.

She smiles.

Lily closes the cooler and struts over to the sectional. She sits down on Sid's lap and puts her hands on his shoulders.

"You did good, killer," she whispers.

"You gonna make good on our deal?" he says, placing his hands on her hips.

She snatches his wrists. "What did I tell you about hands?"

"Sit on them," he says, placing them back where they belong.

"That's right," she says, undoing his belt buckle. "Don't make me call Big Dave in here."

Lily puts her hand on his face as she rises up, then comes down, impaling herself on his rock-hard cock. She squeaks as it enters her. It hurts for only a second. She takes a deep breath and begins rocking like a ship on the ocean.

This is what she owes him, but she enjoys it too much for that.

Her eyes are closed when she feels his hand around the back of her head, pulling her down to his level.

"No," she whispers. She can't fight him, but it's not because he's so much stronger than her.

She feels his lips against hers, his tongue pushing in, penetrating her in a way more intimate than she has ever known. She opens her mouth to accept him fully. His tongue tickles against hers. She likes this. She wants this. She wants more.

"I—" she starts. She looks back into those void-like eyes. What did Quint say? Lifeless eyes, black eyes, like a doll's eyes . . .

It's better with no words, she decides.

She keeps kissing him, and letting his hands go

where they want. She climaxes twice before he can endure no more and releases inside her.

She flops down on the sectional next to him.

"I feel like a Bond girl," she says, sighing deeply.

"I don't know what that is," Sid says. Of course he doesn't.

"Our time's almost up."

"So this is it?" he asks. "You're a stripper now."

"Oh, I'm just doing this to pay for college," Lily says, fluttering into an impression of an ultra bimbo.

"Really?" he says.

"No!" She punches him in the shoulder. "Ass!" She falls back on the sectional and chuckles.

"I'm saving money to produce a slasher film," she says, digging through her clutch for her Marlboro cigarettes. "I've already got twenty grand."

"Is that a lot?" he asks, putting his pants back on.

"Yeah. That's a lot." She laughs. He's like a space alien sometimes.

He stands up from the sectional and buckles his pants.

Lily draws a cigarette from the box as he walks away. She holds it in her hand, staring at it. There's something missing. She doesn't feel the compulsion she once did. She puts the cigarette down.

"Sid?" she calls. He stops in the doorway and turns back to her. "You want to see a movie with me?" she says.

FADE OUT

Directed by MIKE LEON

Story by MIKE LEON

Screenplay by MIKE LEON

Produced by TYPING

Executive Producers MOSTLY DO NOTHING

Director of Photography IS A REAL THING

Art Director RACHEL LANG

Costume Design ARE YOU READING THIS?

Set Design YOU SHOULD LEAVE THE THEATER

Music by OTHER PEOPLE ARE LEAVING

Visual Effects Supervisor SOME POOR BASTARD WHOSE STUDIO WE DROVE INTO BANKRUPTCY

Casting by HUGE PACKAGING AGENCY

A Basement of Doom Production

A Mike Leon Film

Second Unit Director YOUR FRIEND IS LOOKING AT YOU

Unit Production Manager IT'S THAT LOOK

First Assistant Director THEY WONDER IF YOU LIKED IT

Second Assistant Director BUT THEY'RE NOT SURE

Gaffer SO NOW IT'S AN AWKWARD GAME OF CHICKEN

Best Boy TO SEE WHO SPEAKS FIRST

Key Grip AS IF THEY MIGHT DISOWN YOU

Animal Handler BECAUSE YOU LIKED THE MOVIE

A Camera Operator NO MOVIE IS THAT BAD THOUGH

A Camera First Assistant WELL

A Camera Second Assistant MAYBE *MAC AND ME*

B Camera Operator I WOULD DISOWN YOU FOR THAT

B Camera First Assistant OR *BATTLEFIELD EARTH*

B Camera Second 6 VENEZUELAN RED LLAMAS

C Camera Operator OH GREAT

Digital Imaging Technician THERE'S ANOTHER SCENE

Camera Loader IT'LL PROBABLY SET UP A SEQUEL

INT. VIDEO TIME – BACK ROOM – DAY

"Christian, come look at this," says Addison. She rifles through the stack of old movie posters sitting on a chipped desk in the back of the store. Most of them are the kind of trash that just feeds the right-wing rape culture in this country, but there's one that would look good in the front room.

"What is it, babe?" Christian says. He steps into the room, sipping a kombucha tea from a bottle. His Morrissey T-shirt has grey filth on it and there's soot on his fingers.

Addison pulls her amazing find from the stack and holds it up for him to see. It's an original poster for *One Flew Over the Cuckoo's Nest.*

"Oh, wow," Christian says, brushing his fingers off on his sarong. "That's great. We can hang it over the vinyl display. Very indie rock. I cleared some space in the corner up front for the reading area with the vegan cookbooks and socialist literature."

"Did you cancel the order for those gluten-free cookies?" Addison asks, narrowing her eyes at him. He has a tendency to forget things. She sets the movie poster carefully back on the stack.

"I sure did." He frowns in disgust. "I can't believe they were made with hydrogenated oil and dairy products. Disgusting."

"That's what you get for listening to ovo-lacto vegetarians." The couple who recommended the cookies still eat dairy. They probably think it's okay to eat the fries at McMurder too. Addison is sick of these kids jumping on the cruelty-free bandwagon just because they saw a Chipotle ad.

"They're such poseurs." Christian rolls his eyes. "They really are."

"Oh Christian, this is going to be the best eco café in the whole city."

"Yeah," he says. "I just keep wondering how we got the building so cheap."

"You can't accept that some people are more interested in reinvesting in the community than being greedy capitalist pigs?"

"Well, I guess," he says, shrugging. "But five thousand dollars? What if it's haunted or something?"

"That kind of pessimism isn't going to win the war against feedlots and fast food."

"Did you hear that?" Christian's head whips around toward the showroom.

"Hear what?" Addison says. She chuckles.

"Out front." Christian leans out into the showroom through the open door and then back into the stockroom with her. "I thought I heard something."

"You can't scare me. I don't believe in ghosts." She bends down to the floor, scooping up some aluminum display hangers. There are hundreds of the damn things back here, mostly just spread around the floor like garbage. "Help me pick up these metal pegs. I don't know what we're going to do with them yet. I don't think they're recyclable."

"Addison?"

She stands up straight. "What?"

In front of them, blocking the door to the front room, stands a man taller than either of them, taller than the door, taller than anyone she has ever met. He's dressed all in black, except for his head. His face . . .

His face is a terrifying mass of ruined flesh, charred and bloody like flash-cooked burger. There are no lips to hide his collection of pointed fangs or blood-dripping tongue. One bloodshot eye bulges with rage; the other is just an empty socket dripping with red slime.

The monster raises a butcher's cleaver over his head, nearly clipping the ceiling. Addison screams as the cleaver comes down, splitting Christian's head in two. Hot blood sprays in her eyes and mouth.

"Fresh meat!"

Here's the first chapter of the next book in the series: *Godless Murder Machine*:

EXT. EGYPT – SHARM EL-SHEIKH – NIGHT

To the infidels, the burqa is a prison, a dungeon where innocents are thrown and kept, never to see the light of day. To the people of faith, it is a cover, a sheath to protect those outside from the lure of the 'awrah, the shameful parts within. To Fatimah, it is a shield.

The burqa shields her from the others and their disgusted stares, from pointing children and laughing men. It hides her flesh and her hate. Under her shield, she is just another faceless woman.

"How many will this make?" The question comes in Pashto from the cold barbarian of a man who accompanies her. Sayyid al-Dhafiri. His head is bald, but his chin supports a lengthy and coarse black beard with a few dyed red vertical stripes. His dull brown eyes are dim and listless, and Fatimah sometimes wonders if his unquestioning devotion to Allah has left no independent thoughts swirling behind them.

"Seven," she answers. The crowd continues through the streets around them, a river of flamboyant transgressors flowing through a dark wood of neon-colored sin. The city of Sharm el-Sheikh is a blight upon the Egyptian land. They have flung modesty to the wind here and the women show their faces and bodies. Men poison themselves with alcohol. Even the women drink. The air is thick with their perfume stink and unashamed laughter.

"Allah is merciful," Sayyid says.

"Most merciful," Fatimah says, but her response is distant, aloof, dead. Most would overlook this, but she knows Sayyid will notice. He can detect even the slightest hint of unbelief and never fails to confront it.

"You have doubts?"

Fatimah tilts her head low as she finds the words. She begins to answer, but a crowd of squealing kuffar women stumbles by, loudly and drunkenly singing of lewd acts. This is not their place. They belong half a world away or fueling the fires of Jahannam, not here in the land of believers interrupting her conversation. She waits for them to pass.

"Each time I pray for death," Fatimah says. "And each time it does not come."

Sayyid nods grimly.

"That is because Allah, may He be glorified and exalted, has a plan for you," he says. "Soon the pain will end, but first you must truly submit to His will."

"I am truly devoted. What more could I possibly give to prove it? Ask any act. Ask any piece of me and I will cut it away in offering."

"I do not doubt you, but Allah, may He be glorified and exalted, does not reward offerings. He does not barter in exchange for your desires. He is not a merchant. He is a ruler."

"What must I do?" she asks.

"You must only understand you are insignificant. Your desires matter not. Only His plan matters. Serve Him. Serve His plan."

"I live to serve Him. If I die, it will be to serve Him." Her answer is stiff, almost sullen, hardly the way it should be.

"Do not despair, Fatimah," he says. "I have already received word of our next great conquest. A great enemy of the caliphate has been found in the United States. You know him. The coward. The demon from the dark. The great pig of strife and suffering."

Even without any other detail, Fatimah knows who he means. For years she has burned with hate for this monster. In the mountains back home, they speak of him—of the devil with skin as black as night and a face like a skull. They tell tales of entire villages murdered quietly in the night, except the young girls, who were carried away to satiate some dark amusement. They still hang wards in the trees near those places to keep him away. They call him Djinn, Ghul, Gallu, Ifrit, and sometimes Shaytan, but Fatimah knows he is none of these things, and she has a much simpler name for him.

"The Beast."

Her heart beats faster and her breathing becomes difficult to stay. This is far too fortunate to be a thing of chance. It can only be her destiny.

"I will do this thing," she exclaims without hearing another word. "Nothing would please me more."

"First, you will finish what you started here," Sayyid says. "Then we will seek out our enemy and destroy him. This is the will of Allah, may He be glorified and exalted."

"Yes," Fatimah says, nodding enthusiastically. "May He be glorified and exalted."

"Go now," he says, turning to depart.

Fatimah is already making her way down the street, past rainbow colored lights dangling from palm trees and windows struggling to contain heavy bass beats. She doesn't hear the blasphemous music, though. She is too consumed with raw emotion—the only emotion that remains within her.

She turns to her right, walking through the open doorway she saw the wretched kafir enter before her.

She steps into a world of bright colors flashing in darkness and wiggling bodies grinding together with sweaty lust. Sparkling disco balls and fish-shaped aluminum cutouts spin on strands of wire above her head. A musclebound and tight-shirted man just inside the door yells at her over the ear-bleeding thumps from the speakers. Fatimah has no interest in what he has to say. She brushes past him and runs for the dance floor.

The dancers gather in the middle of the club on a waxed wooden floor surrounded by carpeted space with couches and translucent bars lit with neon colors shaped like fish. Near the edge of the mass of teeming bodies, Fatimah spies one of the drunken women from outside. She only has to push through one or two other people to reach the wicked non-believer. A man in a loose fitting white shirt snarls as she scrapes past him, knocking a green-tinted glass from his hands to shatter on the floor. The woman only squints and looks at Fatimah through one glazed eye, as if teetering between laughter and total disregard, as Fatimah reveals the detonator and screams.

"Allahu Akbar!" Fatimah shrieks.

The ground-rattling bass thump of the speakers is lost like a gentle whisper amidst the deafening detonation thunderclap of forty pounds of ammonal. The pressure compresses her and the heat sears like fire on her skin. It feels like she's been crammed into a baby coffin and set aflame atop a funeral pyre. Fragments rake her arms like razor rain. To open her eyes would be to lose them. To scream now is to breathe fire and steel.

It ends in blackness, as it always does. A blindfold of acrid smoke fills the room, obscuring the broken bodies and leaking blood. The screeching ring left over from the blast makes all the crying and screaming sound miles away. The only sense left is touch, and the crowd uses it liberally to claw and crawl, scurrying over the slow and the dead like a swarm of terrified rats.

Fatimah emerges from the front doors into the street. Onlookers have already begun to gather. The stupid ones rush inside and the cowardly ones stand and watch. They don't know her from any of the dozens stumbling from the smothering cloud, choking and clawing at their faces. She wishes she had another bomb for them, but all her explosives were spent.

Outside, she is exposed. Her shield was shredded in the explosion, as was intended. The burqa was lined with sheets of glued-together ball bearings as shrapnel. The tattered remains of the blue fabric cling to her head and shoulders, where the force of the blast was not as intense. She counts her nine blood-drenched fingers as she hurries away from the scene. The blood is likely her own, from the dozens of scrapes and cuts that crisscross her body, but no more digits were lost this time.

They will say it is impossible to survive this thing she has lived through. They will say she left the bomb and triggered it from afar. They will say she was completely vaporized in the blast. They may say she does not exist at all. In a way, that is true. There is nothing left of her—at least not of the person she once was. Now there is only hate. It burns within her, building, expanding, threatening to explode like the suicide vests she has used to kill so many. Soon it will break free and engulf her. She will finally die destroying the person she hates most: the coward who left her this way.

Fatimah will go to America and she will destroy the Beast. She will destroy Sid Hansen. It is the will of Allah.